PRAISE FOR JAMES A. MOORE!

James A. Moore's work "recalls vintage Stephen King."
—*Publishers Weekly*

"Fans of *The Shining* and *Phantoms* will welcome James A. Moore into the ranks of horror master."
—*Midwest Book Review*

"Moore's work stands toe-to-toe with the best of King, Koontz or McCammon. He's simply one of the best ten authors working in the field today."
—*Cemetery Dance*

"Here is a talent. Here is someone to watch."
—Bentley Little, author of *The Return*

"Add a pinch of Stephen King, a dash of Dean Koontz, a flowering of Peter Straub and one part Bentley Little and readers will have an idea what a horror novel by James A. Moore is like."
—Harriet Klausner, *Baryon Magazine*

James A. Moore "leaves the reader breathless at every turn...a master of suspense."
—*RT BOOKclub*

THE TRANSFORMATION

The house was as quiet as ever. Chris opened the door and the two of them went inside.

"Show me."

Jerry nodded and took off his shirt. His undershirt had short sleeves and he held up his arm for Chris to study. Sores ran down the flesh, just like the ones that had been there before, but much more prevalent than previously. Jerry flexed his fingers a few times and looked at the hand hard, his mouth pressing into a thin line.

And his fingers changed. They grew longer, the nails extending into wickedly sharp claws and the skin darkening, growing coarser. Chris looked at his friend and then sat down hard on the sofa, no longer able to feel his legs. For that one moment his entire being was focused on that damned hand.

The sores that covered Jerry's arm darkened, until they matched the color of the flesh on his hand. At their very centers the skin rippled, moved as if someone had thrown pebbles and the flesh there was water....

Other *Leisure* books by James A. Moore:

NEWBIES
FIREWORKS
POSSESSIONS
UNDER THE OVERTREE

JAMES A. MOORE

RABID GROWTH

LEISURE BOOKS   **NEW YORK CITY**

A LEISURE BOOK®

April 2005

Published by

Dorchester Publishing Co., Inc.
200 Madison Avenue
New York, NY 10016

ISBN 0-8439-5172-9

The name "Leisure Books" and the stylized "L" with design are trademarks of Dorchester Publishing Co., Inc.

Printed in the United States of America.

Visit us on the web at www.dorchesterpub.com.

RABID GROWTH

Chapter One

I

The grocery store was a nightmare and Chris Corin wished it were the sort he could just wake up from. Sadly for him, it wasn't. It was the type that happened while you were fully conscious. He usually didn't mind going to the Acme just down the road from his house, but today the people wandering around inside the place seemed to be in particularly foul moods. Like he needed to share their disappointments with the world around him. He had enough of his own, thanks just the same.

Just of late his life had hardly been peaches and cream, but he was doing his best not to throw it back at everyone around him. His little sister, Brittany, was doing enough of that for everyone as it was. She was pitching bitches about damned near every imagined slight in her life, and in the meantime he was using the money that was supposed to be for his summer trip to Europe in order to pay the bills. Said trip was a goner. Instead of meeting a few new faces while hiking through Italy and France, he'd spent most of his summer recovering from the explosion that almost ended his life just after he'd graduated from high school. Physical therapy for his knee, and a slew of doctors trying to understand why his eyes had gone from blue to green at the same time. Detective Martin Callaghan—slightly less terrifying than Frankenstein's monster but not as jovial—was still sniffing around from time to time to see if maybe, somehow, Chris had remembered a little more about the accident that had leveled the abandoned building he'd almost died in. Callaghan was also doing his best to find out what had really happened to his partner from the local police department: Walter Crawford, a man who had vanished six months before and then mysteriously taken the case for Chris after a simple breaking and entering that became the start of a sordid mess.

That and other catastrophes. In the three months since he'd finished school and turned eighteen he'd lost his mother to a stupid accident and been forced to take on his little sister as a new burden in his life. The rest of what had happened was a little more freakish than he wanted to actively think about.

He sorted through the stacks of Hamburger Helper in his cart and kept the ones that looked most appeal-

2

ing, fully willing to pretend that they didn't mostly all taste the same, despite the promising pictures that adorned the boxes. Next he went over to the part of the store that sold hamburger meat. The cheaper the better. In theory he was going to be a very, very wealthy man some time in the future. He'd won the lottery and had over forty million dollars coming his way. But first he had to deal with the bureaucracy that ran that sort of thing, and so far it had taken a while. In the meantime the last of his money was going into buying enough cheap supplies to keep him and his sister from starving to death. With puberty kicking her butt, Brittany had become a human eating machine.

He did a quick mental calculation of funds and decided that what he had would suffice. With the ramen noodles still stocked in the pantry, he could get a week or so out of it. It would have to do.

Chris started toward the front of the store, smiling at a pretty blonde girl who was about his age. She was tired and the smile she returned was weak. When he saw the toddler near her leg he understood the reason for her exhaustion. *Her kid? Her little brother? Is she a nanny somewhere?* It didn't matter. Not really. But at least she was a pleasant distraction from the teeming mass of frustrated hausfraus milling around the Acme.

She turned away and he went about his mission to buy groceries and leave the store as quickly as possible. He'd made it to the checkout lines—which were as ugly as the mood at a Saddam Hussein fan club meeting in New York City—before he got the first strange sensation. He couldn't exactly call it being nauseated, but it was similar. His skin felt tight, almost drawn toward something in front of him and to the left. He looked that way but didn't see anything. He was fully aware of the people around him—the man whose deodorant had given up; the cute blond girl coming up from behind with her toddler firmly attached to her hip; the dour-looking cashier whose face looked specifically designed for sucking lemons under her too-thick layers of makeup—but for the moment they were almost insignificant. The off feeling running through his flesh made them dwindle to mere sensory input.

He focused instead on the sensations coming his way, the odd pulling that almost demanded his awareness. Through the large windows at the front of the store he saw several cars, mostly parked, a few of them in motion, and he saw a few people here and there as well. From behind the sign that offered him "Hamburger at $1.19 per pound," he saw two figures moving fast in the direction of the Acme. One was obviously running away from the other, judging by the frantic actions being taken—the way the partially obscured form weaved and moved indecisively, as if trying to find an escape route. Wherever he might have been running, the figure finally decided the grocery store was his best refuge.

Chris felt his entire body tense as the legs and lower body he'd seen past the white paper banner stuck to the window came into view. The man was hardly in perfect shape, either physically or, apparently, financially. His clothes looked like the sort that Goodwill just threw out, and the filth that covered his flesh looked to have been accumulating for at least the last month. The man's face was gaunt and partially hidden behind a thin black beard shot with gray. His hairline had receded, but what hair he did have was long and unkempt. His flesh, what could be seen beneath the layers of dirt and facial hair, was pasty and feverishly sweaty. That last part could merely have been due to the overwhelming heat.

The man following behind him looked to be in slightly better shape, with broader shoulders and less emaciation in general—though he, too, looked like he'd last met with soap sometime in the last century. There were a few differences beside merely his bulk, the largest of which was the nearly homicidal expression of rage on his face. Whatever the skinnier bum had done, it hadn't made him friends with the one in hot pursuit. Even as Chris watched, the one doing the chasing lunged abruptly forward and shoved the skinnier target in the shoulder hard enough to send him rebounding off a support post hidden in a brick façade. The bum let out a grunting noise and hit the edge of the post with bruising force. His head slammed against the chipped brick hard enough to leave a gash and he fell to the ground, stunned.

Chris started forward, intent on stopping the brutal attack, and then made himself stop. It went against his nature to let someone get the crap kicked out of him while he merely watched, but he also had to remember that Brittany was now his charge. He couldn't very well get himself into trouble with the police if he intended to keep his sister safe and out of Child Protective Services.

The taller of the brawling bums, completely unaware of Chris's dilemma, kicked the smaller, wounded one on the side of his head. Several people inside the Acme had taken notice now, and most of them merely made comments under their breath and watched as the fight progressed. Chris bared his teeth and again thought of intervening. He even took a few steps in that direction before he caught himself the second time. He'd only gotten out of the hospital a little over a month ago and, frankly, couldn't exactly afford to go back in again. Nor, for that matter, could he afford gaining the attention of the police. There was a blown-up building in his not-so-distant past that at least one detective was still examining. Detective Callaghan—not Harry, but just as scary—hadn't really bothered him too much in the last few weeks, but he didn't feel a sudden need to remind the man that he was alive.

The smaller of the two combatants scrambled across the dirty concrete and half-crawled into the grocery store, his forehead bleeding a trail of dark red across the ground to mark his passage. His pursuer yelled something incoherent and charged after him, apparently set on finishing the task he had started.

The short, shaggy man apparently didn't feel like

being hit again and Chris couldn't blame him. This time around the man pushed himself into a display of Ragú sauces and sent the jars of sauce cascading across the linoleum floor. Some of them shattered on contact with the ground, but a surprising number managed to remain intact. Somehow, through the avalanche of glass and pasta sauce, the wiry man managed to regain his footing properly. He spun himself around in order to avoid another attack from behind, and several of the people who were near him backed away as if his smell alone could cause sudden blindness.

Shorty panted and whined at the same time, his teeth bared in a feral, frightened expression. Closing in on him, the larger man—the aggressor—charged again. Shorty reached into his voluminous collection of clothing and pulled out a handmade knife. The shaggy man chasing after him barely seemed to notice, at least until the thin blade cut into the clothing covering his stomach. The man backed up quickly, clutching a hand at the gaping wound in his shirt and hissing—not a little hiss of pain like one might make when stepping barefoot on glass. Oh no. This was a *HISS*, like the sound of air exploding from a slashed tire.

Most of the people in the Acme were screaming or protesting the sudden violence that shattered the calm of shopping at the local grocery store. More than a few were actually backing away from the conflict to avoid becoming collateral damage. Chris watched, and maybe he was the only one who noticed when the recently cut man's face changed. For just a moment the features buried under the thick beard and mustache shifted, warped from what they were supposed to be. The mouth opened wide and Chris saw the teeth in that gaping maw as they did the impossible and changed, widening and flattening before they reverted to normal. The nauseated feeling that had been crawling through his flesh since the moment the two bums came into his visual range flared, grew far, far worse for a few seconds, and then subsided as the wounded man's features went back to something approximating normal.

Most of his features. Chris had the misfortune of looking into the man's eyes as they blinked and reopened. He got to see the flares of light and the odd swirling flashes that clashed within the overly dilated pupils. The effect was damned near hypnotic and he stared, his mind not quite willing to accept what he was seeing. It wasn't a trick of light, and it wasn't a funky pair of contact lenses. He was seeing something that should have been impossible, and the sight was enough to bring back memories he was doing his damnedest to forget.

His skin tingled, the sensation only worsening as he looked at the freak in front of him. What had been merely uncomfortable was rapidly becoming painful, especially on the parts of his body that had been most grievously wounded in the explosion that had put him in the hospital.

Chris stared into those eyes and

The ice he felt growing on his hand—not truly visi-

ble, but he felt it there, sinking deeper and deeper into his body—spread itself to his mind and Chris Corin looked on as the thing began to speak to him without words.

It spoke of endless suffering, torments that would go on for eternity and beyond, and the new and interesting tortures it would find to deal with him if he harmed any more of the Keys. The images it vomited into his very mind in order to communicate were vivid enough to leave Chris staggered far worse than the explosion had managed. He'd felt soiled and filthy when the entity had looked over his life's memories, but this . . . this was far deeper. There was nothing, no part of the alien mind that spoke to him, that he could consider remotely human. He tried to look away, to close his eyes, but it was no good. The darkness of those pupils seemed to draw him in deeper, to suck his will away and leave him to drown in a cold void.

remembered more than he wanted to about what happened in that damnable house. The eyes he stared into brought it back in a violent torrent of dark memories. He made himself look away and stared instead at the shorter of the two men.

Shorty got bold and swung his blade again. This time the other one was ready for him and caught his wrist, squeezing so hard that Chris could hear the bones creaking from ten feet away. The knife fell from a hand that suddenly had no strength and the shorter man cut loose with a wild scream as he bucked and threw himself from side to side, desperately trying to escape the no doubt immense pain. The bigger one was having none of it. Chris saw the man's eyes go back to normal, felt an odd lessening of the weird sensations that were coursing through his body, and at the same time heard the smaller man shriek again as something snapped in his wrist.

The man apparently lacked in finer fighting techniques, but he made up for it by lunging toward his enemy and biting down as hard as he could on the bearded face of his taller opponent. The tall man went berserk right around the same time his shorter adversary sank teeth into his cheek. He let out a howl and started using his limbs the way Indiana Jones used a bullwhip, flailing and slashing in a seemingly chaotic but oddly graceful assault. He hit more often than he missed.

The two brawlers stumbled and staggered across the front of the store, knocking a few displays over—the second cascade of Ragú spaghetti sauce that hit the floor caused a few people to scream louder than the actual fighting had managed to so far—and coming closer to Chris. He would have backed up and kept his promise to stay out of trouble, he really would have, but then the kid got in the way. He wasn't very old, maybe three or four at the most, and he looked at the two strange men with absolutely no comprehension of how much trouble they could cause him. He may have started catching on when they fell in his direction. The short one was still grabbing the taller one's face with his teeth as they started falling and Chris reacted without thinking. He reached out and grabbed the blond-haired boy by the arm, hauling him out of the way of the two combatants.

He half expected the little kid to scream or struggle, but instead the child just looked at him with wide blue eyes and then ran away. Right around the same time the little munchkin was splitting, the two men fighting each other ran into Chris. He staggered back, his eyes wide, his heart pounding. The men disgusted him. Not because they were dirty, which they were, or even because they were bloody, which was also true, but because they seemed to be the source of the strange nausea he was feeling, and he didn't like it. Hell, part of him wanted to run away and part of him wanted to just lash out at the two men until he could make the weird sensations vanish.

He was still toying with actually getting into the fight himself when the police showed up and stopped him from being stupid.

He backed away quickly, leaving room for the cops to do their business, and then went back to his groceries while the officers sorted everything out. One of the policemen kept staring in his direction, a short, broad-shouldered man who couldn't have looked more Irish if he'd tried. He stared long enough that it made Chris nervous, but beyond that they had no interaction. The police didn't bother questioning witnesses. They had all the information they could possibly need from the employees of the Acme and from the security tapes that were handed over.

Chris was home twenty minutes later. He dropped the grocery bags on the scuffed old linoleum kitchen table and sorted and put the groceries away. He'd forgotten to buy milk, but at that precise moment he couldn't have cared less.

There was something about the fight that bothered him, aside from his own knee-jerk desire to join in, that is. The shorter of the two men had looked familiar. He couldn't have told anyone why, or when he might have met the bum before, but there was definitely something familiar about him.

That odd sense of déjà vu surrounding the man lingered through the rest of his day and into his troubled sleep as well. Chris Corin's sleep was almost always troubled these days. The nightmares had started when his mom died and simply hadn't gone away since then.

II

The next day was better. The next day he just stayed at home and stayed mellow. Brittany was even in a pretty good mood—meaning no sudden emotional explosions and she hadn't called him an asshole even once through the course of the day. He didn't have plans and he didn't really want any. Instead he chilled and waited to see what the day would bring.

This time around, it brought an unexpected party. It started when Courtney St. Clair came over unannounced. He and Courtney had dated for all of a month a few years ago, and in their short history she had been one of the most exasperating women he'd ever known. But with an easygoing smile, dark green eyes and her short dark blond hair, she was always fun to look at. She'd been showing up sporadically ever since his mom died. She was one of a very small contingency of friends that had been there for him and Brittany during that dark time, and while he doubted they would ever date again—though a cynical part of him kept expecting her to move the idea forward now that he was about to be very rich—they had sort of become friends. Today she wasn't really planning on hanging around. She was just supposed to meet up with Katie Gallagher and go off shopping. Somehow his house had become their fairly regular meeting ground and that was okay.

While Courtney was over—and looking as good as ever and in a good mood, which always led his mind down dangerous paths that were most definitely best avoided—he broke into his emergency funds and ordered three pizzas from DeLucci's. He figured, what the hell, he could use the treat and the leftovers would take care of breakfast in the morning. Katie showed up around the same time as the pizzas and footed the bill while he was in the bathroom. Next thing he knew two of the best-looking girls around were sitting down with him and Brittany and eating pizza. Jerry showed up like magic to derail any more bad thoughts about how fine Katie was looking and he brought along beer. Just why Jerry brought beer was a mystery, but Chris was in no hurry to examine the reasoning. And somehow from there, it just sort of quietly exploded into an actual party.

Jerry and Katie were a cute couple, despite the recent efforts that had left them with a few injuries of their own. Katie had long brown hair and deep, dark eyes and a body designed for wet dreams. Jerry was tall and lean and had an easygoing smile and a sense of humor that was as laid back as he was, if a little on the risqué side. Like Chris and Brittany, they had both been at the house fire. Jerry got the worst of the bad things that had gone down in that place, and had the scars to prove it. Most of them were under his clothes, but one scar on his right cheek was still new enough to stand out. Jerry was just lucky it looked more like a dimple than anything else. Chris would have been perfectly pleased if the gathering had stopped with them, but it didn't.

It wouldn't be fair to say that the entire block showed up, but there was a decent percentage of the neighborhood at the very least. Sam Hardwicke and his daughter Diane, cute, blonde and decidedly not interested in Chris, came by. They were sort of just checking in to see how he and Brittany were holding up after their mom had passed—there were a lot of people doing that and he did his best not to take any offense at the idea because their hearts were in the right place. Somehow they managed to stay for a little over two hours. Bill Hollister, whose family had moved away three years ago, made a cameo in the neighborhood and relaxed for most of the night. And so it went on and on, with probably twenty people showing up all told. And it was nice, damn it all, just to forget for a while that his life wasn't exactly going anything at all like he'd planned for it to be going. It was nice to feel like a real person again, even if it was only for a short while.

Somewhere along the way, several of Brittany's little girlfriends showed up, though he couldn't really call half of them little anymore. Every time he turned around one of her friends was suddenly getting curves where there had never been any before, and a few of them were casting looks his way that would get him into serious trouble if he ever thought about acting on them. The law frowned on three years' difference when the definition of legal adult came into play. But he had to remind himself of that fact several times throughout the course of the night.

If he caught his little sister acting that way, he was going to lock her in her room for the next decade. He thought about it for a few seconds and decided maybe it was time to have a talk with her about birth control—preferably abstinence—and also about making sure whatever guy she was with believed in condoms. Though it was tempting to just make her stay home, the idea of dealing with her full-time along with her mood swings did not appeal very much.

He also noticed that a few of the guys he had graduated from high school with were looking at Brittany with a different sort of eye than they had in the past, and he didn't like that one little bit. If any of them

15

made comments, he might have to make a few of his own. The fact that Brittany was hanging with a group of girls who looked like that wasn't easing his mind. He wondered how his mom had managed to put up with it all the time.

While he was contemplating what to do about the entire Brittany affair, Courtney came over and sat on his lap. They'd fooled around a few times when they were dating, but she had grown up a lot since then, and having her derriere resting firmly on his bulge was doing nothing to make him comfortable. Courtney—who loved being the center of attention as much as some people loved the ability to walk or breathe—only made matters worse by deliberately sliding herself around in his lap several times. She knew what she was doing and was having a blast at his expense. He didn't mind now, of course, but the cold shower later was going to be pure hell.

"Where have you been all my life, stud?" She made her voice extra sultry as she slid her ass along his front side and blew in his ear. He knew better than to take it seriously, but if the room hadn't been full of people he just might have tried his luck anyway. It had been far, far too long since he'd gotten laid.

One of Brittany's friends—*Kara? Lisa? Monica?* He could never keep them separated in his mind—wrapped her arms around his neck and hugged him from behind. She had definitely been growing and apparently so was he, because when she rested her cheek against his face and smiled, Courtney threw out a deep chuckle and whispered, "Easy, Tiger."

Oh yes, far too long.

Brittany was flirting with David Hines, a jock who had been on the football team with Chris. Good ol' Dave flirted right back until he saw the murderous look Chris threw his way. By the time Brittany caught on and looked in her big brother's direction, he was back to enjoying the far-too-flirty actions of Courtney. They weren't dating and it would never work out. He knew that, honest. His body on the other hand didn't care. Courtney kept torturing him for at least another twenty minutes, by which time he'd almost had to change his shorts. She was not blatant when she moved her body over his, but she was very good at keeping his soldier at attention and ready for combat. It was wonderful and it was pure hell.

As the night progressed, everyone mellowed out. It wasn't really the sort of party where they were going to be dancing in the streets or anywhere else. Most of the neighbors said their goodnights, as did a few of his buds from high school, and Brittany and her little jail-bait contingent slinked themselves over to another part of the room and settled in for a juicy gossip session.

Courtney had moved back over to sit next to Katie, her feet propped on Jerry's lap, which Katie was good enough to ignore. Chris sat nearby, but not actually in the middle of the conversation, reveling in how much he'd been missing just sitting around and shooting the shit. Several people Chris barely knew, and a few he was pretty sure were complete strangers, had made themselves at home, and somewhere along the way more pizzas showed up and the beers were replenished. The place was just sort of pleasantly buzzing with a few quiet conversations and the occasional joke that was passed from group to group.

The only sour note during the entire party was Jerry, and that wasn't really sour so much as a reason for worry. Chris was sitting on the couch and talking to a couple of his chums from high school whom he hadn't seen since graduation. Brad Henreid was talking about his plans to go into a vocational school and become a mechanic—not because he couldn't have done anything he damned well pleased, which he could have, but because he loved cars. And next to him John Constado was moaning about going to a local college instead of out to Cal Tech where he really wanted to be.

Jerry was sitting only a few feet away, chatting with Katie and grinning ear to ear, his hand automatically rubbing Courtney's bare feet—and again he was amazed that Katie didn't want to beat the crap out of her best friend. It was rare when Jerry wasn't at least smiling a little. He looked pale, but then he'd never exactly been a slave to the sun's rays. Pale was practically his usual color. Everything was going along fine until Bill Hollister patted him on the back and Jerry damned near passed out. His face went from lazy grin to a wide wince and his color went from pale to stark white. The Heineken in his hand fell to the floor, the bottle rolling and dribbling the last few dregs rather than shattering. At that precise moment, Katie was whispering in Courtney's ear and having a conversation about God alone knew what. Probably no one in the room but Chris and Bill saw Jerry flinch. Bill stepped back as if he'd accidentally shot Jerry with what he thought was a toy gun. Jerry sat perfectly still, his teeth bared and his eyelids closed and fluttering. It was a look that said he was processing the pain and trying to get past it. Before Chris could really absorb the entire thing, it was over, but he started to stand up and check on his best friend anyway.

Which was when the blond girl from the Acme the day before intercepted him. He recognized her immediately, with her long, pale blond hair and broad smile—an expression she had not had the day before, but which made her, if anything, even more attractive—she caught his attention as easily as a barbed hook catches a greedy carp.

"Hi, you're Chris, right?" Her voice was light and husky and made him think about the sort of things that weren't supposed to be considered in polite company. He laid part of the blame on Courtney, as he hadn't yet recovered from her earlier lap dance.

"Guilty as charged." He smiled at her, noticing out of the corner of his eye that Jerry seemed better now. He'd check on Jerry later if there was still a problem. "Do I know you?" He made a mental note to work on his subtlety techniques.

"Not really, but I needed to thank you for what you did yesterday." He went over a quick assessment: he'd met her, smiled at her and gone on his way. That was pretty much all he could remember doing.

"Well, you're welcome. But could you tell me what I did to warrant thanks?"

Her smile broadened, and she rolled her eyes in embarrassment. He liked the flush that came to her cheeks and the dimples that pulled at the corners of her lips. Yep. She was a cute one. And she wasn't even wearing any makeup, or if she was it was very, very subtle.

Her mouth moved, and he remembered to listen to the words that came out of it, instead of just staring at the gentle changes in the shape of her lips. "Well, yesterday at the grocery store? You pulled a little kid away from the two freaks that were fighting?" He nodded. "That was my little brother, Jason. You saved his butt from getting hurt by those creeps, and I wanted to thank you."

Chris blinked, taken aback. He hadn't really even given thought to the kid he had grabbed, he just grabbed and then ignored. "Well, you're welcome. But I really didn't do anything but move him. He wasn't really in any danger, I don't think."

"He would have been squished at the very least. So thank you." She smiled again and Chris tried to think of something witty to say. Nothing was coming to mind.

Just before the silence could become awkward, Jerry

20

let out another yelp of pain and Chris turned his head to see his best friend rising from his seat, his arms wrapped protectively over his ribs. The tendons in Jerry's neck were strung so tightly under his skin that they looked like suspension wires holding a bridge in place. His skin was pasty white and sweating heavily. Bill Hollister was backing away, his eyes showing confusion and a little fear.

Chris said a quick "excuse me" and took off, moving to Jerry's side with almost the same speed as Katie. Katie beat him by a heartbeat, putting her hand on Jerry's shoulder. Jerry didn't even seem to think about it, he just swung his arm at whatever was touching him and damn near knocked Katie sprawling across the sofa he'd just vacated. Katie fell back, her eyes wide, her face almost comically shocked. It might have been funny if Jerry hadn't looked so enraged at the moment. Jerry, who was about the most laid back human being Chris had ever known, looked dangerously angry, like he was perfectly willing to move over to Katie and finish what he'd started by, say, taking an ax to the side of her head.

Chris intercepted before Jerry could do any of the things he seemed to be thinking about. "Yo, Jerry. Calm down, man. Everything's cool." Jerry looked murderously in his direction for half a second, his eyes dark and furious, then abruptly calmed down. He shook his head and looked over at Katie, his face suddenly apologetic.

"Oh, shit, Katie. I'm so sorry." Now, it's fair to say

21

Chris had seen a few fights between Katie and Jerry over the years they'd been dating. After three years together it was pretty much inevitable that he'd have seen at least a few skirmishes. So he knew to back up before Katie got off the ground and was fast enough to warn Bill away before things got ugly.

Katie managed to rise from her semi-prone position, half on the couch and half on the floor, to a full standing battle ready stance before Chris could do anything else. Jerry was so busy being apologetic—and Chris could see he meant it—that he didn't have time to react either. Katie planted both hands on his chest and shoved hard enough to send him staggering backward. Brittany of all people managed to defuse the situation. Her thin little body slithered between Katie and Jerry before they could reach a complete meltdown stage and she spoke calmly and pleasantly to the both of them while she planted one hand on each of their chests. That worked for her. If Chris had planted a hand on Katie's chest she'd have knocked his head off his shoulders and Jerry would have kicked his testicles from where they were to Texas.

Brittany, his little sister, and the number-one pain in his ass, managed to calm the two down and in a few minutes even had everything else smoothed out. He had to remember to thank her later.

Somehow the party continued without further incidents. It was nice to actually relax and not have to worry for a change of pace. There was still no money and they were still on the dregs of what could be called their food supplies in the Corin household, but he didn't figure to worry about it just then.

Chris mingled for a while and spent some time talking to the new girl he'd inadvertently made friends with. Her name was Laura, and they had a few things in common, mostly a serious case of financial straits and a decided indecision about what they were going to do regarding college. In his case there was Brittany. In her case there was her little brother and running the family business. Her parents were alive but neither of them was in very good shape after having been caught in a house fire at the beginning of the summer. Her mother was in a coma and showed no signs of improving. Her father had been blinded in the incident and was still trying to figure out the simplest things, like getting to the bathroom without killing himself on every piece of furniture in the house. The idea of him actually running the store was beyond merely ludicrous. If her parents were recovering at all it was very, very slowly.

Her family owned a bookstore, and currently she was running the place most of the time with the occasional help of a rather unreliable cousin. Today was a rarity; said cousin had shown up and seemed inclined to earn the money she paid him. He could hear a lot of bitterness beneath her pleasant tones. He could also understand the cause of the sour attitude. She'd likely had plans. They had been changed when life threw a hardball and hit her in the back of the head.

Before they really had much time to speak, she was

gone. While she trusted her cousin to a moderate degree, she didn't trust him to tend to her parents's needs. Laura left before the party started breaking up. After that Chris went from small group to small group and played catch-up with several of his high school chums. It felt strange, and even in some cases, forced, to speak with them. Their lives were moving on. His was at a standstill and there was nothing he could do about it at the present time. They had college or in one case the military ahead of them, and he had his house and his little sister and thoughts about, someday, actually going ahead.

He tried not to be bitter, but it wasn't always easy.

Eventually the party faded. Most of the people left and a few—like Jerry and Katie, who were now on the rebound from their earlier conflict—stayed around to help clean up the mess. Surprisingly, the mess wasn't as bad as he'd have expected even a few months ago. Maybe that was part of growing up. Maybe it was just a happy accident.

When they were all done, Chris sat back and opened a second beer. He'd considered having more, but there were those damned responsibilities in the way again. When they were mostly done cleaning and Jerry had settled in the chair across the battered old table from him, Chris did what best friends do and asked him what was wrong.

"Nothing's wrong, man." Jerry looked at him with his head lowered and his eyebrows raised. It made him look a lot younger than he was. "Who said there was anything wrong?"

"Dude. I was talking to a really cute girl and I actually had to leave that talk because you and Bill looked like you were gonna go round and round." Chris shrugged and took a sip of Heineken. "You're normally most likely to just let an insult slide but you looked like caving his face in wouldn't have hurt your feelings any."

"He didn't say anything to hurt my feelings, Chris. He slapped me on the back and his hand hit my ribs." Jerry looked at him and made a motion with his arm that encompassed the sides of his rib cage. He looked like he was talking about a bad case of the crabs, as if the wounds he'd gotten on his rib cage were the embarrassment of his entire family and not for social discussion. "Where I was hurt this summer."

During the insanity that had taken over Chris's life for a short time, Jerry had been taken captive by the strange cult that had been seeking a necklace, of all things, to bring changes to the world. Through a method that Chris couldn't hope to comprehend, they had plugged his best friend into a plant and made a duplicate to deceive him. The plant would have slowly eaten Jerry away and had actually done enough damage in a few hours to leave Jerry in the hospital for most of a week. Their method of using Jerry had involved literally plugging him into the plant that made a copy of him. He had several scars on his rib cage where he had been plugged in place. There had been eight of the damned things stuck in between his ribs, and when they'd been pulled out Jerry had moaned and writhed across the ground as a long series of roots had been yanked from his insides.

Jerry had been in agony, but was still intact. Several of the people the rootlike things had been inside of had suffered much worse. They'd been there longer and the things had been eating them from the inside out. Chris remembered looking at one woman who had been consumed by the things, her flesh rotted away, her muscles and internal organs exposed, and remembered how she had thrashed inside her organic prison. Her death, he kept telling himself, had been a mercy. It helped to think that way because it was really his decision to leave her and several others behind to burn when the house they were in caught fire.

He shook that thought away and thought instead about Jerry. "So, what? It's still tender there?"

"Not quite." Jerry looked away from him, flipping his head so that his overly long bangs slid away from his eyes. "It isn't healing right."

"Jerry, dude. That was almost two months ago. What the hell are you talking about?"

"I mean there's some kind of infection and it won't go away." Jerry looked back at him, his eyes half lidded, like he was trying to bluff his way through a weak poker hand.

"Why didn't you say something earlier, man?" His heart fell. Christ alone knew what the hell those things had been or how they might have affected Jerry. He could still remember pulling the heavy gray filaments from Jerry's sides and seeing the thick blood flow spilling from the wounds. He remembered the way Jerry had screamed when the first of the vines was tugged from his side.

"Not really the sort of thing you just mention in conversation, Chris." He took a sip of his beer. "Besides, that was my main reason for coming over today."

"You've been to the doctor, right?"

Jerry shook his head, irritated by the comment. "No, Chris, I thought I'd just fucking let it sit and fester, maybe see what grew there."

"Okay, dumb question." Jerry nodded enthusiastically. "What did the doctors say?"

"They don't know what to say. They've got me on buttloads of antibiotics and they've taken samples for examination. Other than that . . ." He shrugged.

Chris was at a loss for words. It just wasn't the sort of thing you expected to run across. It wasn't the sort of thing that happened to people you knew. He shunted his mind away from the thought that your mother wasn't supposed to die in a flaming car wreck, either. He tried hard not to think about that. It was too painful to deal with.

Jerry sighed and shifted in his seat. "Here's the thing. They know it isn't cancerous. It isn't growing or changing, it just doesn't want to heal the right way and it itches like a bitch. Mostly it's a lot of scar tissue, but there are a couple of spots they've had to cut out for examination and those are the places where the infection is worst. So long as it doesn't suddenly become contagious or something they're cool with me being out of the hospital. Not happy, but cool. If it changes, I might get put in a room and kept there until they can cut it all out of me or whatever the hell they think they have to do."

"Shit, Jerr . . ."

"So basically, I get to hope it gets better and they get to try to decide what it is."

"Does it hurt?"

"Not really. It isn't really comfortable and it itches, like I said, but it isn't like it's crippling me."

"And you've been dealing with this since the—since the fire?"

Jerry shrugged. "Yeah, but it's not like it's the only thing in my life or anything, man. It's just something that's going on."

"What's Katie got to say about it?"

"Nothing." Jerry looked over at Katie and Courtney and Brittany, his face going into poker mode again.

"You haven't told her, have you?"

"She knows it's sore. That's about all."

"Shit. What the hell are you thinking?"

"I'm thinking she doesn't need to worry about this crap; she's got enough to worry about already."

Chris found he once again had no answer to that. Mostly because he didn't know what was going on in Katie's life. He'd been a little too absorbed with what was going on in his own.

Eventually everyone went home. For the first time in weeks, Chris went to bed genuinely tired. But a good tired. He'd had a day with little to worry him except for Jerry's injuries, and while they were troublesome, they were less of a concern than they might have been, because even Jerry seemed almost at ease about them.

He settled himself into his bed and turned on the TV as he did most nights lately. A cold can of Pepsi and little else was there to see him through the night. On the television a man with perfect hair and a thousand-watt smile was reciting the latest news. He finished a story about an apartment fire—they lost everything they had, but no one was seriously injured—and the picture situated next to the man's face switched to a different scene; two policemen were dragging a wildly struggling man out of a squad car and toward a decidedly institutional building. Chris had been there before, though he never liked it. It was a police station.

But the building was of little consequence and even the police didn't much matter. What was far more significant was the face of their captive. The last time he'd seen the face had been the day before, when the lower part of the very same face was covered in blood and the beard had been matted with the thick, drying fluids. The image was still burned into his mind and it wasn't likely to go away anytime soon.

Curious, he turned up the volume. The news anchor's face turned solemn as he spoke about the man being arrested as a suspect in the murder of several homeless people in the city. ". . . Authorities believe that Arthur Hall could be responsible for as many as eight murders in the area within the last two months. Hall himself was reported missing by his family last April, and has only recently been identified by fingerprint evidence. He has so far been unwilling to cooperate with the authorities and has refused to answer any questions.

"Only fifteen minutes after we initially aired this story, the suspect, Arthur Hall, was found dead in his holding cell. Police spokesman Everett Cartwright has declined to comment, save to say that an investigation into the suspect's death has become a priority."

Chris blinked sleepily, and turned down the volume on the television to a mere whisper. His mind did a few slow loops as he ruminated over the death of a man he'd seen alive only a day before. He turned off the lights in the room and closed his eyes, leaving the glare from the TV as his only source of illumination as he drifted off to sleep. The man's death was uncomfortably close to home, but not enough to make him rest uneasily. There was still something about the man that seemed very familiar, but he couldn't place it and he was simply too tired to care at the time.

IV

The sun in his eyes was what woke him. The glare finally got through Chris's troubled dreams and rather rudely tapped his conscious mind on the shoulder until he finally made his way lazily to consciousness.

Getting out of bed was the last thing he wanted to do.

Still, the day would hardly be well spent if he did nothing but sleep, and his mother would surely roll over in her grave if he did. Remembering the desecration of her grave a few months ago and the decidedly unpleasant experience of looking down on her mortal remains, he shuddered at the notion. Definitely time to get out of bed.

He pulled on the jeans he'd worn yesterday and stumbled groggily from his room. Breakfast would be good. Or, judging by the position of the sun through the window, maybe brunch would be a better definition.

Despite his own efforts—and to be honest, those of Katie, Courtney and his own sister, the house looked pretty much like a disaster area. The kitchen sink was full of dishes, the furniture in the living room was just plain dirty, and the coffee table had accumulated a plethora of rings from the bottoms of glasses and a few piles of cigarette butts were scattered all over the wooden surface.

He thought about it for all of five seconds and then reached for the remote control. After turning on the TV, Chris went on to the kitchen and started on the dishes. They would not, he'd noticed, wash themselves, no matter how hard he willed it. The news made good background noise, and he hardly needed to look at the anchors to hear them talking about what was going in the city or the suburbs around him. It didn't take all that long for him to finish in the kitchen. He opened the refrigerator and then the freezer, found one of the dollar-and-nineteen-cent concoctions his sister called "cardboard pizza," and threw it into the oven at the appropriate temperature before he started in on the living room. By the time the pizza was ready, he'd finished with damage control. He sat down on the couch and sank his teeth into the first slice, letting himself focus on the news.

The dead man from the grocery store was on the news again and the story had gotten strange enough that Chris sat with a mouthful of half-chewed imitation pizza in his mouth, watching with the sort of focus he normally reserved only for very attractive women.

The man's body was missing. They'd had it nicely locked away in a meat locker, waiting, no doubt, for the coroner to give it the once over, and somehow they'd managed to lose the body. The police were understandably upset, but they were also convinced it was merely a clerical error, at least according to the portly man in the business suit who was answering questions for a handful of reporters.

The picture on the tube flashed to a different-looking man than the one Chris has seen at the grocery store. Different, but obviously the same man. He was clean shaven for one thing. He was fleshier, bordering on fat. His face was smiling and he had his arms around two little girls and the woman with them in the picture. The faces of the innocent had been blocked out by whatever amounted to Hollywood magic in the area, leaving thick, luxurious hair and a blurred, shadowy blank slate behind. He could see that this was the same Arthur Hall, but he would have never made the connection if he'd spotted the man walking down the street in that state.

"Arthur Hall is survived by his wife and two children, who have declined to speak with the press at this time. Our thoughts are with them." The man on the TV intoned his solemn words and managed to look almost sincere. Chris looked at Arthur Hall's round, jovial face until it was replaced by two hockey teams sliding across the ice, their sticks held high like swords.

He thought again of the tall, thin man whose face changed in front of him at the store, who had taken a bite out of his victim's flesh like he was eating an apple, and had trouble accepting that the nice-looking business type on the screen, complete with receding hairline, could have been the same man.

In the long run, it couldn't be too important. The man was dead now and it wasn't like he knew him or anything. But that damned voice in the back of his head begged to differ. It insisted that Chris had seen the man before, that he knew him from somewhere and that while they had never exactly been friends, he'd met him more than once. He swallowed his pizza without any pleasure whatsoever and then looked up as Brittany came into the room.

Anyone looking at Chris and Brittany next to each

other would have to look hard to convince themselves that the two were siblings. Chris was stocky, muscular and dark-haired. He had been quite the little halfback on the football team and had spent a few summers learning how to box from the sort of men who believed the best way to stay in shape was to lift iron all day. He was muscular to the point where it was almost embarrassing. Brittany, in contrast, was tall and thin and starting toward elegant. Her face was pretty enough with full lips and bright blue eyes, her hair was that shade of red that almost always seemed to come out of a bottle, but in her case didn't. She was starting to look more and more like her mother, and that meant—as far as Chris was concerned—that she was going to be stunning when she finally finished going through the changes of puberty. Just six months ago you'd have been hard pressed to believe she had breasts or ever would. These days she was wearing a real bra as opposed to that training thing he always called her slingshot. The thought always left him a little uncomfortable. Both of them had fair skin—a side effect of being Irish, he supposed—and both of them managed to endure growing fields of freckles wherever the sun found their flesh, but that was about all they had in common physically.

Brittany looked at his pizza and leaned over, grabbing two slices before he could have stopped her. Her hair was pulled back in a ponytail, which was a blessing in his eyes because otherwise the rest of his brunch might have been covered in the fallout from her tresses.

"Morning." She spoke around the bite of pizza she shoved into her mouth.

" 'S'up, squirt?"

"Cost of tea in China." She looked around and wrinkled her nose. "And the fumes from yesterday. This place still smells like beer." He sniffed and nodded, feeling a quick wave of nausea. Ever since the events earlier in the year he had hated the scent of stale beer. It was too close a reminder to things he was trying his very best to forget.

"I gotta get some Lysol. I hate that smell."

"Well. Don't drink." She smiled like a perky little cheerleader and he mock-scowled in her direction.

"Didn't see you ignoring the stuff." He grabbed up another piece of his meal before his sister could finish inhaling what she had in her hands. She'd already killed off the first slice and was eyeing the remaining slices. "I shouldn't let you do that. You aren't old enough."

She stuck her tongue out at him and then took a bite from the other victim in her hand. "Neither are you."

"True that." Brittany sat next to him on the sofa, in easy reach of his cardboard meal. He ate faster and so did she, in silent acknowledgment of the contest that had begun. They continued eating in silence until the picture of Arthur Hall showed up on the screen again as the broadcaster recapped the news stories.

"I keep getting the idea I know him. Does he look familiar?" Brittany looked at the TV and reached for the last slice of pizza at the same time. She picked up the slice and held it in her hand as her face got a little paler.

"Yeah. I do." That was as far as she got when the phone rang. Before he could ask her where she knew him from, she bolted off the edge of the sofa where she had been perched and lunged for the phone. Her panty-clad hip bumped him and he had to scramble to catch his last piece of pizza before it fell to the ground. She'd managed to bump it out of his hand with the greatest of ease.

"Hello?" Brittany nodded, looking a little puzzled. "Yes, this is Brittany Corin. Who's this?"

Chris watched Brittany's face get even paler, her blue eyes widening. "You're who? My grandmother?" His sister's voice sounded as stunned as it should have: They had never met the woman who was on the phone. They had seldom even heard about her from their mother. Their grandmother was, like virtually every member of their family aside from their now deceased mother, a complete mystery. That was the way Eileen Corin had always kept it.

Chris turned his head so fast he pulled muscles in his neck. There were few things he could have expected less. He looked at his sister and watched her closely as she spoke into the phone.

"What? Oh, yes. No, we're doing all right." His sister nodded, her lips thinning as she pressed them together. "No. No . . . No. Look, I don't even really know you, why would I want—?" She shook her head and closed her eyes and her face paled even more. "That's not true. No, I have Chris to watch over me; and besides, I'm not five, I'm fourteen." Brittany shook her head angrily and blinked her eyes at around a hundred miles per hour. "No. I don't want to come stay with you and I don't even want to meet you. Where were you when my mother was dying? Where were you when Chris was in the hospital?" Her voice was increasing in volume to the point where she was basically yelling into the receiver.

Chris reached over and plucked the phone from her hand as Brittany started to cry through her screaming session with the voice on the other end of the line.

"Hello? Who is this?" He already knew, of course, but that didn't stop him from making her tell him.

"Christopher?" The voice was old and cultured, blue-blood New England through and through. Thurston Howell the Third was alive and well and a woman, apparently. She didn't sound like the millionaire's wife on the phone; his grandmother sounded more like a man in timbre and confidence, even if her voice was feminine. "Christopher, this is your grandmother."

"Which one?" If she was expecting a friendly reaction she was mistaken. He had never known any of his grandparents and wasn't suddenly feeling the need for a family reunion.

"I'm sorry?" She sounded both confused and amused by his brusque tone.

"I said 'which one.' I have two grandmothers and I've never met either of 'em. So who are you?"

"Young man, there's hardly any reason to be so curt."

"My ass. I see my sister going into tears on the phone and I want to know why. So who are you and what can I do for you?"

"You're a very direct young man. I admire that. Very well. My name is Rebecca Carlysle Corin, and I am your maternal grandmother. I called because I want to see about visiting you. My intentions are simple: I want to meet your sister, and you, of course, dear boy, and I want to offer my help to the two of you. I imagine by now your finances are virtually non-existent and I think I can provide aid to the both of you. You are blood, after all, despite whatever stories your mother might have told you."

"No thanks. Not interested."

"Christopher, I can only imagine what you must think of me. I have never been a part of your life and I want to rectify that. Your mother—my daughter—and I had our differences, but that never meant I didn't love her and it certainly never meant that I didn't want to be a part of your lives. I was respecting your mother's wishes." Her voice didn't sound plaintive or the least worried. She could have been discussing what canapés to have at a dinner party.

He sighed and closed his eyes. Maybe he was being too harsh. All he had to go on was the little his mother would say about the woman on the phone, and most of what she had said had been about her early child-hood. She never discussed why she and her mother didn't speak. It was one of the taboo subjects in the house. Eileen Corin had seldom raised her voice to her children, and she had seldom needed to. She had never yelled about how horrible her mother was or anything along those lines, she had merely never given answers about the woman, even when Chris or Brittany had asked.

"Okay, so what did you have in mind?"

"I was thinking I could come down and see you, see how you're making out and possibly offer a little financial assistance. I wouldn't want to stay with you; I know that would be inconvenient and I don't want to impose. But perhaps we could meet a few times and we could discuss the best way to get your sister adjusted to the idea of coming to live with me."

"Excuse me?"

"Brittany. She's far too young to be on her own and the last thing you need is the burden of raising a teenage girl when you're barely an adult yourself and ready to head off to college soon, I'm sure."

Chris looked at Brittany. She was looking right back at him, her pale face wet from where tears had fallen and a desperate look on her face. He knew his sister very well, knew her as only a sibling can know a sibling in a tight-knit family. She wanted to head off to live with their grandmother about as much as he wanted to run razor blades up and down his penis for fun.

"That's not going to happen."

"I'm sorry?" Her voice sounded like she was having trouble with the notion that anyone would ever deny her anything she wanted. Apparently it just didn't happen. Well, it was time for the old bag to learn how things worked in the real world.

"It's not happening. You aren't going to get custody of Brittany. She doesn't want to live with you and she isn't going into protective services and she isn't going to live on the street. I'll take care of her, just the way our mom would have wanted."

"Christopher . . ."

"You want to come down and visit, maybe we can arrange that. But Brittany isn't leaving this house." He felt his jaws clenching and forced himself to relax a bit. "That's the closest you're getting to having custody."

"I could force the matter, Christopher. I don't want to, but I will if I have to. Your sister needs a stable environment and a chance to get properly educated in the finer ways of life."

"Brittany needs to stay right where she is, lady."

"I have lawyers, Christopher. I will use them as I find necessary."

"What a coincidence. So do I."

"Christopher, why are you being so unreasonable?"

"Because Brittany doesn't want shit to do with you, Mrs. Corin. Neither do I, for that matter. I don't know what happened between you and my mother and I don't really care. All I know is she probably would have done everything she could to keep you away from my sister. That's as good a recommendation as I need."

"You're being unreasonable, young man." Her voice had grown far more aggressive. She sounded like a general preparing to bark orders to his troops, and she sounded like she intended to destroy anything that got in her way.

"You're being annoying. Don't call again. Don't bother to visit, don't bother to send a fucking Christmas card; not that you ever did. You're not a part of our lives and we don't want anything to do with you. Understood?"

"Clearly. You'll be hearing from my attorneys within the next few days."

"Bring it on, Grandma. You just do what you have to do and I'll take care of my sister the way I see fit."

He slammed the receiver into its cradle and closed his eyes. The opportunity he had longed for, to have someone else to take care of his financial woes and to handle making sure Brittany was safe, had just been waved in his face and summarily slapped by his own hand. And why? Because he loved his sister, even if she was a pain in the ass and a pizza thief. And because there was no way she would ever be happy with their grandmother.

"Chris?" Brittany's voice was plaintive.

He looked over at his sister and pulled her into a one-armed hug. "Don't sweat it. I sent the old hag packing."

"I don't want to live with her. She sounds like a doctor."

41

"A doctor?"

"Yeah, the kind that tells you you have cancer and hands you a bill for half a million dollars at the same time."

"She sounds like an old mule with an attitude." Brittany hugged him briefly before pulling back. "Don't sweat it, Brit. I'm not letting her take you anywhere you don't want to go."

"Good. Because I don't want anything to do with her." Brittany looked at the shabby rug under her feet and then over to the sofa. She flopped down with all the grace of a boulder, the springs of the old sofa protesting weakly beneath her.

Chris looked over at the phone like it might suddenly rear up and bite at him. "Me either."

He thought about college and about how much easier it would be if he could pass the buck regarding his sister. Then he swallowed the thought down like a bitter medicine. That just wasn't going to happen.

Still, it would have made life so much easier. . . .

He walked into the kitchen, looked at the corkboard near the phone, and found his lawyer's number. Of course the law offices wouldn't be open today, but that hardly mattered. All he wanted to do was leave Sterling Armstrong a message about the possible custody problems. His attorney was supposed to be one of the best, and he was also one of the most expensive. If Jerry's dad hadn't vouched for Chris, the man would have never given him the time of day. So far his work was all gratis, but that would change the instant Chris got his first check from the lottery.

He dialed and closed his eyes again. He could feel the headache building inside his skull and hoped it wouldn't be one that lasted all through the day.

Chapter Two

I

Sometimes he thought his sister was a raving lunatic. Other times he was sure of it. As if his words meant in reassurance had instead convinced her that Chris was going to immediately send her off to live with their grandmother, Brittany went into all-out bitch mode. She spent the rest of the morning pacing around the house and then all but kicked down the door in an effort to get out as quickly as possible just after noon.

Chris paced around for about an hour before deciding to give her some space. What he wanted to do was grab her by the back of her neck and drag her scrawny ass all the way back to the house. Instead, he waited. If she pulled another stunt where she was gone most of the night he would work out a suitable punishment, but for now he had to give her some space.

He wondered how it was his mom hadn't just dumped them both at an orphanage. He could remember a few times when he'd been almost as much of an ass. He let himself think over a few of the worst occasions and felt himself get flustered. Being a legal guardian to his little sister had never been on his plans. Damn, but it would have been easier just to say yes to his grandmother.

Jerry came through the front door about twenty minutes after Brittany left. He didn't knock, but Chris didn't exactly expect him to. Jerry wasn't looking his best. In addition to being a little green around the old gills, he had an expression on his face that said all was most definitely not going the way he would like it to.

Jerry nodded and dropped a brown bag on the table. Chris's stomach rumbled when he caught the scent of a seriously greasy cheese steak wafting from the innocent looking package.

Bribery. It had to be serious. Chris nodded a hello and pulled one of the wrapped sandwiches from the depths of the bag. Even as he did that, Jerry set down two bottles of Stewart's root beer. Chris and Jerry ate in silence for a few minutes, reverting to nearly savage states of mind as they inhaled food and drink alike. When the food was gone, Chris leaned back and nodded his thanks. Jerry returned the gesture and sighed mightily.

"So, what did you do this time?"

"Katie's pissed off."

"Like I said. What did you do this time?"

Jerry shook his head and shrugged, which could have meant *I don't know*, but which Chris interpreted properly as *wait a minute, I have to figure out how to answer that without seeming like a complete asshole.* Chris waited. What else could he do? Jerry was his best friend, and besides, he'd just been properly bribed. Cheese steaks and Stewart's went a long, long way toward improving his patience.

"We had a fight about me not telling her what's going on. She said she knows I'm hiding something from her and it's pissing her off." He looked at Chris and shook his head. "Man, I don't want to tell her what's going on. I don't want her worrying that much."

"How bad is it? The infection, I mean."

Jerry pulled his shirt up and exposed his torso. Heavy gauze and tape covered most of his chest, but there were several spots where seepage had discolored the previously sterile cotton. With his lips pressed tightly together, as if anticipating the sting of pulling tape and maybe taking with it a few layers of skin, Jerry caught the lowest square of bandage and adhesive and pulled it free.

Chris flinched in sympathy and then flinched a second time when he saw the wound that lay beneath the wrappings. The scar wasn't a perfect circle, but Chris hadn't really expected that. It looked more like a cross section of thin wood placed against Jerry's skin and then carefully covered with makeup. The rough edges of the wound were raised and puffy. The scar tissue looked shiny and tight, and here and there small red sores ran close to the surface of his scarred flesh. The patches of red were dark, almost bloody in color, and reminded Chris of the time Brittany had managed to get ringworm. These were not perfect circles, but the had the same sort of hollowed out appearance.

"Damn, Jerry." He thought about touching the spot and changed his mind.

"Yeah, I know it isn't pretty. What bothers me is it won't go away." There was something more there, and Chris knew it. Jerry wasn't saying something significant and was trying to be casual about whatever he was hiding. Chris let it slide. Jerry would talk about it when he was ready.

"Dude. You think these little sores are worth ruining what you and Katie have?"

Jerry looked down into Chris's face sharply, turning his head so he could see the man near his rib cage. "Of course not. Don't be a dumbass."

"Then I think you better get off your ass and tell her what's going on."

"You don't get it, man. She didn't really take well to what happened."

"The house fire?" He could see the problem: Jerry was his best friend, they'd been through a lot together, but even now neither of them wanted to talk about what had happened at the derelict house earlier that summer. Neither one of them wanted to remember the fire or the events that led up to it. Surely Jerry had no desire to remember all of the things his doppelganger had done.

Jerry put the bandage back over the scar on his chest, careful to lay it out as smoothly as possible. "What else? If you think that hasn't been a fun subject to avoid, guess again."

"Look. I know what happened sucked. And you know I can never say how grateful I am to both of you." Chris felt himself get flustered. Even thinking about the things they'd all seen and his confrontation with whatever it was that had tried to force itself into this universe was enough to make his stomach ache. "But you guys need to talk about it if only to get past the shit that's happening between the two of you." He looked at the bandages on Jerry's chest. "Maybe you need to show her just to let her know that you're still healing. I mean, I know you two are . . . intimate . . . Maybe you should show her without the bandages after the next time you two . . ."

"Get nasty? Have wild and crazy sex? Bump uglies?" Jerry looked down at the rug under his feet and started putting his shirt back on, the bandages hiding the play of his muscles. Thinking back, Chris realized he hadn't seen his best friend without a shirt all summer, and that was probably the longest he'd ever seen Jerry not take off his shirt when the heat was high enough to allow it. It was almost as weird as everything else that had happened. Damn, even the little things in his life were messed up from what had taken place. How could he think it hadn't affected anyone else as badly?

Jerry looked at him. "That hasn't happened in a long while, dude."

"Say what?"

"Katie and me. We haven't been intimate for over two months."

"Because of the bandages?"

"That's part of it." Jerry looked at him again, his eyes half lidded. This was not something he wanted to talk about and it was obvious.

"What else?"

"Like I said, we've been fighting a lot."

"Jerry. That's crap and you know it. You two fight, yeah, but I've only seen a couple of blow-ups between you. Mostly you've both been right as rain."

"Sure. Like you and Brittany have been just chillin'." His voice was more than a little bitter.

Chris blinked and slid from his crouching position, back onto the edge of the coffee table. "You two haven't said anything."

"Yeah, Chris, we haven't. Katie decided you were going through enough shit of your own without us adding any more."

Chris felt his blood pressure rise and clenched his teeth. He knew Katie was trying to do the right thing, but it hurt just the same. He had always been there for his friends and with very rare exceptions—Jerry and Katie not among those exceptions—his friends had always been there for him.

"Well, that shit stops now."

Jerry smiled wryly at the tone of his voice. "Why do you think I'm here, oh great marriage counselor?"

Chris smiled. "Okay, point taken. So, have you thought about what you're gonna tell Katie?"

Jerry dropped a fifty-dollar bill on the table. "Yeah, well, I was sort of hoping you'd take her out to lunch and argue my case."

"Shouldn't we all go out together? So you can be there?"

Jerry looked away from him again. "I have something I really, really need to take care of. Another appointment, with a dermatologist this time. I think it might go better if I wasn't there."

Chris studied his friend for several seconds. "You said something that bad, huh?"

"Yeah. I did. Chris, if you can't make this better I'm gonna lose her. I screwed the pooch this time, man."

"What did you say?"

"Let's just say my temper has been getting pretty crappy. Lack of sex, I guess. But I can't keep myself in check anymore."

"What did you do?"

Jerry Murphy looked at him with the most miserable expression Chris had ever seen on another person's face. "I hit her, Chris. I just reached out and hit her. I didn't want to, I didn't mean to, but I did. And I don't know if she'll ever forgive me."

Chris nodded slowly, not saying a word. He didn't know if Katie would forgive him either. Or if Chris himself could forgive him. There wasn't a person he knew and cared about who took to that sort of crap. That was one of a small handful of things that Chris couldn't abide. Despite many times when he wanted to, he'd never even hit Brittany, and that was practically allowed since they were siblings—though, granted, if he had, his mother would have beaten him to death.

Chris looked at Jerry until Jerry looked away. They both felt the same way and Jerry was feeling every bit of guilt that he should have.

"So. I'll talk to her. If she'll talk to me. And then I'll give you a call."

"Thanks, Chris." His voice sounded very, very relieved. "You're a life saver."

"We'll see about that." He looked away from Jerry. "And Jerry?"

"Yeah?"

"You know if I find a bruise on her, I'm gonna kick your ass, right?"

"Yeah. I know, Chris."

"Good. Long as we're clear."

II

Chris and Katie met in her neighborhood, at the restaurant of her choice. Oliver's Pizza was not exactly the location Chris would have chosen, but the food was inexpensive and tasty, even if the neighborhood left a lot to be desired. Not that Chris should be judgmental. In the long run it wasn't that different from his own neighborhood, economically speaking; it was just a little closer to the city proper so the run-down buildings in the area were a bit more prominent.

Katie had been reluctant to meet with him. She knew what the meeting was about and made it clear that she wasn't at all happy about him playing advocate for Jerry. As far as she was concerned, that meant that Chris had chosen sides.

In a way, he supposed he had, but he really wasn't thinking about it that way. Mostly he was thinking that two of his best friends—people he pretty much took for granted would one day get married—were having a fight and he wanted to make it right. Contrary to what Katie might think, he hadn't chosen Jerry's side at all. He'd chosen the side where they were still together.

They ate in silence for a while, with Katie looking around the restaurant and occasionally nodding to one of her neighbors, and Chris looking out the window at passersby. Most of them looked perfectly normal, but now and then he saw a bum wandering past. Chris wasn't used to seeing quite that many of the homeless in his own neighborhood. The city was not always pretty and clean, contrary to the ads on TV and in the paper.

Katie broke the silence first. "So what did Jerry tell you?"

Chris shrugged. "He said he blew it with you. That he hit you. Is that true?"

She nodded and he felt his lips press together. He muttered an expletive under his breath.

"It wasn't like a fist or anything. It was a slap."

"Doesn't make it right."

"That's why I haven't answered his calls."

"Do you want to be together with him?"

"Not if he's gonna hit me again." She shook her head and he watched her dark hair sway like a wave around her head. Technically there was probably something wrong with Chris looking at her hair and thinking about how attractive she was when he was trying to get her back together with his best friend. But it would only be really wrong if he let the raw thoughts get in the way of his mission.

"Safe to guess you know he's sorry?"

"He better be, but that doesn't mean I'm going to forgive him, not without a damned good reason for the way he's been acting." Her voice was tense. When she bit into her slice of pizza—and one of the things he liked about Katie was that she didn't nibble like a fish with a flake of food but actually ate instead—her teeth gnashed together with an audible clack. She was definitely not amused by Jerry's actions, or feeling very forgiving.

"Look, I'm not supposed to tell you all the extenuating circumstances . . ."

"Quit talking like a damned lawyer and tell me what's going on, Chris. I get enough of that crap from him." He looked back out the window, because it was easier than looking at her when she was angry and disappointed in him.

Outside he saw a small gathering of homeless men. All of them dressed in layers and layers of clothing as if in defiance of the baking heat. He couldn't imagine willingly being out in that weather with more than jeans and a T-shirt, and these men were all dressed like it was fast approaching winter. Two of the men passed a bottle between themselves and several others looked at them as if thinking it wouldn't be too hard to get the bottle away.

"Jerry has been hiding something from you because he says you're already going through enough right now. I don't really know what that means because you haven't felt you could share with me." He looked away from the window and back at her, fully aware of the expression on his face. He was about to get a lot of bitching thrown his way so he felt it best to get his one gripe off his chest first. "I'm gonna say this once and I want you to pay attention. If you have a problem, you can come to me, too. It's not one way. Okay?"

She nodded, looking a little guilty. That made him feel a bit better, but only a bit.

"Jerry has a few problems from when he got hurt . . . at the house."

Katie blinked, her body actually jolted as if he'd been the one to slap her, not Jerry. "What do you mean?"

"There's some sort of infection where he was . . . stuck to that thing around him." She flinched almost again, not a large flinch, but it was noticeable. Katie really didn't like to think about what had happened, and that was made very obvious by her reaction. "I'm not supposed to tell you, like I said, because you're not supposed to worry about him, but it hasn't cleared up and they don't know what's causing it. So he's been a little edgy."

"What? Why didn't he—?"

"Okay. Pay attention. He didn't want to worry you. Now, you and I know it doesn't work that way, but there it is. He was afraid you'd worry."

"That's the dumbest thing I've ever heard!"

"Don't shoot the messenger, I only found out a couple of days ago."

Katie fumed, looking away from him and staring at the wall, processing and trying to remain calm, which, frankly, had never been her strong suit when it came to Jerry.

Chris looked away, staring out the window again. Two of the bums were passing a bottle back and forth, taking swigs from it. The wine looked dark as midnight inside the green glass, but managed to take on a red color when they spilled it all over themselves, drinking as if the fluid in there was too important to avoid having right now, no matter how much they managed to spill it on themselves. Not far behind them another man dressed just as poorly was opening a bag from McDonald's, his eyes looking into his take out sack as if they were looking at the map to El Dorado.

"I don't know if it excuses what he's done, Chris. I

know where you're coming from, but he hit me. He's never hit me before and I don't think being nervous is a good reason." She finally looked back at him, her eyes narrowed and angry. "My father used to hit me. He also used to hit my mother. He was always sorry afterward, and he was always sincere, but he still used to blister my butt over little things, a lot of them I didn't even do."

"Katie, you told me yourself your dad was a heavy drinker. You told me he got on the wagon and stayed there. Has he hit you since then?"

Katie looked away, shaking her head. "Here's the thing, Chris. Jerry was sober when he slapped me."

"I'm not saying that he was right, Katie. I told him if I found a mark on you I was going to kick his ass, and I meant it and I still mean it." He leaned closer to her, looking into her eyes hard. "I'm just saying that there are extenuating circumstances and maybe once this is under control he'll stop being a prick."

She looked dubious about it. He couldn't blame her. There was a tension between them that had virtually never existed before and the worst part of it was, the tension was caused by a person who wasn't even there. Sometimes he wanted to knock Jerry's teeth down his throat.

Katie looked away again, trying to choose her words. There was a part of Chris that wondered if she was as careful with her words when she spoke with Jerry. Familiarity breeds contempt; that was the old saying, wasn't it?

Rather than stare at her, Chris looked out the window again. A lot could change in a few seconds. The two men with the wine bottle were facing off against the bum with the McDonald's bag. He had the sack clutched to his chest, his eyes wary as the others came closer, pointing at the bag and saying something to him. One of them even appeared to be offering the now mostly-empty bottle of wine in exchange.

"So fine. I'll meet with him, Chris. But I want it to be at your place and I want you there. It's that or I'll bring a knife big enough to cut his balls off, just in case he decides to get punchy again."

Chris kept looking out the window. With little warning one of the two bums shattered the bottle against the temple of the one with a solid lunch. Before Chris could do more than blink, both of them fell upon the man with the Happy Meal and took it from him. He crawled on the ground, his scalp bleeding profusely, and tried to regain his feet as they took his prize away. Chris had to do something. It wasn't in his nature to sit by and do nothing at all.

Unsettled, Chris looked back to Katie. "That's great. Listen, hang on a second, okay? I'll be right back." Watching the fight had distracted him from the queasy feeling in his stomach and had also kept him busy enough that he didn't let himself think. He wasn't going out there to break up the fight. He wasn't a cop and he was more than a little tired of getting himself questioned by the cops. Instead he walked over to the pay phone near the rest rooms and dialed

911. As soon as the voice on the other end answered he named the location, said there was a stabbing and that an ambulance and police would be needed, and hung up. Down in the part of himself where he didn't like to look, he thought he saw the shadow of a coward huddled in a corner, avoiding a chance of being noticed, but growing more malignant inside him. A cowardice cancer as it were.

That was as far as he was willing to go. *Wuss.*

It wasn't his problem. *Loser. Coward. Would you be sitting by if it was a pretty girl out there instead of a helpless old man?*

He kept asking himself that all the way back to the table.

Katie watched him as he walked back, her face almost managing to remain neutral. "What's wrong, Chris? Was it something I said? I know Jerry and I both act like school kids sometimes . . ."

"What? No. No, nothing like that." He glanced out the window. It wasn't looking good for the man who brought his fast food into the area. "You just say when you want to have the talk with Jerry, okay? Whatever you say, I'll make sure he's there and very, very apologetic."

"Shit!" Chris slapped the tabletop, watching as the two bums wailed their frustrations onto the man they'd already stolen the food from. "I'll be right back."

Chris walked toward the door at high speed, almost bowling over a couple that was trying to enter

Oliver's. The traffic was sparse, but several cars had slowed to watch the Beating of the Bum Show on the other side of the street. Some looked on, shaking their heads, and one particularly special loser was actually laughing about it.

Chris punched the side of the BMW with Laughing Boy behind the wheel, lowered his head, and charged at the two assailants like a bull.

Somewhere behind him, Katie called out his name with a panicky edge in her voice. Just ahead of him, the two bums looked his way, distracted by her urgent tones. The one on the left, the one he had already decided to knock shitless first, looked right at him.

He was supposed to be a dead man. Chris had seen him two days earlier eating his buddy's face. The one who was helping him with the ass kicking. The one whose dirty face looked just fine now. The nausea he'd felt before was stronger, but at the same time more distant. As if his mind was queasy now, not his stomach. He slammed into Arthur Hall with a violent gusto. He had tension burning through his body and much as he hated to admit it, a good fight was just the thing to help ease his troubled mind.

Arthur Hall let out a scream of surprise and lifted off the ground as if jet propelled. Chris carried him for a dozen paces in an awkward fireman's carry before heaving the man over his shoulder like a bag of dog food.

He turned around and jumped over Hall's prone body. The man was already trying to get back up.

Hall's friend looked at him with a strange expression, completely oblivious to the fact that Chris was about to cave his face in.

Chris tucked his fist in next to his body and moved quickly, waving his left hand in front of him. The bum did exactly what Chris hoped he would and looked at the waving fingers in front of him. Chris put his weight into the right hook he used to hit the man. There was something satisfying in the way the words the man uttered were suddenly cut off. One second he was saying "Hey, I know you," and the next he was dropping like a quarterback stiff-armed by a mountain of a lineman.

Arthur Hall was standing again, but he was not at all steady on his feet. His skin was sweating and pale and looked a little like it had been soaking in water for a few hours. The man with the hauntingly familiar face was not looking good at all. That suited Chris just fine.

He looked at the poor bastard they'd bum rushed—no pun intended—and saw that he was breathing. He guessed that would have to do. What Chris new about medicine was limited to Icy-Hot for sore muscles and aspirin for damned near everything else.

He looked at Hall, who had stumbled closer to the freak he'd come with. "You sit your ass down, Hall. I already called the cops."

Hall looked at him and his eyes went wide. "I know you! You're the one who did this to me!"

Chris scowled and shook his head. "You did it to yourself. Sober up."

He turned and started back toward the restaurant, his body twitching with an adrenaline rush. Katie was standing almost directly behind him, her pretty eyes wide and worried.

"Are you okay?" Even as she asked the question, she backed up from him a pace or two.

"Yeah. Fine." He looked down at the ground, his face going red with embarrassment. Christ, she probably thought he was trying to be macho. "I just couldn't sit by and let them kill the guy . . ."

"I called the cops. They should be here soon."

"Fine. Let's pay up and leave before they get here. I don't like cops." He didn't say that Detective Walter Crawford had soured him on the police forever. He didn't have to. Katie knew all about what Crawford had put Chris through in order to get a necklace that had belonged to Chris's mom.

"I already paid the bill."

"Damn it, Katie, I'm the guy. I'm supposed to pay."

Katie, smiling, punched him lightly in the arm, amused by his exasperated tone of voice. "You trying to say this is a date, Corin?"

"Oh hell no. I know better." Katie looked almost wounded. She hid the expression quickly. He smiled back, winking at the same time. "Last thing I need is you and Jerry mad at me instead of each other. I might not survive the fight."

She punched him again, a lot harder this time. She had a smile on her face, but it was tight and not overly amused. "Smart-ass."

"I'm just saying." He raised his hands in mock surrender. "Besides, if we were dating, who would I have baby-sit Brittany when I go out to pick up chicks with Jerry?"

He opened the door to his station wagon, flinching when Katie made another move to hit him. The girl had arms like a steelworker's, only shapelier. She'd been working in a posh restaurant for longer than he cared to think about, and he guessed maybe carrying all those trays made for some serious muscle tone.

The station wagon was a piece of crap and the hood was a mess to look at. After the little incident when Jerry's doppelganger had quite literally driven his fists through the hood, Chris had managed to reassemble the engine but hadn't had much luck with replacing the hood yet. But it still ran.

Down the street he heard the sound of sirens and got his ass in gear faster; he wanted nothing to do with questions about why he'd gotten involved or anything else. *Let the cops handle it,* he decided. *I have better things to do, like listening to the screaming match between Jerry and Katie.* Katie strapped herself into the passenger seat and did her best not to look at all worried about his driving skills.

Naturally, their exit took longer than he wanted. The cop car that pulled next to his wagon and parked, lights flashing and siren screaming, had blocked Chris in.

Katie tried hard not to laugh at the look he shot toward the squad car. It took her a few minutes, but with a little cajoling and a few snide comments, she had him smiling again. A day after a massive fight with Jerry that was still not resolved and minutes after watching him get into a fight and she was busy making him smile. The girl amazed him sometimes. He made himself get off that track of thought at high speed, and resolved to find a girlfriend in the near future. Falling for Jerry's honey would not do him any good at all.

The cops brought Arthur Hall past the car and Chris got a good look at him in the strobing lights from the three cop cars and two ambulances that had arrived. The other bum was there, too, and Chris and Katie got an eyeful of both of them. The exposed flesh on their bodies was covered with small blisters. They weren't everywhere, and they were mostly approximately the size of nickels, but the skin around the blisters was raised and puffy. Toward the center of the afflicted areas, there were small red marks that looked almost as if they had been hollowed out.

They looked a lot like the wounds on Jerry's rib cage that refused to heal.

Chris watched silently until the men were placed in squad cars. He didn't point out the wounds to Katie. She'd likely see similar ones soon enough.

"Jesus, Chris. Did you see that guy?"

"Yeah. Couldn't really help but see him . . ."

"No. I mean did you *see* him? Did you look at his face? I know him."

Chris looked sharply her way. "From where?"

Katie's face was pale and her lips trembled. "From that place. That house where everything went so bad."

"Say what?"

Katie's hand clutched at his forearm, her nails scraping lightly as she made a loose fist around his flesh. "That big one, the one you punched out. I saw him at the house." Chris felt his stomach drop. "Chris, he was one of the guys we pulled out with Jerry."

Chris didn't say anything. He couldn't think of any words that would make sense of the chaos spinning around in his head.

A policewoman tapped at the window of the car. She wore almost no makeup, had her dark brown hair pulled back in an efficient ponytail, and was not at all happy about being there. She still managed to look good. Maybe it was the uniform. Maybe it was just having an authority figure around and being comforted by the thought while he let his mind scurry around in places he didn't like to study too closely.

He rolled down the window and asked as politely as he could what he could do for her.

The officer asked them if they'd seen anything. After hesitating, Chris nodded. Katie looked at him, surprised as he reported what he'd seen. She was even more surprised when he gave his name and address.

After the attractively stern policewoman had gone away and told him they might call later with more questions, Katie couldn't wait any longer. "I thought you said you don't trust the police."

"After Detective Crawford, I don't."

"Then why did you give you real name and address to them?"

"Because this time I don't have anything special. I'm just one of half a dozen people who saw what happened."

He looked away from her, watching the squad car transporting Arthur Hall pull away.

"Besides, if I want to keep Brittany, I have to look like a good, upstanding citizen."

That brought up another can of worms, and they talked about his grandmother's phone call as Chris drove Katie home.

Chapter Three

I

The alarm clock went off far too early in the morning for Chris's comfort. The sad fact of life was that he was never meant to be a morning person. He reset the clock for another half hour and let himself drift for a while. Then his bladder reminded him that now and then the fluids he put in had to come out.

Twenty minutes later he got himself dressed and crept over to Brittany's room. He opened the door carefully and peered into the semidarkness of his little sister's bedroom. She was in there, sleeping. It was a good sign. He was trying to be patient with her, but there had been a few times now when she simply wasn't where she was supposed to be, and those instances never sat well with him. He kept remembering the time he'd found his sister with a stranger on the couch, her hand in the man's pants and his hand groping her teenaged breast. It hadn't gone well.

She'd become decidedly unpredictable since their mother's death. Chris made some coffee and managed only to scorch the French toast as opposed to actually turning it into cinder. He put half of the toast on the table with a paper plate over it and wrote Brittany's name on the plate with a felt tip pen that had long since started drying out.

After a very fast breakfast he pulled on his shoes and stepped outside to wait for Jerry. Jerry had another appointment with a doctor. Chris was going along for moral support. Katie couldn't make it; she had to work the day shift.

After almost two hours of fussing, bitching and later hugging and kissing, Katie and Jerry were back on speaking terms. The two concessions she insisted on were that he never hit her again—a promise that Chris hoped his friend meant to keep—and a visit to another doctor. She made the phone call from Chris's place, just as soon as Chris told Brittany to get off the damned phone, and set the appointment up for first thing in the morning. She was the only girl he knew who could pull a stunt like that and have it work. There was no such thing as getting a doctor's appointment quickly in Chris's memory. Most of the time when he was forced to go see Doctor King, it was a day or more after the phone call was made that the actual appointment took place.

The air was refreshingly cool, and Chris reveled in it. Lately it seemed that the only weather in the area was hot, followed by hotter. Jerry pulled up within ten minutes. He climbed into the Mustang with Jerry and nodded his good morning. The radio was too loud, the music raucous, and the car's engine was a dull roar of thunder as Jerry accelerated away from the curb in front of Chris's house on Longfellow Avenue.

Jerry threw him a bag with two Egg McMuffins in it. Chris had already eaten but decided he could eat more. He chewed while his best friend drove.

Jerry looked his way a few times, his expressive face about as nervous as Chris would have expected.

"So, you and Katie still okay?"

"Yeah. But I swear I don't want to go to another fucking doctor, bro."

"No one ever wants to go to another doctor, dude, but if it'll keep you on Katie's good side, you're smarter to just do it."

Jerry nodded and drove toward the center of town. "She's worth the grief, man. You don't have to tell me twice."

Chris nodded and looked out the window. There were few words spoken for the rest of the trip. Much as he hated it, there was a tension in the air between the two of them and he doubted it would fade away very quickly. Both of them were skirting around what Jerry had done to Katie and until the current crisis was resolved, they would likely continue to avoid talking the subject over.

Chris waited in the outer office while Jerry went in to see the doctor. The offices were in a stand-alone building with an actual parking lot. They were close to the hospital but not located in the oversized collection of offices directly across the street. Elevator music ran through the air and despite whatever hopes he might have had, there was not even a good-looking receptionist to look at. The woman behind the desk was portly and heading over the hill at high speed.

It was almost inevitable that he fell asleep. And just as inevitable that he dream.

Chris sat on a beach, one he wasn't familiar with, his eyes half closed against the glare and his fingers intertwined with the smaller, more delicate-seeming fingers of a woman. The wind was a gentle caress and the sun far above was a nice counterpoint. From time to time he could hear Brittany's voice carrying over the shore, tinkling with laughter. It was a good sound. It seemed like an eternity since he'd heard true happiness in his little sister's voice.

Off to the right he could hear the sound of seagulls squabbling and calling to each other and he looked that way. The big gray birds were fighting over something that had washed ashore, but there were too many of them for him to make out what their prize might be.

A shadow stole the sun's light from him and Chris looked to see a silhouette dwarfing his own. The dark shape had wild unkempt hair and from behind him where the shadow originated, he heard deep, phlegm-filled breathing.

James A. Moore

"Damn, Corin, I thought we were friends." The voice jolted him. The cold wet hand that clamped down on his shoulder did worse. He felt things in that grip, wet and slippery things that ran across his flesh and seemed to seek a way into him.

Chris turned his head and saw the decayed flesh of the woman behind him. Her slim body was rotting, a gaping hole in her abdomen left a hundred wet, red trails across the shore towards the ocean. The dark brown hair covered her features, but he knew her well enough. Chris started to scream, even as the fingers sank into his arm.

"Why did you kill my babies, bro?" The wet voice of the shadow sounded hurt and angry. The fingers sank deeper still as Chris turned to face the source of that voice.

Jerry shook him hard enough to make his head move and Chris damn near vaulted out of the comfortable office chair. His eyes flew wide and he let out a small scream before he could clamp his lips shut.

"Damn, bro." Jerry smiled at him, his dark eyes looking amused and worried at the same time. "You all right?"

Chris gasped, sucking in a breath, his heart thumping along at twice the normal speed and perfectly aware of two little kids looking at him and smiling nervously. He ignored the kids and looked at Jerry, blinking the remaining sleep from his eyes. "Yeah. I'm okay." He stood up and Jerry caught him when he lost his balance.

"That's good to know. 'Cause you weren't acting it."

"How are you? What did the doctor say?"

Jerry's good humor faded fast. "That he's never seen an infection like that. He took some different tests. The man has almost every device I could think of and a few more. Guess maybe he doesn't trust hospital techs, 'cause damn, Chris, this place is wired with it all." Jerry looked away, his eyes searching for something he could pretend to study.

"So what is it?" Chris put a hand on Jerry's arm, drawing his attention. "Come on, fess up."

"I'll show you outside."

They left a few minutes later, walking into a hot summer glare that made Chris wish for the beach, only not the one from his dream.

"Okay. So this doctor took a zillion tests and he showed me the results. He still doesn't know what it is. He doesn't like the look of it and he said I should be in the hospital. I told him that isn't going to happen." Jerry looked around and made sure no one was immediately in their line of sight. Without any preamble he pulled up his shirt, exposing his chest to Chris.

Chris bit his tongue. One girly scream a day was his limit. The sores were much worse. Whatever was causing them had apparently decided it was a good time to go forth and multiply. From the main source of each sore a dozen smaller infections had shown up, each livid and red and looking a little wet.

Jerry kept talking as Chris looked, amazed and horrified by the growth of the things. It was like someone with poison ivy. At first there's just a small red patch and then if you scratch, there're a few hundred areas of flesh perfectly willing to get just as red and angry. "Here's what I do know. It isn't spread by contact and nothing shows up in blood tests. I've had every poison you can imagine checked for and nothing. The sores don't have bacteria or viral infections and antibiotics seem to slow them down but even that may not be true anymore."

"There's got to be something we can do about it." Chris looked away, staring at the street beyond the doctor's offices. "Look, somebody somewhere has got to know what those things were. The ones that took you." His voice dropped to just above a whisper, unconsciously doing his best to avoid anyone hearing about what was going on. "Maybe we should look into different ways of finding out."

Jerry snorted. "What? Consult a psychic?"

"Why the hell not, Jerr? What do you have to lose?"

"Not much anymore, bro." Jerry spit and looked Chris in the eyes. "I don't figure I've got much at all if this shit doesn't stop soon."

"Let's get out of here. I have to make sure Brittany's okay and then we have to see what we can find out."

They left, Jerry sliding into the driver's seat as soon as he'd tucked in his shirt properly. The inside of the Mustang was hot and Chris decided to blame that intense heat for the nausea he felt. Seemed like he got queasy around Jerry a lot these days. Maybe it was guilt. He couldn't decide.

The usual heavy metal was missing from the radio when they started off and Jerry ignored the words being spoken on the news. Chris would have, too, but he caught a line about "missing" and "murdered homeless" and tuned himself in to the news. ". . . sources in the police department claim that the increase in crimes against the homeless is nothing new. According to one source, the indigent population is always going to be a source of victims for some people. So far no less than seven bodies have been found in recent weeks, and there are a few who claim that the population of indigents has been steadily decreasing for some time."

Chris switched the stations. The news gave him a freaky feeling that did not sit well with his current troubled stomach.

II

Brittany was just getting ready to leave when Chris got home. Jerry gave her a quick grin and moved into the house while Chris cornered her and played interrogator. "Where ya goin'?"

"Off to see the wizard?"

"Ha ha, deep inside I'm laughing. Where are you going?"

Brittany rolled her eyes and sighed. He resisted the

urge to drop his fist on the top of her head. "I'm just going over to Kelly's place, okay?"

"Kelly?"

"Yeah, Kelly Hampton? Blonde, cute . . . you saw her at Flavor of the Week?"

He nodded. Kelly was, in fact, blonde and cute and rapidly turning into jailbait, but he didn't recall her being into any of the shit he wanted to keep Brittany away from. "Fine. Be back for dinner, okay?"

"Whatever." She sauntered out the front door, her attitude once again in full bloom.

"I mean it, Brit. I'm not playing with you."

"I know! God, get a life!"

Chris backed down. He figured another word and she'd just go postal. It wasn't worth the grief.

The phone rang five minutes after he and Jerry had settled themselves in the living room. Sterling Armstrong was on the other end.

"So, Chris, what's this about your grandmother?"

Chris sighed. "She wants custody of Brittany. Brittany doesn't want custody of her."

"You don't think she'd be a good candidate for raising your sister?" The man's deep voice sounded puzzled.

"Sterling, she's never been a part of our lives. We don't know a damned thing about her, except our mother hated her."

"Well, I guess we could call that a negative recommendation. Okay then. I've already started the paperwork, so your bid for custody is already in place. The thing now is to make sure she doesn't beat us to the punch."

"If our paperwork is in place, how could she do that?"

"You'd be amazed what a good lawyer can do. Fortunately, you already have a good lawyer, so I'll get things moving on this end."

"That's great. Thanks."

"Don't thank me yet, Chris." Sterling Armstrong was supposed to be one of the best. When he spoke, Chris tended to listen. "You need to make sure you keep your sister out of trouble, all right? All it will take is a few incidents to make it look like you're not old enough to be a proper guardian to her. She manages to get that point across and it'll be an uphill battle."

"I'll talk with her."

"Make sure you do. We still don't know what happened at that house fire you were witness to, but I bet there are a few reports floating out there that point a finger in your direction. It doesn't matter if you did anything or not. What does matter is that you were at a site where a house fire leveled a building and several people were found stumbling around with serious injuries." He paused for just a moment before continuing. "With a good enough team on her side, that could be spun into a serious situation. All your grandmother has to do is make you look worse than her, and I can tell you right now that won't be hard to do."

"You know my grandmother?"

"No. I don't need to know her, all I need to know is

that she has money and she has good representation. I've never gone up against her heavy hitters in court, but they aren't exactly known for losing their cases."

"Last I checked you weren't considered a slouch, Sterling."

The man chuckled into the phone. Even his laugh sounded confident and cultured. "I'm not. But that doesn't mean I assume I'm going to have an easy time in court."

They said a quick good-bye and Chris looked over at Jerry, who was watching him with an amused expression on his face. "Jeez, bro. You sound almost like you're serious."

"No shit, Sherlock." He shrugged. "She's my little sister."

Jerry nodded, not speaking for a moment. When he did speak, his voice was subdued. "Listen. I gotta run. I'm supposed to meet Katie for lunch."

Chris nodded. Five minutes later, he was alone.

He'd gotten to the point where he hated being by himself. The company was lousy and he had too much time to think.

He turned on the television and switched to a local channel that had early news. One of the city's local roving reporters was busy interviewing a man who was most definitely down on his luck and probably had been since before Chris was born.

The man spoke with surprising eloquence, and Chris forced himself not to think about all of the homeless as being solely drug addicts. "You just have to listen to hear the gossip. I've heard half a dozen people telling each other that they are being hunted." The man looked away from the reporter and into the camera lens, and Chris wondered if he hadn't been an actor at one time. He seemed to be playing up the drama. "A few of them swear they are being hunted by something that isn't human."

The picture on the TV changed to a reporter in the studio speaking, with a reporter standing out in front of an abandoned building that was criss-crossed with crime scene tape. The reporter out in front of the derelict structure spoke in a professional voice, though it was obvious that something near where she stood had made her nervous. "That was the scene this morning, Linda. This afternoon, Michael Porter and two of his friends were found inside the remains of the building behind me. All three of them had been murdered and, according to a source privy to what occurred inside the abandoned warehouse, they had all been dismembered."

The anchorwoman, Linda, he assumed, nodded and cleared her throat. "That brings the total deaths among the homeless in this area to ten in the last month. Police aren't willing to confirm or deny if there are any connections, but word on the street is that there are, in fact, distinct similarities in all cases."

Chris turned down the television's volume and lay back on the couch. He was asleep before the next commercial break.

III

He awoke to the sound of the telephone screaming in his ear and sat up in a nearly complete darkness. The only illumination came from the TV that was now playing reruns of *The Andy Griffith Show* in black and white. Despite his disorientation, he answered by the third ring.

"Hello?"

"Chris?" It was Brittany. She sounded like she was in tears.

He was fully awake in an instant. A lot of his personal nightmares involved getting a phone call from his sister when she was in tears. A good number of the others involved a policeman calling to tell him his sister was dead and asking if Chris could come to identify the body. "Brit? What's up?"

"I'm at police station . . ." Her voice started to hitch in a series of short, gasping breaths. "I'm in trouble."

"What? What happened?"

"Just . . . just get down here, Chris, okay? I need you to come down here."

He demanded information and she gave it to him, crying more noticeably by the minute. Chris's blood pressure felt high enough to blow the top off of his skull. He left the house a few minutes later, making sure to drive as carefully as he could.

At the police station he identified himself to a man behind a desk who looked about as bored as was humanly possible while still being conscious, and then waited as patiently as he could for almost an hour before a police officer brought his sister out of holding. Brittany had been crying. That was just fine with Chris. Before he was done she'd have many more reasons to cry.

There were a lot of questions about where her parents were. Chris was prepared for them. And had the paperwork he needed to verify that he was, currently, her acting legal guardian. Just in case there were any questions, he offered up Sterling Armstrong's card, which he had been given for just such emergencies.

There was paperwork to fill out. Sometime before midnight, they left the building, Chris standing rigid with suppressed rage and Brittany doing her best to make herself smaller.

Chris kept his calm, not yelling, not taking it out on the road, all the way home. Brittany in turn sat huddled in the passenger's seat, staring straight ahead, afraid to open her mouth unless she might set him off.

His calm faded about twelve seconds after they entered the house. Chris tucked the car keys into his front pocket, walked into the kitchen and came back into the living room where Brittany was waiting. He held a bottle of Jack Daniel's left over from when their mother was still alive.

He tossed her the bottle. She caught it mostly out of reflex.

"Drink up."

"What?" Brittany looked at him as if he'd suddenly sprouted a few carrots from the top of his head.

"I said drink up. You want to get drunk so fucking bad, you go right ahead and do it." His face was dead calm.

"I don't. I don't want to drink." She put the bottle down on the coffee table.

"Yeah?" Chris looked around the room and she could see the transformation in his features. He went from being as stoic as a statue to just short of as violent as a hurricane in an instant. "You have a funny way of showing that, Brit."

Brittany shook her head, not really arguing, but not wanting to get into an argument. Chris scared her when he got that way.

"You mean to tell me I got a call to pick you up at the police station and a nice long grilling by some asshole in a suit because you *didn't* feel like getting drunk? Because I guess maybe I owe you an apology if that's the case. Hell, I just sort of figured they might have a reason for hauling your stupid ass out of a goddamned liquor store and taking a fake fucking driver's license from you." His voice got louder and angrier as he spoke. "Maybe you were just there and the fake license just fell into you hand along with the fucking bottle of scotch, is that it?"

"Chris, stop it." Her voice was very small.

"I keep asking myself if maybe they're right, Brittany. Maybe I'm not the right person to be your legal guardian if you can't even listen to a few simple rules." He crossed his arms, looking at her from under heavily knitted brows. "Silly me. I thought you wanted to stay here."

"I do! You know I do!"

Chris closed his eyes and made himself count to ten, trying to remain as calm as he could despite the shattered nerves that were turning his stomach into a volcanic pit of acid. "Then why the fuck am I having this talk with you? Why can't you get it through your head that you can't be pulling this sort of shit."

"Chris, I just wanted—"

"What?" He reached down near her and grabbed the bottle of whiskey. "If it wasn't a goddamned drink what the hell did you want?" He gripped the bottle so hard he was afraid it would break and slash his hand into ribbons.

"I wanted to have a normal life."

"Well get over it!" He hurled the bottle across the room. It hit the wall and exploded into a shower of glass and alcohol. "You're not going to get a normal life, Brittany. There's no such thing. You get me or you get the granny from the black lagoon or you get a foster family. Those are your choices!"

Brittany started crying and he looked away from her, not wanting to feel any guilt over her tears. He'd decided it was time to get a little sterner with her. "You'd better make up your mind fast, little girl. Because the shit you just pulled? That's exactly the sort of shit that will get you taken away from here!"

"Chris . . . I'm sorry, okay?"

"No! It's not okay! I'm doing my part here, Brittany. You fucking do yours or I won't be able to help you! You have to behave if you want to stay here. It's not up to me, it's up to a fucking judge who doesn't give a shit about your feelings. He only cares that somebody is protecting you and if I have to fucking bail your ass out of jail because you want to buy shit that even I can't buy legally, then he's going to decide on our grandmother!"

Her tears came back with a vengeance and as much as he wanted to actually comfort her, he made himself stand still. "You get up to your fucking room. You're grounded. No phone, no TV, and no computer unless I say otherwise."

She didn't even argue. She just went up the stairs. Chris sat down and stared at the television, which seemed to be what he did most of the time these days, even when it was turned off like it was right then.

He only noticed the answering machine flashing that there was a new message a few minutes later. There was one message. It was from Sterling Armstrong. His lawyer had been in contact with his grandmother's lawyer. There was going to be a fight. His grandmother had kept her word and filed for custody of his little sister.

For just a minute he was tempted to let the old bitch have her.

IV

The next two days passed without incident. Chris relished them. Brittany behaved herself and actually listened when he explained what was going on with the petitions for becoming her legal guardian. She was upset but managed to act her age instead of her shoe size. It was an improvement. Despite having grounded her, he relented a little and let her have a friend over.

Kelly Hampton came over dressed in jeans and a T-shirt that were roughly four sizes too small for her. Part of him looked at her as jailbait. Most of him decided to look at her as a potential problem for his sister. It was a bit weird trying to think like a parent.

While Brittany and her friend hung out in her room, Chris tried to phone Jerry. It wasn't like his buddy not to at least call. His sister Ronni answered the phone, sounding, like always, as if she were waiting for the most important phone call of her life and the idea of answering for any other member of the family was extremely inconvenient. In person she was a sweetheart and an insatiable flirt—and had been the object of a few of Chris's fantasies when he was younger—but on the phone she remained a bitch. Jerry wasn't home but had his cell with him. Chris thanked her and tried the mobile phone Jerry was almost never without. He left a message for Jerry to call him when there was no answer.

It wasn't like Jerry not to answer his cell phone, a thought that refused to leave Chris alone as he paced around his living room. It was seldom that he worried about Jerry. For the most part Jerry was the most competent person he could think of. There were maybe a handful of times in his entire life that he could remember Jerry falling down or even stumbling. He was almost unnaturally graceful, and when it came to luck, well, his best friend had it in spades. He had a great girlfriend, he'd been raised into money and success, he was apparently easy on the eyes—even when he was out with Katie he had girls flirting with him—and he was damned sharp.

Chris walked up to his room and pushed pass the disaster his floor was littered with—said disaster in the form of laundry that he was trying not to think about—and lay back on the bed. He didn't want to think anymore. Thinking was going to give him ulcers at the current rate.

Just as he was ready to drift off to sleep, the doorbell rang. Chris sighed and got out of bed and made his way down the stairs to open the front door.

It was Jerry. He'd looked better. Chris stepped back, shocked by the condition his friend was in. Jerry entered, nodding his head instead of speaking. His skin was pale and he was sweating.

"Jesus, Jerry. You look like death warmed over." Chris's face knitted into a concerned scowl and he watched his friend carefully, afraid he might fall down and crack his head as he stumbled toward the couch.

"Not really feeling my best, bro." His voice was as shaky as his hands.

Chris finally gripped the feverish arm of his guest and settled him on the couch. For an instant, he thought Jerry was going to pull away from him, his bicep tensed and then relaxed as he held him.

"I'm definitely getting that. What's happening?"

Jerry snorted and the short gust of air became a body-wracking cough that left him looking even worse. When he was done having his breathing fit he looked at Chris with dark eyes and moaned. "It's getting worse." He shook his head and leaned back against the couch. "I'm getting the weirdest muscle spasms, and I swear to you someone's crawled inside my head and is whispering shit to me."

Chris felt his stomach fall out and plummet into an abyss. He'd lost his mother only a few months ago and had enough sense to know he hadn't even finished dealing with that tragedy yet. He didn't want the same thing happening to his best friend in the world.

"Look, Jerry, this shit is getting way too serious now. I know you don't want to go to a hospital, but damn, dude. It's time to go."

Jerry shook his head and scowled. "No way, man. There's nothing they could do with all the damned blood they took from me or the fucking biopsies, and I'm not rotting away in a goddamned hospital." Chris started to protest and Jerry held up a hand for silence. He wasn't finished. "Look, all I know and all you know is this shit started with your mom's necklace. Why don't we focus on that, okay? Nothing personal so don't take it that way. I'm not blaming anyone, but maybe if we find out something about the damned thing and what it did, we can find out how to fix this."

Chris shook his head. "I can do that, Jerry, but it isn't going to make what's happening to you any better."

"And neither are the fucking doctors, Chris!" Jerry's voice was like a bullwhip, harsh and sudden. "I've been to five different doctors and taken ten-plus different pills and injections and nothing is working." He stood up from the couch, his muscles tensed and damn near vibrating. His face was angrier than Chris could ever remember seeing it, and everything about Jerry Murphy was as far from normal as could be.

Brittany chose that moment to come flying down the stairs, her face alarmed. She wasn't used to the sounds of Jerry yelling. She was far more accustomed to that from her brother.

Jerry looked at Brittany and relaxed noticeably. He might be willing to blow a gasket in front of Chris, but apparently he didn't like doing it in front of Brittany and that was fine in Chris's book.

"Is everything okay?" Her voice was tentative. Brittany's eyes were wide in her pretty face and her hair was loose, making her look enough like his mother at that moment that Chris could have wept if the circumstances had been different.

Instead he forced a smile and nodded. "Yeah, we're just having a bitch session, Brit. What did you need?"

For a second he thought she'd start a bitch session of her own, but apparently she decided not to push her luck. She was allowed to have someone over and that was enough for her. "I just wanted to make sure everything was cool. You two sounded like you were gonna start swinging."

Chris nodded and Jerry shrugged his shoulders. "Hey, we can't let you have all the fun when it comes to screaming, can we, peewee?"

She rolled her eyes at Jerry and flounced back up the stairs.

Chris paced the room wanting to grab Jerry and shake some sense into him, but he knew better than to try. "Damn, Jerry. Okay, I'll see what I can find out about the damned key thing. You just do me a favor and try to stay calm."

"Hey, cool as a cucumber, bro."

"Seems like that would be a first lately." If Chris came off as being a bit angry, that was too bad. Jerry had hurt his feelings, and as pouty as it sounded he was annoyed by the sudden outburst. He'd never been the type to force a smile when he was pissed and didn't feel the sudden need to start.

"Chris?" The voice was tentative and Chris looked back at him feeling a dreadful pang of guilt. The problem with being a hard-ass is that you have to actually be a hard-ass. It wasn't in his genes to get away with it for long.

"What's wrong, Jerr?"

Jerry sat back down on the old couch's armrest and

looked at Chris with fear in his eyes. He looked all of
ten at that moment. "Chris, bro, I'm hearing voices."

"Say what?"

"I'm hearing voices." Just as quickly he looked
away, ashamed to admit that maybe his mind wasn't
what it should be. "Not all the time but it's getting
worse."

"What are they saying?"

"I don't know. It's like trying to listen to a whisper
in a foreign language, man. I can hear it, but I can't really understand it." Jerry's hands moved around in
aimless circles, anxious for something to distract
them. "You ever hear a sound that wouldn't stop and
was just the right kind of sound to make you want to
scream?"

Chris thought of Brittany on a tirade and nodded.
"Yeah."

"That's what this is like. I can hear it almost all the
time now, sometimes so faint it's like a sigh and sometimes it's like I have a fucking Kiss concert going on in
my head."

"Have you told the doctors about that part?"

"No."

"Shit, Jerry . . ."

Jerry stood up and stretched like a cat, a talent
Chris had always envied. He shook his head and dug
in his pocket for the keys to his Mustang.

"You leaving already?" Chris was surprised. Jerry
seldom felt the need to rush anywhere.

Jerry gave him a brief flash of a smile, a real smile,

and headed for the door. "Gotta see a lady about a horse or something." Whatever he'd hoped to get from Chris, he'd been disappointed. Chris couldn't help that, but if Jerry was right, maybe he could do something about the rest of it.

There were more bookstores than he would have expected in the city and Chris had to call most of them before narrowing down the places he would search. He spent almost two hours before he decided on a small list of shops to try.

A little-known fact that Chris Corin caught onto with ease: Bookstores are not exactly the best places to go for an easy time looking up information, unless you have long hours to spend and large amounts of money. Another important fact Chris learned that day: Talking to the person in charge of the bookstore can be very, very helpful. After wasting another four fruitless hours he finally promised himself he would actually ask for help at the next location he came across.

He drove into a part of town he would rather have avoided—not far from where he'd tried to get himself properly blown up earlier in the summer—and looked carefully at the shop fronts along Whelan Avenue before he finally found the store he was seeking. Dark Harvest Books claimed to have an extensive new age and occult specialty selection and he aimed to find out if they were blowing hot air up his pant leg or if they were sincere in their promises.

The front of the store was unremarkable, save that

the windows had been cleaned and the bricks on the outside of the building were remarkably free of graffiti. He opened the door and walked into the scent of musty books instead of patchouli and felt he was on the right track for a change of pace.

The interior was crammed with more books than shelf space, but that meant nothing. The last three stores had proven that when it came to bookstores—especially used bookstores—there was something of a premium on space. The long row of used romance novels that lined the side wall next to him didn't do anything to make him feel better about his chances at this location.

He walked up to the long glass counter a few feet past the piles of damsels in distress and muscular men who apparently couldn't keep their shirts buttoned to save their lives, and felt a little better when he saw a few of the titles behind the glass. He didn't know what the old books were all about, but they were definitely not romances. "*Book of Counted Sorrows, Malleus Malifecarum* . . ." His eyebrows knitted as he tried to read a few of the others. "I'm can't even work my tongue that way."

"Well, some of those titles aren't exactly in common English." Chris looked up and allowed himself a smile when he saw the girl. "Nice to see you again, Chris. I didn't expect this."

"Hi. I wasn't expecting to see you either, Laura. I forgot you said your folks ran a bookstore." She was just as cute as he remembered, and maybe even cuter with her hair pulled back in a functional ponytail. She was dressed in jeans and a men's blue button-down shirt. Extremely casual and oddly fetching, the look fit Laura as far as he could see.

"So what can I do for you?" She smiled warmly, her eyes still looking a little tired, which was a feeling he understood all too well.

"Well, I'm looking for information on a necklace that I heard about that's supposed to have . . ." He looked away and made himself look back. It might not be the best way to impress the woman in front of him, but he needed to know if she had any books that could in fact tell him about the damned source of Jerry's illness, even if it was only in a roundabout sort of way. "It's supposed to be linked to a lot of other necklaces and be something pretty special in a cult."

"A cult? Like an Aleister Crowley sort of cult?" She lifted one thin eyebrow and her lip curled into a half smile. It looked good on her face.

"Yeah." He felt his skin flush a little red and tried not to think about it as he grinned. Coming from her mouth the idea sounded ludicrous. Then again, she hadn't exactly been there when he ran across his first cult experience. She couldn't hope to understand what went on. Hell, he'd been there and he still wasn't really getting a good grasp of what had happened. Mostly he tried to avoid thinking about it.

"Well . . . My dad swears he has one of the best collections in town. If anyone around here could find an answer for you, it would be him." She frowned a little as she spoke.

"Oh. Is he doing better? Your dad I mean?"

"A little. He still can't get around, but I could ask him if you like."

"I would like very much." He nodded, unsettled by how flustered Laura made him feel. "I mean, I can't tell you how much."

"He's asleep right now. I just gave him his medications and they just pretty much knock him into tomorrow . . ."

"Oh, don't wake him. I can always come back later . . ."

"You don't mind?"

"Come on, you told me he's had a bad time. Let him sleep."

"Well, if you want to come by tomorrow, I can ask him in the meantime. Why don't you tell me about this necklace thingey of yours and I'll write it down." She looked around herself for half a second and then snatched up a pen from near the register.

"Okay, it's called the 'Western Key,' and it looks like a gold coin, with some silver fringe work and three small gems in it."

Laura looked up at him. Her face wasn't smiling anymore. "Seriously?"

"Yeah."

"My mom used to have a necklace kind of like that. I remember it from when I was a kid."

Chris felt a deep chill spread through his stomach. "Weird. Maybe it'll be easier than I thought if she had one like it. Maybe your dad already knows about them." His voice sounded tinny in his own ears.

Laura smiled again. It wasn't the same bright smile he'd seen before, but instead a nice, polite smile like you'd expect from a stranger. "Well, I'll ask him when he wakes up. Was there anything else you needed today, Chris?"

"No. Thanks, Laura. That should just about handle it." The tension grew in the air and he wondered, briefly, if he'd made a mistake. Maybe it was just the thought of her mother or a necklace that she was looking for and couldn't find. Either way he moved toward the door. "I'll swing by tomorrow. Take care until then, Laura."

He left the store as calmly as he could unable to get rid of the feeling that he'd just screwed up in a big way.

V

Jerry was trying to be calm. Damned if he wasn't trying, and hard, but the voices seemed intent on making him as miserable as possible and there didn't seem to be too much he could do about it.

Maybe it wasn't really right to call them voices. They were more like static and white noise, only with a personality. The personality of a sociopath, true, but personality just the same.

In the car next to him, Katie was talking about

Courtney's latest conquest. A month ago she'd pretty much ruined a nice but stupid kid named Stu and now she was hanging with a kid named Donnie Mickle and was likely going to nuke him within a week. He liked Courtney, even went so far as to have an occasional fantasy about her and Katie getting together with him, but damn, the girl was a full-scale bitch.

He shifted lanes smoothly, letting the powerful engine sing to him like a lullaby. He loved the purr and feel of the car in motion, even if the car had been a sore spot in his relationship with Katie.

She could be a little strange sometimes.

Right now, she was acting strange . . . that, or his mind was playing games with him again. She was right there next to him, speaking animatedly, but all of the words coming out of her mouth sounded like gibberish.

And the sound of those nonsensical little syllables was annoying the hell out of him. He was tempted to put her in her place, and to make himself behave, Jerry clenched the steering wheel harder and nodded his head.

Damn, but he wished she'd just shut the fuck up.

He was just turning to tell her as much—and a part of him that was far more rational was telling him to calm down in a voice that he ignored—when the Cadillac scraped the side of his cherry red Mustang.

He heard the sound of metal hitting metal and then he heard the whispering nonsense that had been filling his head expand outward, pulsing into his skull like a mushroom cloud exploding across the horizon. Jerry Murphy closed his eyes.

When they opened, it wasn't Jerry who looked out of them. Jerry had become, for the moment at least, an annoying hiss of static in the back of the mind that was running things.

VI

Chris went back home after hitting the rest of the bookshops on his list. Most of the occult specialty stores seemed to carry tarot cards, incense and around fifty books from major publishers that dealt with ghosts, witches, teenage witches and past life regressions. A few of the dynamic ones, the ones that went way out on a limb, actually mentioned aliens and had a few books on government conspiracies. Had he wanted any of that crap he could have hit a Barnes & Noble. He was looking for serious information and the only place that looked like they might have it was run by a girl who didn't seem thrilled with him at the moment.

So much for his first day of hardcore research the old-fashioned way. He stopped on the way home and grabbed a sack of burgers at a McDonald's that had double cheeseburgers on sale. Brittany would have to be happy with them. He was too tired to cook and too frustrated to hear her bitch.

He got home just after seven at night, with the sun

still up and threatening to set sometime before midnight. The summer months always threw him like that. Brittany had apparently decided to make amends for some imagined slight. She'd cleaned the living room and even put away the dishes he'd washed the night before.

He sat down on the couch and called her name. A minute later she came out of her room, looking freshly scrubbed and smiling brightly. She was dressed in clothes he considered more appropriate to her age than half the crap she left the house in these days. It was nice to see her smile. She hadn't done a lot of that since their mom had died. Mind you, he hadn't either, but he wasn't quite as moody as his sister, at least not normally. Right now he felt like a bad mood waiting to happen. There was that line from Pink Floyd's "The Wall" that seemed appropriate; he could feel one of his turns coming on.

Seeing his sister happy took a lot of the threat away. They ate in relative peace, with Brittany talking about how Kelly was thinking about a slumber party. Chris let her do most of the talking and decided he'd let her go to the party, but only after he called Kelly's parents. The fact of the matter was he could make all the rules he wanted and Brittany might obey them sometimes, but he'd feel guilty as hell if he didn't let her have a little fun. It wasn't easy, he reminded himself, to be a teenager. He was still technically a teen, but these days he had a few more rights.

Besides, he could use a night off from babysitting.

He was getting ready to tell her as much when the

phone rang. Brittany flew across the couch and grabbed before he could even blink. "Hello?" Her face stormed over for an instant and then she smiled. "Yeah. Hi, Katie! Yes, he's here."

She handed him the phone, sitting under the cord a few feet from him and nibbling on her burger.

"Hi, Katie. What's up?" He wanted little more than to close his eyes and sleep, but he always had time for Katie and Jerry. They were the exceptions in his life.

"Hi, Chris." Her voice had that tone she could manage so easily. She sounded happy to hear his voice and simultaneously annoyed at life in general. But this time there was a serious undercurrent that made Chris's neck hairs stand up. Two words and he'd caught the tone. That couldn't be a promising thing.

"Katie? What is it?"

"Chris, it's Jerry. What else? He screwed up."

"What happened?" Brittany was listening intently, her eyes focused on the burger she was eating but every part of her body seemed to lean toward him.

"We had a car wreck."

"You're both okay?"

"No. We are definitely not okay. Chris, the guy came off a side street and smacked the Mustang. It's a few scratches, that's all. And Jerry jumped out of the car just about ready to kill the guy."

"What happened?"

"Jerry beat the shit out of him. The guy was trying to apologize, it wasn't like he did it on purpose, and Jerry went postal all over him."

97

"Well, I mean, how bad can it be?"

"He broke the guy's face all over the front of the Mustang, Chris! The poor man was bleeding all over the place and unconscious before I pulled Jerry off!"

"Jesus." Chris got a shiver down his spine. Jerry was not exactly a fighting machine, but he could be nasty in a fight, Still, Chris wouldn't have expected that sort of thing from his best friend. From Bryce Darby, the local psychotic, sure, but not from Jerry.

"Did anyone call the cops?"

"Yeah, Chris. They did." Her voice sounded exasperated and as tired as he felt. "But by the time that happened, Jerry had run away."

"Excuse me?" Chris was feeling worse about the whole situation by the second. Unless Jerry was pretty sure he was going to get himself creamed by a substantial number of seriously nasty characters, he didn't run from a fight and he also did not run from his responsibilities.

"He was looking around and screaming something, Chris, but it wasn't in English. I don't know that I've ever heard anyone speaking like he was. It was like he was doing that religious thing . . . talking in tongues or something. Chris, I swear it was like he didn't recognize me. I tried to calm him down and he looked at me like he'd never seen anything so disgusting in his whole life."

"Okay, Katie. Where are you? I'll come get you."

"No, Chris. I'm already getting a ride. I just wanted to let you know about what's happening."

"Oh, okay. I'll go looking if you want me to."

"That would be great. Listen, I'm just going home. My mom's coming out to get me and I'm just going home. I've already been talking to the police for the last hour . . ."

"Go get some rest, Katie."

Chris hung up the phone and sat on the couch for a while contemplating where his best friend might run off to if he wanted to be alone. When they were kids it was easier. Back then they'd both lived in the same neighborhood, before Jerry's dad had decided to move the whole family to greener pastures. Three blocks away was where Jerry would have gone back then. Three blocks away to the playground that even then was all but forgotten by the neighborhoods in the area. These days he doubted half the kids even knew about it.

Chris looked at his sister and managed a weak smile before he explained what was going on. They finished their meal in near silence and then went out to the station wagon to look for Jerry.

Brittany was remarkably calm. If Chris had been in a clearer state of mind that might have worried him.

Chapter Four

I

The air was cool and clear, with a breeze that felt almost perfect. Chris would have enjoyed it a lot more if the pretty girl next to him was any pretty girl but his sister and if he'd been out cruising for fun instead of looking for Jerry.

They'd been driving for close to three hours and the station wagon was running on empty. Chris knew basically where they were, but only because he'd stuck to the main roads. He tended to stay in his own little corner of the city, and this was definitely not his regular stomping ground.

And he hated it. He hated every second of it, because he fully expected something to go wrong.

Isn't it great when the world lives up to your expectations? He expected things to fall apart, and life opted to give him what he expected a short time later.

Brittany was in her own little world, not five feet away from him. He decided to bring her back to home. "So, if I let you go to this slumber party over at Kelly's, you know you'll have to actually stay in her place, right? None of this shit about going out to the Club of the Week or anything."

She looked at him in complete silence for almost a full minute, her pretty face unreadable. Then she nodded. "Okay, but I have a condition."

"You have a condition?" He was moderately amused, so decided to hear her out before shooting her down. "Like what?"

"You're off the hook for watching over me, right?"

"Yeah. . . ."

"So go out and do something."

"What?"

"Go out and do something. All you ever do anymore is stay at home. Go out and do something. Go to a movie or go get laid."

"All I ever do is stay home?"

"When was the last time you actually got out of the house besides doing something for Katie or Jerry or me?" She wagged a finger in his direction. "And I don't mean going off to the bookstore or whatever you did this afternoon, either. I mean going out to do something fun."

"I do things, Brittany."

"No you don't. Ever since . . . Ever since that

damned house, you stay at home and hide in the living room and watch TV."

"I'm not hiding."

"Hell you aren't."

"I just haven't had anything I've wanted to do."

"You've been hiding." She looked out the window, dismissing his protest as nothing but hot air.

"I have not been hiding."

"You have, too."

"Brittany."

"Hiding." Her voice was a bored sigh. He hated that she was so damned good with the casual melodrama. "Been hiding since you got out of the hospital."

"What have I been hiding from?" Even to his own biased ears he sounded defensive.

"Near as I can tell you've been hiding from anything that might be fun." Brittany looked his way without moving her head. Just her eyes moved, tracking across his way with a look that said she was already beyond bored with the conversation.

"I don't know what the hell you're talking about."

She did a passable imitation of his voice. "I don't know what the hell you're talking about." Brittany sighed. "Look, the last thing in the world I could care about is your social life, Chris. But you haven't done anything since before you went into the hospital, and I don't think it's healthy for you to spend all of your time in the house. It's like you're trying to forget that you have a life. So now I'm going out for the night and you don't have an excuse anymore. Go out and do something tonight. Anything; just get the hell out of the house."

Chris drove in silence again, Brittany looking away from him, her head resting against the passenger-side window. He didn't want to speak, he wanted to lean over and swat his sister in the head because she didn't get it. He couldn't have a life any more. He had to take care of her and that took precedence over college, over his trip to Europe, over pretty much everything.

She didn't get it, and she probably never would.

He pulled into a Citgo gas station with a convenience store and counted the money in his wallet. Five dollars would not go far. Brittany reached into her jeans—and Chris made a note to take her shopping for clothes when he finally had money, because she was growing like a damned weed and the jeans looked about three sizes smaller than were comfortable, not that she seemed to mind—and she pulled a small roll of money out. She fished two twenties out of the wad and handed them to him. He nodded his thanks, and decided not to ask where she got the money. He'd figure it out later.

Chris filled the tank and Brittany went into the store, coming out a few minutes later with two Pepsis and a bag of Cape Cod Salt & Vinegar chips. Chris put the cap back on the gas tank and started toward the store. Brittany opened her mouth to say something to him and then let out a scream instead as a man grabbed her by the shoulder and spun her in a half circle. The chips and sodas went sailing and Chris looked over at the creep grabbing his sister, his blood pressure already swinging higher.

The man was short and dirty, covered in more clothing than would have been comfortable in winter, and almost as pale as a corpse. That wasn't too surprising, really, considering that he was supposed to be dead. Arthur Hall's fingers dug into the flesh of Brittany's biceps as he bared his teeth and shook her hard enough to make her ponytail flip around on her head.

Brittany took a wild swing with her right hand and managed to clip the man on his bearded chin. He barely even noticed. Chris moved closer, ready to grab the freak and put a hurt on his sorry ass for touching Brittany.

"I know you." The man's voice was raspy, and his eyes were narrowed down to mere slits in his face, which had looked better the last time Chris had seen him in person, despite the blood that had been dripping down his bearded chin. He shook Brittany hard, his arms pistoning back and forth as he screamed at her. "You did this to me! You ruined me, you bitch!"

Brittany kicked her assailant square in the balls, her foot slamming hard enough to make Chris wince in sympathy. Hall let out a yowl of pain and staggered back, dropping Brittany in the process. Chris saw his skin for first time, saw how far gone the man was. His flesh was splotched with heavy red marks to the point that he made Andy Carter—the pizza face from his junior year, look like the "after" part of a Clearasil ad. Even from ten feet away the sores were livid. From five feet away they were angry and he could see that they were seeping vile fluids. From punching distance, they were worse and felt hot and squishy when his fist slammed into the man's head. Hall grunted and staggered back. Chris hit him again. There wasn't really much anger in the action, more a need to get the man to just go away.

He didn't fit into the world Chris wanted, and looking at Hall up close was doing nothing to settle him down. The sores were too much like ones he'd seen on Jerry, only worse.

Chris got so damned distracted he never even saw the right hook coming until it was in his face. But he felt it. Felt his lips break and his teeth rattle in their sockets and most assuredly felt his head snap back. There was no finesse in the allegedly dead man's style, but he more than made up for it with brute strength. Chris didn't have time to recover before he was hit again, this time in the solar plexus. He'd gotten cocky and now he had to pay for it.

The short man backhanded him and Chris fell down this time, not at all certain he could remember anything like how to stand up. Instead of kicking him, Arthur Hall dropped down and landed with a leg on either side of Chris's hips, pinning him in place. Then he started swinging fists, raining down a flurry of blows that felt like hammers slamming into Chris's face.

Chris reached up and locked his fingers around the man's neck, clenching his hands together as best he could through the flurry of blows. He felt skin slide under his fingers, felt the greasy wetness that ran down his hands from the blisters that popped under the pressure he applied and worst of all felt things moving—*writhing*—at the core of those ruptured sores.

He might have pulled his hands back and started screaming if it hadn't been a matter of whether or not he got to stay alive. Instead he squeezed even harder, taking a certain amount of satisfaction from the dark red color that swept up Hall's previously pale face.

Hall didn't slow down. He coughed and hacked and turned damned near purple, but he didn't stop swinging, even when his eyes bugged wide in his head. And Chris got a good look at his eyes, which, really, was probably a very bad thing. They were dark gray, the irises grown so wide that no whites showed at all. The pupils that should have been in the very center of those eyes were in the process of splitting like cells halfway through fission, but the process was not as clean. Where the division was taking place trickles of bright red blood ran like connecting spiderwebs. He could actually see the pupils splitting farther apart as the man he was strangling coughed and strained to breathe.

He might have gone on that way until either Hall was unconscious or he was knocked into a coma, but Brittany decided to interfere, God love her. Now, it's fair to say that even though he was not a tall man, Arthur Hall was heftier than Brittany. On a good day she might weigh in at around a hundred pounds. Hall, if Chris was judging right, was closer to a hundred and sixty-five. That didn't stop her from dragging him off her brother. Brittany grabbed a double handful of thick, greasy hair on the back of the allegedly dead bum's head and threw her weight into it. Hall rolled back, screaming incoherently. Chris started to go with him before the skin he had in his hand slid free of his grasp. Most of it at any rate. A layer or two stayed firmly glued to Chris's fingers.

Brittany backed up quickly, her eyes narrowed with the sort of spiteful glare she normally saved for Chris, and kicked the man in the face as he started to get up after her, still coughing and gagging from the punishment Chris had delivered to his trachea. The man staggered to his feet, blood flowing from mashed lips where Brittany had tried punting his mouth to the other side of the parking lot. There was blood on his neck, too, and something red and stringy was moving in that blood, as if seeking a source for its sudden exposure to the air.

Chris slid himself into a sitting position, trying his best to actually regain his balance. The blows he'd taken were not making his equilibrium function like it was supposed to, and everything wanted to shift to the left. Bed spins were more fun when you'd gotten drunk first, instead of punch drunk. His ears were ringing and his head felt almost as bad as Hall looked.

Hall grabbed Brittany again, growling deep in his throat as he yanked her closer. She screamed in his face, her voice a shrill wail, and started swinging wildly with her hands and her feet.

Chris managed to get to his feet right around the same time the man hauled off and punched Brittany in the side of her face. Her head snapped to the side and she let out a sound Chris had never heard from his little sister before. He hoped to never hear it again.

It was a noise that was enough to make him see red. Chris charged, putting his body weight into the shoulder that slammed into Arthur Hall. Hall was not a big man, and he proved it by trying to reach escape velocity as he lifted off the ground, screaming incoherently until he hit the side of the gas station's convenience store. The man slid down the rough brick with a grunt.

Chris moved toward him, breathing hard, his eyes narrowed. He might well have killed him right there, but the clerk came out from inside the store, looking more than a touch nervous.

"Hey. Umm, I called the police. So, you might want to leave." Chris looked his way and the nervous-looking teenager took a step back. "Look, I know you didn't start it, and I'll tell the cops that. Just give me the cash for the gas and get out of here."

Before Chris could come up with a proper reply he got a boot heel in his crotch. That pretty much took all of the fight out him. Chris dropped to his knees, coughing, as the pain did a tactical nuclear explosion through his privates and moved in fast, nauseating waves through the rest of his body.

Arthur Hall stood up, his funky-looking eyes shooting around in all sorts of directions. Apparently he wasn't really in the mood to deal with cops or to fight with Chris and Brittany any longer. He took off down the street at high speed.

Chris didn't even think about following. He was far too busy trying not to puke. Brittany managed to pull money out of her jeans and told the man to keep the change. She pulled on Chris's arm until he finally stood up and staggered toward the car, while he prayed the pain would please, God, just go away.

They left quickly, ushered away by the sound of police sirens in the distance.

Brittany kept looking around the entire time back to the house on Longfellow Avenue. Katie's car was there in the front of the house and Courtney's little VW Bug was there as well. They helped Brittany pull Chris inside. He wasn't feeling much like company and staggered off to the bathroom, where he spent a while praying to the porcelain god.

II

Waking up to the sounds of women talking was becoming a part of Chris's life of late. He would have enjoyed it a lot more if they were talking about happier things. Brittany and Katie and Courtney were in the living room, downstairs from his bedroom, and they were speaking about Jerry and about the dead man who had kicked Chris's family jewels into the next week.

109

He sat up in bed and listened for a while. They were talking about Jerry, not surprisingly, and Katie was worried half to death. Chris was worried, too, and the more he thought about the entire situation, the more anxious he grew. On top of everything happening to Jerry, he'd had another of the sort of encounters that left him wanting to duck his head in the sand and hide away. And he'd had Brittany with him when it happened.

He got out of bed, feeling a little tender in several spots, and took off the T-shirt he'd been wearing. He switched it for another shirt that wasn't too dirty and made a mental note to get to the laundry sometime soon.

A quick pit stop in the bathroom told him more than he ever wanted to know about how he was looking, which was like someone had been beating the hell out of his face and doing a fine job of it. His lips were split and had scabbed up, leaving dark red striations behind that hurt when he winced. His skin had several bruises darkening his jaw and cheeks, and the left side of his face was swollen from the whupping a dead man had slammed down on him.

"Shit on this."

He limped a little on his way down the stairs. The girls heard him long before he made it to the living room. Courtney looked at him with genuine concern in her eyes. Somehow that affected him more than the same expression from Katie and his sister.

"Hi." His voice sounded scratchy, which didn't really surprise him. He looked from Courtney to Katie and then to Brittany. When he saw the shiner just under her left eye he let out a sigh and moved closer.

Brittany's pretty face looked just fine until you got to the black and purple mark on her cheek. He reached out and touched the angry bruise lightly and she pulled back, looking annoyed. Silly of him to forget that they weren't allowed to be civil to each other.

"I'm fine." Her tone said otherwise. She stepped back and moved toward the kitchen and he let her.

"Anyone hear from Jerry yet?" Katie just shook her head, her eyes downcast. And he hated that expression. He hated it so much he wanted to scream. She was a sweetheart and she was a good friend and damn it all, she had done so much for him and for Brittany that seeing her looking that distressed was enough to hurt.

Because his legs still felt awkward under him, Chris sat on the couch. Courtney sat next to him a moment later, and rested her head on his shoulder. She still smelled as good as ever and was looking better all the time. He smiled, carefully, and leaned into her, grateful for simple human contact. He hurt all over and he was exhausted, even after all of the time he'd spent sleeping.

Katie shot a look that was one part anguish and a double ration of pissed-off at Courtney, who promptly leaned back away from him and then stood up. Chris didn't ask why. He didn't even blink. There were probably reasons enough—like their failed relationship a few years back—without him asking about any of the other possibilities.

111

The silence would have been awkward if it had been allowed to happen at all. Brittany started talking and the phone began to ring at the same time.

"Chris, that lawyer called today, the one you hired? He said he needs to talk to you about the probation of mom's estate or something like that and about the disposition of your winnings from the lottery."

Chris nodded, half listening, and answered the phone. "Hello?"

"Chris?" The voice was feminine and it took him a second to recognize it.

"Hi, this is Laura, from Dark Harvest."

"Yeah, hi Laura." Hearing from her made his heart beat a little faster. It had been a while since he'd actually developed a crush on a girl, but there it was.

"I won't be able to help you with finding out about that necklace."

"No?"

"No. I don't know what the Western Key is, but when I mentioned it to my father he got very upset. He said never to speak of it again." She paused for a moment, as if expecting him to have a counterargument. "I think it would be best if you stayed away from here, Chris. He didn't like it when I mentioned your name, either. He said you were marked."

"What? Laura, I don't even know your father."

"Well, he seems to know you. Please don't come around again." She hung up before he could say anything else. Chris looked at the phone as if it might sting him and shook his head.

"You know what? That's just fucking fine with me. Thanks very much for nothing!" Chris slammed the headset down into the cradle, practically wincing at the possible damage he'd caused. Fuck it, it just didn't matter.

He wanted information and his one good source, potentially at least, had just dried up. So he'd have to get the information some other way. When in doubt there was always the Internet, but he'd already tried that route before and instead of knowledge on the necklace his mother had always worn, he'd gotten himself about a trillion listings on the Florida Keys and the best spots to vacation there.

So he would have to get more experimental in his research, but for now that could wait. He needed to find Jerry and see if his best friend was surviving the world away from Castle Corin. Aside from a few vacations, this was probably the most time his bud had spent away from the place in a long, long time.

"Okay. I'm going to go look for Jerry. I've had about enough of this place. I figure I hang around any more and I'll take root to the sofa." Brittany nodded and Katie shot him a grateful look. She was Jerry's girl and every one of them fully expected the two to get married at some point, but it was a simple fact of life that sometimes guys told guys things and sometimes girls told girls things, and if any guy on the planet knew where to scout for Jerry, it was going to be Chris.

Chris pulled out of the driveway a few minutes

later, heading no place in particular. He didn't have any plans, just to look and see where his mind took him. Where the demented little lump of gray matter chose was DeLucci's Pizza. DeLucci's was the best, hands down. It was also the site of his last sane day, and maybe Jerry was feeling a little sentimental as well. If nothing else, it was a destination.

He pulled into his usual spot at the pizzeria and climbed out of the car, doing his best not to think about his mother's death and focusing instead on the many good times he'd had at the dive. The smell of garlic and cheese permeated the air and probably the building itself after so many years. Chris smiled to himself and walked inside.

What he found were a lot of memories, mostly pleasant, and a bit of a surprise in the form of Jerry's older sister, Carmen. Carmen looked a lot like her brother. Too much so, really, to ever be called beautiful. But she was pretty, and when she smiled she could even manage cute for a few seconds. Her body, on the other hand, was the stuff runway models and playmates are made of. Three other girls with decent looks and mostly nice bodies were sitting with her.

Carmen looked his way and did a double take. They hadn't seen each other in over a year, and he guessed the rough nature of his life of late was showing on his face. She pushed her chair away from the table and her friends, murmuring something about being right back. Then she moved with more speed than grace and ran over to him, hugging him lightly in a way that made him remember she was a member of the opposite sex and not just the sister of his friend.

"How're you, Chris?" She looked at him with almost maternal concern, though she was only a few years older than he was. That was fair enough. She'd been stuck with the dubious task of baby-sitting her brother on many occasions and had been forced to put up with Chris at the same time. "I mean aside from the bruises. What ran into you?"

"I'm okay, Carmen. I came over to see if maybe Jerry was hanging around." He broke the hug but let his hands rest on her shoulders. "I just had a run-in with a mugger. He didn't come out any better. How are you? How's college life?"

"I'm good, Chris. Really good. But better if that little shit brother of mine would get his ass home."

"Still no word?"

"Not since they found out he was terminal." She looked away for a moment, her face clouding over with worry and maybe regrets.

"*What?*" The word flew out of his mouth before he could stop it and the volume guaranteed that everyone in the place looked his way. He managed to reopen the split in his lower lip at the same time and winced at the sting. "Terminal? What the hell are you talking about?"

Carmen looked at him with a sadness he wouldn't have thought her capable of a few years earlier. "Chris, I thought he'd told you. Whatever is happening to Jerry, it's not going to get better. The doctors haven't said exactly what sort of cancer it started as, but the sores and the lumps, honey, it's metastasized. He might have a few weeks to live."

Somehow Chris managed to find a seat before he sat down. He wasn't a hundred percent sure, but he thought Carmen might have grabbed it for him. "Shit, Carmen, he told me they didn't know what it was. He said they couldn't figure it out."

Carmen nodded, her eyes blinking rapidly as she tried to hold back any grief that might want to show itself. "He hasn't been home much to talk about it with anyone, Chris. Hell, he hasn't been home in the last few days. My dad's been talking about hiring a detective to look for him, but Mom shot that down hard and fast." She snorted a little huff of almost-laughter. "Mom thinks he needs time to sort it out. The rest of us think he needs to be in the hospital. There's got to be something they could do for him."

Chris nodded, barely hearing the words. Mostly he heard the pain in her voice. "He's good people, Carmen. Your brother's one of the best, he doesn't deserve this shit."

She looked away and nodded and he reached out and grabbed her hand, squeezing the fingers. She squeezed back. It felt a little strange giving comfort to the girl who used to have to baby-sit him, but it was all right. They'd known each other for most of their lives, even if they'd never been really close.

He left a few minutes later, after her friends called her back to whatever she'd been doing. He'd actually been thinking about buying a pizza, but that notion was shot down by the lack of money and the sudden loss of appetite.

III

Chris tried every place he could think of. He went back to a part of town he never wanted to see again, amazed that the area could have degraded even more in just a few months. He even went all the way over to Tillinghast Lane and looked over the remains of the house that had stood there before he helped destroy it. There was nothing to see there and the memories were the sort he wanted to forget, but he made a connection as he was standing there.

His mind wandered over everything that had happened lately and he damn near jumped when he realized what Laura from Dark Harvest Books had said to him. Her father and mother had been injured in a house fire. They'd been in bad shape, her father bedridden and blinded and her mother in a coma. Not that unusual, unfortunately. It was almost commonplace, even in an age where smoke alarms were mandatory. But earlier today, the cute girl he'd helped, who'd seemed so friendly and willing to get to know him better, had sounded hurt, almost angry when she'd called.

And her father knew about that damned necklace that had screwed his life up. The Western Key. It sounded so mundane, like the damned websites said it should. Like it was maybe a vacation spot where families went when they had spare money and were really, really in need of a good sunburn. It sounded like it should be absolutely harmless, and really, he couldn't think of too many people who would know about it and about him, unless they were at this very site when it was used to rip a hole in reality and let something nasty into this universe. Chris's skin rippled with gooseflesh and his stomach churned when he remembered the thing that had basically raped his mind while seeking information. As long as he lived he doubted he'd ever get over that feeling.

And Laura's father had been there. Been hurt in the fire, but lived through it. Knew who he was, and maybe now, knew where he lived. "Oh, shit. Shit, shit, SHIT!" Chris ran back over to where he'd parked his station wagon and climbed back in, his heart thundering in his chest.

"Okay, Corin, calm down. Time to get your ass in gear and work this out right now." Giving himself a pep talk was useless, but better than nothing. It also helped him think. This was a complete fuck up and he knew what he was going to do, but was trying very hard not to let the thought reach fruition in his head.

He was going over to Dark Harvest, and he was going to talk with Laura's father. That was the plan. Well, that and not getting his ass thrown in jail while he was doing it.

Chapter Five

I

Chris came up on Dark Harvest Books and settled in to wait for a while. The place was still open and that part didn't bother him, but there were customers inside and that would not do. Not when he intended to get himself into all sorts of trouble if he had to in order to learn what he needed to know.

Laura was inside, looking tired, and carrying her little brother on her hip. Somewhere above her, the man Chris needed to see was lying in a bed and not feeling his best. Chris didn't care anymore. The man—if he was a man at all—had information that Chris needed. More important even than that was the fact that Jerry needed that information if he was going to survive whatever the hell was happening to him.

Laura seemed nice enough. That was just too damned bad. Jerry was practically family. The only thing that separated them from actually being family was a matter of genetics and he was damned if he was going to let his best friend die because some crotchety old bastard in a bed didn't want to talk to him.

He waited for almost an hour before the last people shopping in the place were done. They must have been hardcore into the occult, because they took a lot of books and none of them looked less than a century or two old. There were three of them in all and not a one of the lot looked much younger than the books. He waited a few minutes more before he walked over to the store and entered.

Laura looked at him and sighed, her eyes noticing the beating he'd taken but showing nothing remotely like sympathy on her pretty face. "I can't help you, Chris. I'm sorry, but that's the way it is."

"I know, Laura. I understand that. But your father might be able to help me and I need to talk to him."

"Absolutely not! He can't have visitors."

"Let me guess why. Does he have a lot of raw red sores growing all over his body?" He took a chance.

She shot it down. "No. He's just at risk from infection, he was burned over a lot of his body."

"Where was that house fire, anyway? Was it pretty close to here?"

"None of your damned business, Chris."

"You remember how you thanked me for saving your little brother?"

"Yeah . . ." She looked down at the ground then, as if ashamed. He felt the same way, because he hadn't done anything all that special as far as he was concerned, but he wasn't above using what she considered his good deed in order to get his way.

"Well, now you can pay me back, okay? Let me talk to your dad for two minutes, just long enough to answer a question or two and I'll leave and you can forget I ever existed, okay?"

"Chris, he's my dad, okay? He isn't well, and I can't let him get any worse."

"I know, Laura, but my best friend is sick, really, really sick because of what the Western Key did. And if I can't find out how to stop it, he won't be around much longer. Laura, please, I'm begging here."

"I can't Chris. I'm sorry for your friend."

Chris shook his head. "I'm sorry too, Laura. But that isn't enough."

He walked behind the counter and brushed past her without looking. Toward the back of the counter area he could see a doorway that he assumed led to the apartment above. He grabbed the handle and turned it. The door opened easily and even as Laura started calling out to him desperately, he started up the stairs that the opening revealed.

Her fingernails slashed across his back, and then her hand grabbed at his short hair. He was glad he kept it short. It took an effort not to turn around and backhand her for the claw marks, but he managed as he kept bulldozing his way up the staircase.

"Chris! Stop, damn you!"

"No! Not until I talk to him!" Oh yeah, he was feeling like a man now, heading up to confront a burn victim.

Laura jumped on his back and he staggered, tried to keep his balance, and fell to his knees, the sharp angle of the stair slamming his kneecaps and sending exquisite shivers of pain through his legs.

"God damn it, Laura!" Her fists slammed into his back and head again and again, until he finally turned awkwardly in the narrow space and caught her thin wrists in his hands. "Knock it off!"

"I'm gonna call the fucking cops!"

"You do that. You go right ahead. I just bet they'd love to know what your folks were up to on Tillinghast Lane before the house fire."

"Laura." It was one word and spoken softly, but they both heard it.

The struggle stopped in an instant.

Chris let go of her wrists as she answered her father. "Yes, Dad?"

"Let the boy up the stairs." The voice was wet with phlegm.

"But, Dad . . ."

There was a deep wheeze, followed by a harsh hacking cough. "Let him up the stairs, girl. You mind me, you hear?"

Laura backed away, her eyes wide. "Go on, Chris. But be careful of his condition."

Chris nodded and stood up again, wincing at the

lingering pain in his knees. "Two minutes, Laura. Then you can pretend I was never here."

Laura didn't respond.

He went up into the apartment, his ears pricking as he listened to the sound of wheezing and harsh breathing to tell him where he needed to go. The rooms that made up Laura's living space were small but neat and well-decorated. The living room was the sort that he expected more from a grandmother in a Hollywood movie than a family of four. There were scattered pictures that dated back at least a few generations, all the way back to when daguerreotypes were more common; most of them showed people with almost stereotypically dour expressions, but a few of the newer ones showed Laura and her brother with a strong-jawed man and a woman who looked like Laura most likely would in another twenty or so years. Mostly they smiled. Sometimes, though, the smiles looked rather forced.

There was a wide dining room and kitchen area set together further back, but before he could go that far his ears finally figured out where the man's wheezing sounds were coming from. Down the short hallway that divided the living room and the kitchen area, a door was open on the left-hand side.

Chris walked up to the opening and looked in without bothering to knock. What would have been the point? He was expected and was already running short on time due to the limits he had imposed on his little Q & A session.

123

"Come in, Mister Corin." That wet voice made his skin crawl and another wave of mild nausea hit his stomach, almost seeming to ripple in the direction of the man lying on the king-sized bed.

Chris stepped in and looked at the source of the voice. Whatever he'd been expecting wasn't what he found. For a man who was supposed to have been badly burned, Laura's father looked remarkably healthy. His hair was short and shot with stark white strands, and his face had more lines than it had in the pictures in the living room, but this was obviously the same face he had already seen in the photographs. His body below the waist was hidden beneath heavy covers that should have had him sweltering half to death in the heat of the room, but he seemed perfectly comfortable. Both of his arms, however, were heavily swaddled in cotton bandages, the arms of his clean pajama top had been cut open to accommodate the thick padding.

"You have questions, boy. Get to them and be quick about it." When he spoke he looked less healthy, as though the effort of talking at all drained him.

"I'm sorry to bother you, sir. But I need to know about the Western Key, and what you meant when you said I was marked."

"The Western Key can't hurt anyone anymore, Corin. You took care of that."

"How do you know about that?" He already knew the answer, of course, but he had to be certain.

124

"I was there." The man smiled then, an unpleasant expression that seemed more like a sneer than any attempt at humor. "I saw you, boy. I saw what you did and I saw what was done to you."

"One of my friends was . . . infected. He was caught by that thing in the ground, the thing that tore the house apart." Chris stepped closer. "What was it? What did it do to him and how can I fix him?"

The man tried laughing and it quickly disintegrated into a retching, hacking cough. For a minute Chris thought he'd keel over dead right in front of him, but when he tried to come closer, Laura's father waved him back. "I don't need you coming any closer to me, Mister Corin." When he had recovered as fully as he seemed capable of recovering, he looked back at Chris again. "You can't help your friend, young man. He is a host to something far more persistent than a flu bug or the common cold."

"What do you mean?"

"Survival of the species is what I refer to, young man. Your friend should have been dead by now, along with the rest of the people who were in that house. They would have been, too, if not for your interference."

"And this was what you wanted?" Chris was having trouble believing his ears. "You actually wanted to let that thing through into this world?"

"Of course. It's what I spent my life waiting for, you miserable ape." He wasn't sounding quite as weak anymore. In fact he was looking positively spry, despite his bandages. Chris swallowed, feeling a wash of sour spittle flow into his mouth as his stomach seethed with new acids.

"You said what was done to me. What did you mean by that?"

"You were marked, boy. You knew that before. You were marked by the very 'thing' you stopped from coming here."

"What the fuck are you talking about?" His knees were shaking a bit now and Chris was ready to leave the room. The man was obviously insane. He had to be.

"You know what I mean, boy. It marked you." The man grinned, his face looking a bit paler. "That feeling in your stomach? Get used to it." The smile dropped from the man's face as quickly as it had shown itself. "Your life is worth shit. You understand me? Your friend got off easy. But you? Your suffering will be nearly endless." Laura's father leaned forward in the bed. "Now get the hell out of here. Go away. You disgust me."

"Listen to me, you sick fuck . . ." Chris reached for the man and watched him flinch before he caught himself. He wasn't here to beat the crap out of an old man, no matter how tempting it might be. "You tell me how to help Jerry or I'll beat you to death."

The man laughed again, this time convulsing and coughing until he was red in the face. Before he could respond further, Laura was there, grabbing Chris by the arm, her nails scraping flesh away.

"You get away from him!" Her eyes were wild, angry and scared. He could understand that. He was feeling that way almost all of the time these days.

"Laura, please!" He wanted so much for this to work out well and knew it wouldn't. Knew that it couldn't, really, because her father was one of them, one of the freaks that had tried to bring his nightmares to life.

"Get out before I call the police." Laura's voice was calmer but her face was just as enraged. "You get out of here and you never come back, or I'll take the gun I have downstairs and blow your fucking head off."

Chris looked at the older man again, watching as something black and rancid spilled from his mouth and ran down his chin. He didn't look remotely threatening anymore, or even like he was capable of rational thought. He coughed again, weakly, and looked to his daughter with confused eyes.

Chris turned to Laura and saw nothing but hatred. Had he been in her shoes he'd have felt exactly the same thing. He left. The old man either wouldn't or couldn't help him anymore.

He was almost home when it dawned on him that Laura was either exaggerating or something was much stranger with her father than she knew about. Laura had said he was blinded in the fire. But he'd looked right at Chris and reacted when Chris reached for him. It wasn't exactly a comfortable thought to have.

He realized a few minutes after that little revelation

that he was actually hungry and made another mental note to himself—to add to the growing list of things he had to do and would never manage to get around to at the current rate—to see a doctor when he had money again.

II

There are only so many places a man can hide if he doesn't want to be found. Jerry had found one where even Chris wouldn't look for him.

It wasn't that he was hiding from what he'd done, exactly. More that he was hiding from what he might do. The voices were getting stronger and much more coherent. They were becoming one voice instead of many and what they said was terrifying him.

Jerry walked along the sewer line, ignoring the stench of raw feces and even more questionable things. At first he'd been afraid of rats, but as soon as any of them got a look at him they bolted, chittering away and looking back at him warily.

They were afraid of him, or of whatever he was becoming.

"Can't really say as I blame you, guys. I'm getting pretty fucking scared myself." He spoke and the hissing voice that was always with him now responded with a surge of gibberish that stuck in his mind like a song title on the tip of his tongue.

He stopped moving, strained to hear the words, but as soon as he focused on them they seemed to recede.

Just close enough to hear but never quite near enough to understand. It was infuriating.

The water around his ankles swelled to a higher level and he knew that something was in there with him, deep in the sewer system that ran for what seemed like a million miles under the town.

He had no idea what was above him. He didn't much care. He just wanted the damned voices to go away so he could hear himself again and be himself again.

Something deep inside of him surged and he grunted, his nerves flaring with pain as whatever was growing in there made more of him its own.

Jerry Murphy sat down in the waters and hugged himself tightly. Something inside hugged back but there was no comfort from it.

Not far away from him a water rat made angry noises about his intrusion and he felt the world grow dim as whatever now sat inside his body and mind sought to take control of him. It wasn't the first time he'd felt the sudden pressure seize him and blanket his senses. But this time it was worse. This time he felt it pushing him down, crushing him inside its growing noises and loathsome malignance.

Jerry closed his eyes and went to sleep. Something else took over then and his body moved, leaping out of the water and charging for the terrified rodent as it sensed whatever was happening inside of him.

Jerry didn't hear or feel or taste what happened next. But the thing growing inside of him did.

III

Katie and Courtney and Brittany were still waiting around when Chris finally got home. Courtney and Brittany had both gone to sleep while they waited and he looked at them in absolute silence as he entered his own home. His little sister was asleep in the recliner, curled up like a cat, her face calm and innocent. He'd have given anything to see her like that more often. Courtney's face was troubled and her lips were parted. She was whispering softly to someone in her dream and her words were lost somewhere along the way. Though he tried, he couldn't make sense of the sounds that came from her. He moved into the kitchen, and there he found Katie.

The look on Katie's face when he told her that he'd had no luck that wasn't bad was enough to damn near break his heart. It wasn't doing much for his morale and he could only guess what she was going through. He'd never been with anyone in the same way that Katie and Jerry were together.

He envied them most times. Not so much at the present moment. Chris had to think about it for all of two seconds before he told Katie about his encounter with Carmen. He waited a moment before explaining the details.

Despite his telling her not to, Katie was cooking a meal with his meager supplies. "Listen, Katie. You know I appreciate you coming over here. You don't have to do any chores. I can wash a dish with the best of them."

She laughed. "No, Chris. You can't. I've double washed damn near everything you tried to clean. Trust me."

He shook his head. "Listen, I ran across Carmen when I was looking around for Jerry."

"Yeah?" She had a tone in her voice that he knew too well. Katie and Carmen had never exactly gotten along. "What did she have to say about Jerr?"

Chris leaned against the counter and wished he didn't have to be the one to tell her. Jerry should have had the balls to handle his own situations and even if he didn't like feeling that way, he liked even less being the one who had to ruin Katie's good mood.

"Shit, Katie. She said he's got cancer. He wasn't telling us the truth about what's wrong. One of the doctors said he's got some sort of cancer."

Katie set the plate she was drying down carefully and looked at Chris, her pretty eyes wide and her mouth pressing into a thin line. Was she going to cry? He didn't know.

"That motherfucker."

"What?"

"That stupid motherfucker lied to me." The venom in her voice would have killed a king cobra. "I swear I'm gonna break his balls when I see him." Her voice trembled, sliding quickly and effortlessly from rage to something even worse. Her voice broke when she spoke again. "He can't leave me, Chris. He just can't."

Katie wrapped her arms around herself and hugged, and Chris moved forward, wondering if he was supposed to give her comfort in this kind of case or if that was considered inappropriate. In the long run he didn't care. He pulled her into his arms and hugged her hard. She resisted for a moment and then hugged back, clinging to him like ivy on a tree.

"Damn, Katie. I wish I could tell you something better. I really do." His eyes stung and he had to hold his breath, hold his eyes closed for a moment to stop from crying. It was killing him, knowing that there was nothing he could do for Jerry.

After almost two minutes, they broke apart and Chris was surprised to see that Katie looked embarrassed. After all she had done for him and for Brittany alike, showing any weakness in front of him embarrassed her. He couldn't believe it.

"I should go home." She looked at the yellowed linoleum like it was the most interesting thing she'd ever seen.

"You don't have to. You can stay here. Mom's room is in perfect order."

She shook her head. "No. I need to think. I need to figure out what the hell he was thinking, the stupid sonuvabitch."

Chris nodded. "You know where to find me if you need to talk, okay?"

Katie finally managed a small smile. "Okay. That's

a deal. Your dinner's almost ready." She nodded to a pot that sat on a low simmer. "I think it's supposed to be lasagna. I added some spices so it would taste like something."

He nodded and gave her another brief hug. "Thanks again. When my money comes in I'm buying you your own restaurant."

"Don't tease the cook." She smiled. "I might poison the next one." He walked her to the door a few minutes later and said his good-byes to a very sleepy Courtney at the same time. Part of him wished Courtney would hang around, but only because he was starting to think a good romp in the proverbial hay would be just the thing to ease his stress.

He didn't like thinking that way. It made him feel like a creep.

Chapter Six

I

The sun was starting its rise and the dark sweet night was being murdered by the growing light on the eastern horizon. The time had come to settle in again. The changes happened best if they had time to rest.

They gathered at the river's edge and stared into the water. There were over twenty of them now, and they were growing stronger and closer together as their bond slowly cemented itself. In the beginning they had hated each other, the very presence of the things growing inside of them had made them feel not kinship, but a deep and abiding loathing.

That had pared down their numbers a bit, but in the long run, they were stronger for the culling. Like weak branches taken from a tree, the dead of their ilk had been slowing down the progress they sought. And now the changes that were happening within them were harder to hide. Now they sought to stay in the dark places.

The river was cool and the sounds it made were soothing to the strange minds that had grown within them. Keeping the minds calm was important. The smallest sign of agitation in the beginning had been enough to send them into frenzies.

These days that was changing. These days they were much calmer, even if they were never really alone with their thoughts anymore.

As one they walked into the waters, making almost no noise as they slipped into the river's embrace. The cold no longer affected them as it had in the past. They barely even noticed the temperature around them. They were stronger than they had been. They were also more tolerant to environments.

They sank beneath the waters of the river and did not float back to the surface. Instead they expelled the air from their lungs and breathed in the murky liquid that had become their new environment. Their eyes adjusted, growing a second lid that protected them and still allowed them to see. There were things beneath the surface of the river that they needed to explore, things waiting for them.

Others came, stragglers, who joined them as they slowly moved deeper into the waters of the Neponset River and sought the source of the new voice that kept calling to them. It was almost time. They didn't want to wait any longer, but knew that certain requirements had not yet been met. This was one of the last.

There, buried beneath the silt, they found it hiding away in the deepest part of the river. They swam or crawled over the debris that humans had left behind and then dug at the river's muck, exposing what they had sought so eagerly.

It was a hunger none of them had felt in a long time, the gnawing, raging hunger of a starved man finally locating a source of food. Their prey was wounded, nearly dead after its months of inactivity. Still, it struggled, thrashing deep below the river's surface and trying to escape from a fate that was sealed when it failed in its previous mission.

They attacked and tore and ate, drinking in the thick black blood of the creature and devouring the wriggling stuff it was made of. Nothing had ever been sweeter in taste, nothing had ever been more suitable to a palate.

And nothing else, not even the wine they'd used to numb the damnable feelings, had ever silenced the screaming whispers in their heads. They ate until there was nothing left of their prey, and when they were done the hunger was gone, the pain was gone for the first time since they had been freed from their prisons.

And at last they understood why they existed, why they were allowed to live at all after they should have been dead.

They knew and accepted and it was good.

Amen.

GET UP TO 4 FREE BOOKS!

You can have the best fiction delivered to your door for less than what you'd pay in a bookstore or online—only $4.25 a book! Sign up for our book clubs today, and we'll send you **FREE* BOOKS** just for trying it out...**with no obligation to buy, ever!**

LEISURE HORROR BOOK CLUB

With more award-winning horror authors than any other publisher, it's easy to see why CNN.com says "Leisure Books has been leading the way in paperback horror novels." Your shipments will include authors such as RICHARD LAYMON, DOUGLAS CLEGG, JACK KETCHUM, MARY ANN MITCHELL, and many more.

LEISURE THRILLER BOOK CLUB

If you love fast-paced page-turners, you won't want to miss any of the books in Leisure's thriller line. Filled with gripping tension and edge-of-your-seat excitement, these titles feature everything from psychological suspense to legal thrillers to police procedurals and more!

As a book club member you also receive the following special benefits:

- **30% OFF** all orders through our website & telecenter!
- **Exclusive access to** special discounts!
- **Convenient** home delivery **and 10 days to return any books you don't want to keep.**

There is no minimum number of books to buy, and you may cancel membership at any time. See back to sign up!

*Please include $2.00 for shipping and handling.

YES! ☐

Sign me up for the Leisure Horror Book Club and send my TWO FREE BOOKS! If I choose to stay in the club, I will pay only $8.50* each month, a savings of $5.48!

YES! ☐

Sign me up for the Leisure Thriller Book Club and send my TWO FREE BOOKS! If I choose to stay in the club, I will pay only $8.50* each month, a savings of $5.48!

NAME: _____

ADDRESS: _____

_____

TELEPHONE: _____

E-MAIL: _____

☐ **I WANT TO PAY BY CREDIT CARD.**

☐ VISA   ☐ MasterCard   ☐ DISCOVER

ACCOUNT #: _____

EXPIRATION DATE: _____

SIGNATURE: _____

Send this card along with $2.00 shipping & handling for each club you wish to join, to:

Horror/Thriller Book Clubs
20 Academy Street
Norwalk, CT 06850-4032

Or fax (must include credit card information!) to: 610.995.9274.
You can also sign up online at www.dorchesterpub.com.

*Plus $2.00 for shipping. Offer open to residents of the U.S. and Canada only.
Canadian residents please call 1.800.481.9191 for pricing information.

If under 18, a parent or guardian must sign. Terms, prices and conditions subject to change. Subscription subject
to acceptance. Dorchester Publishing reserves the right to reject any order or cancel any subscription.

JOIN NOW!

II

The phone screamed and Chris joined it, his mind still locked into whatever dark place it had been visiting in his dreams. He reached over and grabbed the receiver, grunting. "Yeah?"

"Chris? It's me, bro. We need to meet up."

He sat up fast, stifling the urge to cry. "Jesus, Jerry. Where the hell have you been?"

"I'll tell you when we get together. Can you meet me somewhere?"

Chris squinted and looked at his alarm clock. "Dude, it's almost four in the morning."

"I know. I was thinking about the White Horse Diner." Jerry's voice sounded ragged.

"Yeah. Okay. Gimme fifteen minutes, all right?"

"Yeah. That's good. I'll see you." Jerry hung up before Chris could say anything else. He set the phone back down and thought about calling Katie. In the long run he decided against it. He could get more information if the two of them weren't trying to kill each other. And after the news she'd gotten earlier, Katie was likely to want to beat her boyfriend to death and then make sure he was okay.

Chris dressed quickly and left a note for Brittany after carefully checking to make sure she was still in her room. Lately he didn't much feel like trusting his little sister. Go figure.

The White Horse was only a few blocks away, and under most circumstances Chris would have walked it. But it was far too late at night and with the way his luck was going lately, he decided to be smart and drive.

The diner had been around for longer than Chris had been alive and even on the worst nights the place was crowded. There were actually several more customers than he would have expected, most of them drinking coffee and finishing off either a very late dinner or a very early breakfast. He had to look around twice before he realized that Jerry wasn't there yet.

Chris pulled out the remaining change from his pants and dove into his wallet. He found enough to actually eat something and ordered a burger, medium rare, extra everything. The waitress had been around longer than he'd been alive, too, but she hadn't changed very much in all of those years. The most astonishing change was that her hair was no longer held up in a massive beehive but was, instead, cut short. She smiled politely and went about her business.

The nausea started a few minutes before the burger showed up, and Chris casually reached into his pocket and pulled out a roll of Tums. Enough was enough. He could have ulcers later; right now he was just too damned busy.

Jerry slid into the booth, facing him. His body was covered in a couple layers of clothing and a baseball cap advertising a brand of beer Chris knew had gone out of business at least five years earlier covered the top of his head.

Jerry smiled thinly, his face covered with makeup.

Chris didn't have to ask why. Even through the flesh tone it was obvious he had more of the sores covering his skin like a freakish version of poison ivy, or zits gone wild.

"You didn't call Katie?" Chris couldn't tell if Jerry was relieved or disappointed.

"No. I figure I can call her later, after the sun's up."

"Good. That's good." He was twitchy, his eyes looking all around, and scanning the rest of the long room for faces he might know.

"What the hell is going on, Jerry?" Chris was no longer in the mood for playing games. He was tired and he was sore.

"I think I'm losing my mind, Chris. Seriously. I think I'm going off the deep end and I don't think I'm coming back."

"Talk to me. Lay it out on the line, bro. You're my best friend and I don't want any cryptic bullshit from you." The nausea was still there, but calmer now that the antacids had kicked in.

Jerry was about to answer when the waitress came by with Chris's food. Jerry ordered the same thing with a look of ravenous hunger. Chris slid his plate across and watched his best friend attack it.

"I'm all for you eating, dude, but tell me what the hell is going on."

"The infection's taking me over, Chris. It's filled me up and now it's trying to push me out of my own head." His words were muffled by the mouthful of ketchup-soaked fries he stuffed into his gullet before speaking.

"Yeah, we already covered that. Is that why you nailed the guy that hit the Mustang?"

"I don't even remember doing that, Chris. One minute I'm with Katie and the next I'm down in the sewers, man. I don't even remember anything besides him hitting the car and me wanting to keep my cool.

"Yeah, well, that last part didn't go so well." Chris took a long drink of water and then motioned to the waitress for coffee. "Katie said you beat the guy half to death."

Jerry looked down at the burger and then all but attacked it, tearing a third of the thing off and chewing rapidly. Chris's stomach actually gave a rumble, the sick feeling finally fading away to a bad memory.

"I talked to Carmen, Jerry. She's pissed off and she's worried." He waited until his friend had finished the hamburger and then started again. "So am I and so is Katie. Especially since Carmen says it's cancer."

"Don't be an asshole. It isn't cancer. It's that shit you tried to pull out of me, Chris. Some of it got left inside and it's growing and it's fucking with my head."

"Yeah, well there has to be something we can do." Chris looked away. "So far I'm not having a lot of luck. The one guy that knows anything isn't talking and every other source I tried was clueless."

"What one guy?" Jerry was trying to sound calm, but Chris knew better.

"There was a dude at the house that night who got away. He was burned, but he lived. He said I was marked and you were as good as dead. That was all I could get out of him."

"Yeah? What's the loser's name?"

"Jerry, I already tried talking to him, it didn't do any—"

"Tell me his name, Chris. Or where I can find him. I'll get the information."

"I don't think he's human, Jerry. I don't think he's been human for a long time. I think he's one of those damned things, those doubles we found. I don't know if you could take him."

"You let me worry about that, all right?"

The waitress set down Chris's second burger. Jerry looked at his empty plate and then at Chris's. Chris grabbed his knife and cut the burger in half then slid part to his friend along with the lion's share of the fries.

"Where, Chris?"

"He owns Dark Harvest Books, that's all I know. I don't even know his name, his daughter is Laura and his son is Jeremy, or something that starts with a J."

"You think his kids are human?"

"Yeah. Probably. I dunno."

"Then I guess I'll find out."

"Jerry . . . what if he doesn't know anything?"

"Whatever he knows is more than you and me right now, Chris."

"Yeah. I guess."

"It's the only option left, dude. That, or we can try pulling this shit out of me, and I don't think I'd survive that."

"How bad is it?"

"Finish eating first, I'll show you outside."

"That bad, huh?"

"Oh yeah." Jerry finished off his hamburger in two bites and then waved for another two to the waitress. She nodded.

"Dude, I have enough for one burger, maybe two . . ."

"It's on me, bro. I got your back." Jerry leaned in closer and Chris caught a whiff of his breath, which smelled all too much like stagnant beer.

They ate in silence and Jerry picked up the tab. He looked like he was a homeless bum, but the American Express card in his wallet still worked just fine.

After that they went outside where the first pale light of dawn was hinting that it would show up properly in an hour or so. There was more traffic already and several cars had crept into the parking lot while they ate.

"I can't show you here."

"So come on back to my place. We'll get a look and see what's happening." Jerry nodded and they rode back in Chris's car. He had to roll the window down; that nasty yeast smell was back with a vengeance and the very thought of it made his stomach roil.

The house was as quiet as ever. Chris opened the door and the two of them went inside. Once in, he checked on Brittany, who was still sound asleep.

"Show me."

Jerry nodded and took off his shirt. His under shirt

had short sleeves and he held up his arm for Chris to study. Sores ran down the flesh, just like the ones that had been there already, but much more prevalent than before. Jerry flexed his fingers a few times and looked at his hand hard, his mouth pressing into a thin line.

And his fingers changed. They grew longer, the nails extending into wickedly sharp claws and the skin darkening, growing coarser. Chris looked at his friend and then sat down hard on the sofa, no longer able to feel his legs. For that one moment his entire being was focused on that damned hand.

The sores that covered Jerry's arm darkened, until they matched the color of the flesh on his hand. At their very centers the skin rippled, moving as if someone had thrown pebbles and the flesh there was water.

"It takes a lot of effort." Jerry spoke through gritted teeth. Chris felt the heat coming off of him like an opened oven door.

"I'm getting that."

His best friend, the monster, grunted and forced his hand back to normal. For the moment at least, even the sores on his arm were smaller.

"So what now, dude?"

"I need the name of your friend from the house fire, Chris."

"I told you I don't know it."

"That's okay. I can probably find the bookstore."

"You want me to come with?"

"I'd love nothing better, but no. I want you to

watch over Katie and make sure she doesn't do anything stupid."

Katie had flawless timing. She knocked and opened the door at the same time and came in on the tail end of Jerry's comment.

III

"Where the fuck have you been?" Katie didn't walk into the room so much as she stormed, tossing the bags of groceries in her arms toward the sofa with frightening accuracy. Without a conscious thought she held onto the carton of eggs, setting it down on the coffee table. Her eyes never moved from where they were locked onto Jerry with laser-intensity.

"Katie!" Jerry lifted his arms, the sores he'd done everything he could to keep out of her view painfully evident. "I was just—"

"I said where the fuck have you been, Jerry?" Her eyes were doing a fast blink and her pretty face was on the verge of collapsing into tears. Chris already knew she wouldn't let that happen. It was just that she was relieved and now that she knew he was all right, she could be pissed off properly.

"Honey, I can explain . . ."

"Cancer? You sonuvabitch! Cancer? And you think I don't need to know about it? I'm gonna break your balls, you bastard."

Jerry looked over at Chris for help, but Chris just shook his head. This time his friend was on his own, though of course Chris would be there to pick up the pieces and stop too much damage from falling on the fool's skull.

Jerry held open his arms and Katie moved into them, hugging him fiercely. He went a little pale, but didn't move away from the pain her embrace must have caused to the main source of his skin rash from Hell.

"I'm gonna kill you, I swear I am . . ." Her words were mumbled into his chest and then she fell apart, crying softly against Jerry. Chris backed out of the room and left them in peace, taking the groceries into the kitchen.

The peace didn't last very long, of course. There were no broken dishes, and at no point did the furniture feel the need to get thrown through the windows, but the peace did not last. Most people having a fight in Chris Corin's house before the sun had risen properly would not have been in the house for very long. Jerry and Katie were the exceptions. Even before they had stood by him and his sister, they were family. There were no sins they had committed to date that would make him remove them from the premises, and not many he could think of that would make it happen.

He was still thinking about how good they were together when the panic attack hit him out of the blue. He'd just finished with the groceries when he felt his skin break into a sweat and his hands started trembling. Something felt like it was trying to tickle its way out of his stomach, and no matter what he did, he couldn't seem to catch a decent breath. Finally he made himself sit down at the kitchen table because he could feel his legs wanting to give out.

Jerry and Katie were still talking, their tones rapid and combative. That didn't matter at the moment. The only thing that did was that

Jerry's a fucking monster! The same sort of weird shit that robbed my mother's grave and fucked up my car!

Jerry was safe and they could still find some way to heal what was done with him if they tried hard enough. There had to be a way. Because Jerry was too important in his life and he'd already lost

He's in there right now, and he's probably thinking about snaking on the old gang or maybe finding another fucking necklace so he can do it all over again and I can't do that! I can't face that shit again, please, please don't let him be

so much and the thought of anything else falling apart in his life made him want to puke his guts out.

He sat and breathed and tried to make himself stay calm, but it wasn't working very well. He wanted to

Run away from this fucking shit! Just get the hell out of town and screw everybody else! They weren't there! They don't know what it was like when that thing ate my fucking mind they can't possibly

be calm and in control, but it just didn't seem to want to happen. He scooted the chair across the old linoleum of the kitchen and lowered his head down as best he could between his knees. His back and ribs were a little pissed about the idea, but screw it. He managed anyway. That was supposed to help with hyperventilation, and while he wasn't getting much oxygen, he sounded like a teakettle having a stroke every time he tried to gulp down more.

Jerry and Katie kept talking and Chris tried to make himself heard, but all that came out of him was a thin whining noise. He was still making the same sounds when the world went black around him.

Chris woke up a few minutes later. He knew it couldn't have been long, because the sounds of his two best friends arguing were still there. He was drenched in sweat and felt like he'd been soaking in a tub of ice water. He thought about calling a psychiatrist, or maybe going to see a doctor.

Then he thought about his financial situation and decided it was nothing he couldn't handle on his own.

IV

Dark Harvest Books was the sort of place that Chris liked. It was an old building in an old part of town and it had a certain antiquated charm. Then again, Chris liked the library.

Jerry didn't much care for books. They had their uses, but they weren't exactly big on his list of things he wanted to cuddle up with. He'd left his number-one most desirable cuddle at Chris's place. Right now Katie wanted to strangle him, but that was all right. If he worked everything out the way he wanted to here, she could strangle away and actually have an impact.

He was pretty sure the shit flowing through his veins didn't qualify as blood anymore and he knew for a fact that he wasn't breathing with his lungs anymore.

Mostly he was sure he wanted his old body back the way it was, and his mind, too. Both of them were changing too much and if he couldn't get this shit fixed, he might find himself lost in places he didn't like to think about. Places where the whispers were in charge again and he became the little voice in the background for whatever the fuck was trying to take him over completely.

The neighborhood was hardly what he'd call upper crust. Then again, neither was Chris's. But he wasn't here to hang out and be sociable. Jerry looked at he building and suppressed the butterflies that wanted to assault his stomach. He needed to be as in control as he could manage if he was going to get through this in one piece.

He also needed ground rules to follow. Like, as an example, he didn't intend to hurt the girl. And if the little kid was there, well, he was off limits too. But the old man? The father? He was going to talk or he was going to suffer.

There was no traffic on either side of the street. That was just fine with Jerry. Fewer witnesses to worry about. He walked quickly around the two parked cars near the building and opened the door to the shop. He recognized the girl the second he saw her. She'd been over at Chris's place and had looked about ready to ask *him* out on a date.

She almost managed a smile and then she must have gotten a good look at his face and his skin. "We're closed!" The words were blurted hastily as she moved toward the door. He wasn't much in the mood to listen. Even if he was, the whispers were back and growing stronger by the second. It was desperation that made him shove her back against the wall. He told himself that again as he drove his fist into her stomach and watched her double up from the blow.

"It's nothing personal. But your dad and me have business."

Her only response was a groan as she slid to the floor. He hated what he'd just done. Hated even more that it had felt good. He resisted the urge to keep swinging at her and forced himself to follow the instructions Chris had given him.

He'd made it most of the way up the stairs before the whispers became screams. Whatever was riding inside his head wanted out. He staggered and bounced against the wall as he kept walking, the noise in his skull reaching a level that was almost blinding. The parts of his body that tended to wiggle of their own volition started dancing a watusi under his skin.

"You may as well come all the way up, boy." The voice was hoarse and strained. "You and I both know what you want." He located the source easily enough. The voice came from the only room with an open door. Though there were no lights and the curtains had been drawn, he could just make out a figure on the bed.

Jerry walked into the master bedroom, the whispers reacting like the ticks from a Geiger counter as he approached the figure on the bed.

"You know why I'm here? Good. Then we can cut the crap and get to business. Tell me how to stop what's happening to me."

The shape on the bed moved with an odd, almost liquid grace, and the bed beneath it groaned in protest. "What makes you think I could answer a question like that, boy?"

"Because you were trying to bring that thing into this world. You were the one who created this mess in the first place." Jerry walked into the room, his hand searching along the wall for a light switch. It was hard to concentrate through the hissing whispers in his skull.

He didn't want to be here. He wanted to be almost anywhere else at all, especially with the way those sounds echoed through his mind, bouncing like rubber balls inside of a steel drum. They couldn't seem to get out, but they weren't slowing down. Perpetual motion made insane, and all of it inside of his own thoughts and memories. The closer he came to the shape in the darkness, the worse it got. And much as he wanted to run, the sounds inside of him seemed to be drawn to the source of the voice on the bed.

"I didn't summon them. They wanted to be summoned. I didn't create the Keys, I was just there to use them. That doesn't mean I know about what happened to you, boy. I don't and I couldn't care less."

"You lying sack of shit . . ." Jerry moved forward into the darkness, giving up on his hunt for the lights. He wouldn't need light to beat the man to death.

Jerry balled his hands into fists and heard the laughter that came from the darkness just ahead. And whatever lay on the bed came at him in return, the laughter changing into a roar of challenge.

Before Jerry could respond, the silhouette on the bed was airborne and knocking him backward, staggering him toward the door of the room and back out into the main hallway.

For a blind guy, the freak from the bedroom had a lot of eyes. They weren't centered anywhere in particular, but were instead growing like freckles on his skin. Jerry had just enough time to notice them before the owner of Dark Harvest Books slammed him into the floor, both powerful hands wrapping around his throat in an effort to strangle him to death.

Jerry let the rage start boiling inside of him, forcing his anger up and into his body like a shot of pure electricity into his muscles. He had a lot to be angry about, starting with the asshole trying to kill him. He forced his own hands up around the man's wattled neck and locked his fingers in place, thinking about the look on Katie's face earlier, the tears and the anger and hurt that marked her perfect, sweet features.

The old man coughed hard, his body shaking as Jerry cut off his oxygen. But that didn't stop his fingers from trying to work their way through his neck. Jerry pushed his chin down against his chest as hard as he could, grunting with the effort. The freak was stronger than he looked.

They might well have stayed that way for a few hours, both trying to get past the other's defenses with little success, but the blonde from downstairs came up and that changed everything. She took one look at what was going on and reached for the closest weapon she could find, in this case a dark brown marble monstrosity that looked like a man with a squid's head.

Pinned to the ground, Jerry wasn't exactly a hard target to find. She slammed the art deco octopus into his head. Less than a second later, her father won the fight by default.

V

Katie settled herself down on Eileen Corin's bed and closed her eyes. She was tired. So damned tired. Jerry was being unreasonable, and Chris was being as strong as he could, but she knew good and well he was close to the breaking point. He hadn't been back from that particular mental location since his mom's death.

She'd snuck into his room a few times to see if he was all right, especially on those occasions when he'd been out lately, looking for Jerry or for Brittany when she was pulling one of her stunts. It wasn't because she was trying to see him naked or anything—not that she would mind seeing him naked, but that wasn't the point—but because she was worried about him.

About how he was holding up inside, where it really counted.

So far the prognosis from Doctor Katie wasn't great. He was still in one piece, but he wasn't exactly holding it together anymore. Then again, neither was she. Jerry was doing worse than either of them, and even Brittany, who had an amazing capacity for ignoring what she didn't like to hear, was beginning to fall into shreds.

Whatever the hell was happening in their lives needed to stop now. Enough was enough.

Somewhere along the way God had forgotten to put a "Pause" button on the craziness. That sort of sucked. But these days there wasn't a lot she could think of that didn't sort of suck.

Her cell phone rang and Katie damned near flew from the bed to answer it. She was hoping it was Jerry, hoping that she could convince him not to go off and do anything stupid like he'd done when his damned car got hit, but no such luck. It was Courtney.

"Hi, Katie." She loved Courtney. The girl was her best friend in the world, bar none. But no one should be allowed to be that cheerful before noon.

"What's up, Court? You caught me ready to take a nap."

"We were supposed to get together and go shopping today. I seem to recall that being the plan for, you know, taking your mind off of shit. But I'm here at your house and you aren't." Ah, that explained the cheerful tones. Courtney was in mild bitch mode. The arctic tones didn't show up until she reached full bitch mode.

"Shit. Sorry. I forgot. I ran into Jerry and we spent like, four hours yelling at each other."

"Jerry? Holy shit. Is he okay? Are you okay?"

Katie shook her head and tried to speak, hating that her eyes were threatening tears again. "No. No he isn't. No I'm not. It's all turned to crap when I wasn't looking, Courtney."

"Where are you, honey? I'm coming right over."

"No, I'm okay. You don't have to do that."

"Fuck you. You're at Chris's place. I'm on my way."

From a lot of people that might have been enough to send Katie into a fit. Courtney was the one real exception. She was not always tactful, and she certainly had her own agenda when it came to guys like Chris, but she was also one of the sweetest people in the world when she wanted to be and Katie could use an ear to bend for a change of pace. She nodded at the phone as if Courtney could see it, and hung up.

Maybe her best friend could see it at that. She was true to her word and came over less than ten minutes later, probably breaking a dozen different traffic laws in the process.

They didn't talk at first. Courtney just knocked, entered the room, closed the door and then gave Katie a surprisingly strong hug. Katie hugged back, letting the to tears loose themselves at last. And Courtney let her cry, not needing any explanations or reasons. She just held her silently and let Katie get it off her chest.

Chapter Seven

I

There were times when Chris just wanted everyone to go away. Not for eternity or anything, just for a few hours so he could think. Right now he was wishing everyone he knew would come on down and pay a visit. It would have taken his mind off Courtney sitting ten feet away from him and looking like she normally did in his fantasies.

He hated that about her as much as he loved the end result. She was dressed casually as ever—which for her meant that the makeup was light and the hair was casual, the clothes of course, were designed to make his hormones rage. She was wearing a pair of jeans that managed to hug every curve of her body and a

James A. Moore

baby doll T-shirt with the legend "Not that innocent." As if he needed a reminder.

He made himself stop looking, but it wasn't easy. Even with half of his mind focused on Jerry and when he would be back, there was a lot of room in his skull for acknowledging how damned attracted he was to Courtney.

She's got to be doing this to me on purpose. There is no way she can sit there and look like that and not know what she's doing to me. But that was a crock of shit and he knew it. Courtney had been waiting at Katie's place. They were supposed to go out shopping or some such crap and now she was over here and barely even noticing him, because Katie was extremely stressed and for all the same reasons as Chris. But it was easy to think that way with Courtney, because she was almost never without her own agenda and most of those revolved around guys.

Chris smiled. "Look. Why don't you two go shopping? I've got your cell phone number and so does Jerry. Get out of here before you both go as crazy as me."

Courtney shot him a weird look and Katie shook her head. So much for plan B. With no one coming over to rescue him from his own libido and Katie shooting down the shopping spree, he was left in his lusty little limbo.

The phone rang and he practically jumped at it. "Hello?" He prayed hard it was Jerry and could tell by the way she moved that Katie was hoping for the exact same thing.

156

So, naturally, it was Sterling Armstrong. "Chris. I just wanted to check in on the situation with your grandmother, keep you abreast of what's happening. As it stands, we're looking pretty good, but I have to warn you again to make sure that Brittany behaves herself, especially because a little bird told me that you're being watched by a couple of detectives."

"Excuse me?"

"There are private investigators in town that were hired by your grandmother." The man's voice was as cool and friendly as if he were explaining that everything was in place for the family picnic.

"You gotta be shitting me!"

"Not in the least. That's why I'm telling you to be extra careful. I can only imagine that there's no other reason for them to be in town but to be looking for dirty laundry. That means you have to watch out for everything you do right now. And for everything Brittany does."

Chris felt the headset creaking in his grip, which was not really a good thing, especially with what he'd already put the phone through in the last few months.

"Chris? Are you still there?"

"Yeah, Sterling, I'm here." He was surprised by how calm he sounded. He didn't feel particularly calm, but he sounded pretty damned good. "Thanks for the heads up. I'll let Brittany know how serious it is."

"Listen, just play it calm and cool and if you see anyone, let me know. I could be wrong on this, Chris, I just don't think you should take any chances."

"I don't plan to. Take care, Sterling."

He hung up before the attorney could say anything else.

Then he looked over at Katie and Courtney. "I'm going for a walk, guys. I'll be back pretty soon."

"If you're going after Jerry, be careful, okay?" The words took him by surprise. He looked at Katie, his face as calm as his voice. Instead of answering, he only nodded.

Chris walked outside into the miserable heat and looked up at the sky filled with a scattering of clouds that didn't promise rain but gave off enough humidity to make breathing seem like an effort. He pulled the car keys out of his pocket and went straight for the station wagon.

"I thought you said you were going for a walk." Courtney had snuck out the door behind him and was squinting against the glare from the sun. It chose just that moment to break from the clouds and ignite her hair into a halo. He wasn't fooled.

"Yeah, well, I said I was gonna walk, Court. I just didn't say where I was going to do that walking thing."

"Are you going after Jerry?" Her normally smooth brow wrinkled a bit.

"Yeah. I am."

"Be careful. Okay? Just be careful."

Chris kept his mouth shut again and just nodded before slipping behind the driver's seat. He looked back in the rearview mirror several times as he left, and Courtney watched him drive away the entire time. She was still standing in the front yard when he turned the corner.

II

It didn't take long to discover that he was, indeed, being followed. That or he was reaching all new levels of paranoia. The car was a lime green piece of shit that made his old station wagon look like a work of art. If someone really was trailing him, they were hardly the greatest when it came to subterfuge.

Chris went by means of the shortest route and drove at a steady pace all the way over to Dark Harvest Books. He passed the place by and drove down two blocks before he parked.

The rattling little coupe went right on past and parked half a block further down the narrow street from where he'd come to rest. The two guys he saw in the car looked like they belonged in a street gang in east L.A. They were dark-skinned and dressed in clothes that just didn't really fit in with the neighborhood Chris normally called home. Near the bookstore and the area where he was now, they were a lot closer to what would be expected.

Chris climbed out of the wagon and headed toward Dark Harvest, doing his best not to look back too often. In the long run, they didn't really matter too much. Chris wanted to know if Jerry was okay. He wanted to see if Laura was all right, too, even if they hadn't parted on very good terms. She had a right to be pissed. He'd have done the same thing she did if someone had come after his mom, even if Eileen Corin had been acting a little weird.

Going inside the store was out of the question, of course. The police would be called before he could so much as push through the front door. But he could look. There was no harm in walking in front of the store just to see if everything looked kosher. He kept telling himself that all the way up to the front of the place.

It didn't seem very comforting when he saw that the store was locked up tight. He resisted the urge to press his face against the glass and look into the darkened interior. There wouldn't be anything to see anyway.

So he walked. He moved up the slight slope of the road toward the next intersection, glancing noncommittally at the different shop fronts as if he might give a good damn about what was inside each store, though whatever he saw faded away from his mind a few seconds later.

There were only a few people on the street and most of them couldn't be bothered to even acknowledge his existence beyond the possible need to step out of his way. Chris took a right at the intersection and then bolted down to the end of the worn brick exterior of the place. His leg let out a few moans of protest as he ran, but it didn't give out under him like he'd pretty much expected.

The only good news was that his jog back to the

small parking lot was all downhill. There was some bad to go with the good, like the piles of debris resting against the short brick wall that marked the edge of the property, and the damned run of litter that simply sat against the overly full Dumpsters.

His feet slipped a few times and he had to practically dance to keep his balance, but he still made good time, all factors considered. When he reached the end of the building he waited as patiently as he could, breathing through his nose to keep the sounds of his panting to a minimum.

And after he recovered he found himself a few tools to make his life easier. First there were the nails. Then, added bonus, a broom handle that looked to be made of good, solid, seasoned wood.

Chris set about his new mission, moving carefully and doing his best not to be spotted. Not yet, at least. Ten minutes later he was finished and leaning against the wall of the building. All he had to do now was wait.

III

They gathered together again, watching the boy as he stalked around the bookstore. It had only taken one phone call to let them know where he would be, and that was a good thing. They no longer wanted to waste effort if they could avoid it. There was enough they still had to do, but chief among the things they wanted to do was let Chris Corin know that he wasn't forgotten. Or forgiven.

The changes were completing themselves within their bodies and even now they could hear each other's thoughts if they were so inclined. The hunger was gone, defeated by their last great meal, but they still had cravings and urges and they still wanted to make sure those were sated before they became significant.

Corin was responsible for so much. If he hadn't stopped what had been planned for who knew how many years, they would have already been dead. That would have been preferable to what they were going through, to what they were becoming.

The hunger was gone, yes, but slowly it was being replaced by a new imperative. They could feel the new need building inside of every cell in their bodies, growing thicker and fatter within them like cellulite on a food-bingeing obese man. There was so little left of what they had been, just memories and a growing resentment for the lack of any kind of normal future.

And then there was the pain. It wasn't constant, but it was there and it was growing. Bobby Johanssen spoke mostly to himself, but they all heard him and they all agreed with the comparison. "It's like the ocean tides. Sometimes it crushes everything and sometimes it backs away, but it always hurts."

Bobby Johanssen had never met Christopher Corin before he was rescued from a slow death by Corin and his friends and his little sister. He never wanted to see any of them again, either, and probably wouldn't have if the changes hadn't started in his system.

Much as he wanted to be grateful for the rescue, especially to the guy's little sister, who was exactly the sort of girl he wanted to get to know much, much better, everything in his life had gone to hell right afterward and the infectious transformations going on in his body guaranteed that whatever remained of his life wasn't going to be a cakewalk.

Just to remind him of that fact, something shifted inside of him, pushing at his stomach hard enough that he could feel the flesh distend. He clenched his hands into fists until the worst of the pain was over. Unlike a lot of the losers around him, he didn't feel the need to pickle his nerves until the worst of the change was over. He'd dealt his share of drugs, certainly given out a few free samples to a few cute little pieces of ass, but he didn't imbibe in that stuff. His lips pulled into a bitter grin. That shit could kill you.

He must have been thinking too loudly. A few of the ones closest to him chuckled at the thought.

One of the latecomers, one of the ones changed by Bobby and the rest of the original survivors, reached into his pocket and pulled out a cigarette. He struck a match and lit it, dragging deeply of the smoke. Only a few weeks ago he would have been coughing half of his lung out after inhaling that way. These days he didn't have lungs to worry about. The nicotine didn't do anything for him but the desire for it was still there, so he savored it while he still could.

After he'd finished the cancer stick he ground it under the heel of his penny loafer. "You want this ass-hole so bad, why are we looking at him instead of grabbing him?"

"Because he's marked, you dumb fuck." That came from Doug Walters. He'd been a happily married businessman until they infected him. Now he acted like he was still in college or maybe even in high school, his mouth spewing obscenities like there was no tomorrow.

Bobby explained, not because he really had to, but because he still liked speaking with his mouth instead of his mind. "The aura around him? See it? That field tells us he's open game but it also lets him know if we're too close by. We have to work out how to hit him hard and fast and take him down before he catches on that we're here."

"Screw that. There's one of him and ten of us. Take him." That said, the man who still smoked ran into the street and charged at Chris Corin as he leaned against the building where the bookstore sat.

Bobby Johanssen looked at the man running toward Chris and nodded with satisfaction. "I was wondering who'd break the ice for the rest of us."

IV

Chris saw the bum rushing toward him at the same time that he spotted the two lowlifes up past the bookstore, coming back toward their butt-ugly car. The dingy guy running his way was moving like a man with a mission, while the two private investigators were doing their best to look inconspicuous. That pretty much settled who he was going to deal with first.

Chris stepped away from the dirty brick wall and reached down to grab the broom handle he'd found earlier. Not a perfect weapon, but it would do if it was all he could get his hands on.

Captain Homeless lunged, his arms outstretched like he was going to tackle Chris. Chris sidestepped as the man went airborne and brought the long wooden dowel down across the back of the moron's skull. He dropped hard, grunting as he slammed into the pitted asphalt. It had been a bad week so far. Chris decided not to wait until the man was up and ready for more before he dished out a second helping of whoopass. Instead he just kicked the man in the ribs as hard as he could five times. The creep grunted with each blow and rolled into more of a fetal position.

Chris barely even noticed the wave of nausea until it was almost too late. He turned toward the strange sea-sick feeling that seemed to lean outside of his body and looked just in time to see the small herd of men and women running his way, their faces set in scowls of anger and determination.

He broke his stick on the face of a man he'd never seen before. The man had the decency to fall to the ground next to the first attacker, his scalp bleeding a thin red fluid.

Chris backed away, holding the remaining portion

of his trusty stick and watching the rest of the people coming his way. He recognized Bobby Johanssen despite the changes the man had gone through. He had a long beard going now, and he looked like he'd fleshed out a bit, but Chris would have known him even under a couple of pounds of thick makeup. It isn't easy to forget the guy you found trying to get into your little sister's pants. He was standing right next to Arthur Hall and a couple of others who held back and let the rest of the geek squad move in for the kill.

They weren't dropping like flies, much as he wanted them to. They just kept getting back up, and there was only one of him. Chris decided he could do without having to get his ass kicked in. He turned tail and ran. The freakfest behind him followed. So much for the easy way out.

Chris ran hard, his knee screaming to remind him that it wasn't very fond of the notion. He did his best to ignore the flares of pain and keep going, but he was moving up the slight hill he'd recently gone down and the pain refused to just leave him alone.

He had just passed the bookstore when he saw the two street detectives coming from around the side of the building. They looked as surprised as he felt and he took advantage of that fact by shooting right past them.

He ran past the two detectives and poured on the speed, adrenaline finally deciding to be generous and give him a boost. It was a good plan, at least in theory. Unfortunately, none of the creeps doing the chase-

Chris-down dance seemed to have bad legs to go with their shitty complexions.

He did cut one big break though. The detectives took one look at the small mob coming after him and decided to run as well. They were a decent buffer against potential disasters. They were also damned good runners. One of them caught up with him in a matter of seconds. The man had gold-covered teeth and half a dozen earrings in each ear. He looked almost as panicked as Chris felt.

"Who'd you piss off, man?"

"I dunno, and I'm not asking."

The guy nodded and kept pace with him. Just behind them the other detective was already wheezing, though he managed to keep pace well enough. Something a little further back let out a burping sort of growl that told Chris more than he wanted to know about the guys following after them. The noise sent his nerve endings into a panic that soon spread through his whole body.

"Okay. I know you're tailing me, and I don't care right now. Those things want me. If you run, they might leave you alone." Chris panted the words, his breathing already feeling labored enough that the coach back in high school would have been tearing him a new asshole on general principals.

"Yeah, I get that." The man nodded his head. "But it ain't happening. If you die, we can't get our money."

The second man let out a gasp behind them and a few seconds later was running twice as fast, passing them both by as if they were standing still. Chris shook his head. He could have told the man not to actually look.

"They're . . . gonna run us . . . down." Chris's lungs reminded him that breathing and talking were most decidedly connected issues. He was winded and his side was starting to hurt.

Gold Tooth looked at him. "Wanna take 'em?"

Chris nodded and put on the brakes. The man beside him did the same thing, both of them turning to face the oncoming wave of

MONSTERS!!!!

people coming their way. Chris lowered his body and watched as the group came closer. The one whose head he'd caved in was front and center, his eyes jet black and the wound on his skull bleeding a thin dark crap that was exactly the wrong color for blood. He came running harder, his head lowered and his eyes narrowed.

Chris swallowed the dry feeling in his throat and waited until the blackheads on the loser's face were close enough to count. Then he pumped his fist into the face under the nasty wound and felt the satisfaction of bone and flesh splitting under his knuckles. The man did a beautiful backflip and landed hard on the concrete.

The next two in line didn't fall down so much as they blew up. One of them tried to stop, his eyes flying wide, and then as his hand moved up in a frantic wave, his head exploded. What came out of the wound was not flesh and bones and brains. It was all the wrong color and reeked of rotted newspapers and far fouler things. The one to his left lost a leg and part of a hip, then his chest exploded and his head followed suit.

Chris let out a massive shriek and backed away from whatever had happened. It was only when Gold Tooth was in his sight that he realized the man was packing a big damned gun. Chris knew exactly jack and shit about guns, but he was pretty sure the thing in Goldy's hands wasn't exactly street legal. The man fired again and Chris saw the tongue of flame that leaped from the muzzle of the monster in his hands.

The heavyset guy came up on the other side of Chris and started firing. His gun looked about as legal as the first one did. The things coming at them still looked mostly human on the outside, but they were starting to change and what was inside of them didn't even come close to passing muster.

Chris backed up a bit and decided to leave the killing spree to the professionals. He didn't know where his grandmother ran across her choice of private investigators but he'd just upped his opinion of her ability to hire dangerous people.

But then the people she'd hired were human. And the things they were shooting at were not. Before Chris could fully understand what was happening, the majority of the small group of attackers was down for the count and if he had to make a guess, most of them would not be getting back up any time soon.

But Bobby Johanssen and his buddies weren't playing fairly. Three of the freaks were waiting a good distance away, watching the action and doing little else.

Johanssen stared hard at Chris, his eyes shaded by the bright sun, but the intensity of his gaze just as potent as the hard stare coming from Arthur Hall a few feet away.

The guy on the left pulled his trigger a few times and came up empty. Gold Tooth fired a few more bullets before he ran out of ammo.

And when the smoke started to clear and they got a good look at what they'd been shooting, the two gunmen stepped back as fast as they could. There was viscera everywhere. Whatever sort of bullets they were using were definitely not the sort you found in police revolvers. They'd blown holes large enough to park cars in on most of the bodies. The thin gruel that passed for blood in the things painted several feet of the sidewalk a pasty red that had nothing to do with hemoglobin in Chris's mind, and the stench was enough to make his eyes water.

The happy gunmen weren't taking it any better; in fact they were handling the whole situation with a lot less grace. Gold Tooth was gagging as he stepped back, and his pudgy friend was making a high whining noise in the back of his throat. The whiner was slapping at his clothes, even as he ejected the spent clip from his handgun. He found what he was looking for and pulled out another load of ammo to slam into his pistol.

The pulped remains on the ground in front of them started twitching, and one of the bodies that was over halfway intact actually pushed itself into a kneeling position, spilling several vital-looking lumps from its chest cavity in the process. That was enough for Gold Tooth. He turned and ran so fast Chris half expected him to break the sound barrier.

The other guy took careful aim and fired again, the pistol kicking in his hands as he unloaded all over the thing trying to stand up. He fired the entire clip, the weapon in his grip actually smoldering by the time he was done.

And while he was plugging away, the rest of them started getting up. Chris shook his head and retreated, refusing to accept what he was seeing. He'd seen worse, tentacles and teeth and every imaginable combination of bodily deformities all rolled into one big damned room burning away around him. But this was too much. Not because they were hideous, which they were. But the thing about it was that the damned things were getting up.

At some point they were supposed to die. Just like the monsters before. This was breaking all of the rules. He tried to shake the thought off, because he knew that was just his mind playing games again, trying to rationalize, but the thoughts kept coming back.

"Okay. Fuck this." Chris stepped back, his eyes still drawn to the mass of flesh that was moving slowly, trying to pull itself together into one or several entities, he couldn't really tell. There were mouths on there that were making all sorts of noises, and there were feelers or tendrils or ligaments moving around in that wetness seeking to grab onto something else. He didn't want to see anymore, but he was drawn to it, morbidly fascinated with the process.

Bobby Johanssen took his mind off of the things on the sidewalk by punching him in the side of his head. The blow was good, but not perfect, because Chris noticed it soon enough to start dodging. That didn't mean it didn't hurt like hell, however. His ear took the worst of it and felt like someone had tried to grill it up for him as he stepped back. Johanssen didn't wait for a snappy comeback. He just hit Chris again. Chris blocked it and pulled his body in as much as he could to cover the important areas. The blow still ran through his torso and made breathing almost impossible for a few seconds.

"What the hell is your problem?" Speaking took more effort than he wanted to think about and drained his lungs of air he was having trouble capturing again. Chris backed away and Bobby followed. His face pulled into a sneer of hatred.

"You're the problem, Corin. You and your sister and your fucked-up friends!" The man's words were hissed out in a spray of spittle, his anger making him look almost rabid.

Chris stopped backing up and took a hard swing, connecting solidly with the man's face. All he had to do was remember what the man's double had been trying with Brittany and he suddenly had no trouble with the idea of turning his head into hamburger meat. Bobby's head snapped back hard and his feet almost left the ground. He should have been down and out by all rights. But of course that wasn't the way it played out. Instead the man just reached out and caught Chris by the neck, his fingers digging at the bruises that were already there.

It didn't take Chris long to figure he'd screwed up. He brought his arms up and tried to break Johanssen's grip, but failed miserably. His wrists felt like they'd collided with a railroad tie instead of flesh. He let out a grunt and stepped back again, but stopped short when he felt flesh pressing against him. He risked a quick look over his shoulder to see one of the detectives his grandmother had sent after him struggling and gagging.

He had good reason to gag. From what little he could see, Arthur Hall had his hand and most of his forearm rammed down the man's open mouth. Whatever he was doing, it was enough to split the flesh on Gold Tooth's face.

The detective was thrashing around like a pithed frog and Chris wanted nothing to do with whatever the hell was happening to him. Chris grabbed the thumbs locked around his neck and pulled savagely. The skin was tough, but the joints were only so-so. One thumb slid away without much trouble. The other one broke with an audible snap and Johanssen let go of him, barking out in pain.

Johanssen charged and so did Chris. If his enemy had expected him to go down without a fight, he was sadly disappointed. Johanssen was strong, stronger than should be possible, but he was also a lousy fighter. His fist scraped across Chris's shoulder—and the scar tissue from his previous encounter with a gun, thanks—and Chris's fist slammed into Johanssen's neck, sliding off his jawline in the process. Instead of pulling back when he was done punching, Chris shoved his body weight forward and knocked the other man off his feet. The anger was coming back now, all of the rage and fear in his body driving adrenaline into his system. He wanted out of here, and now. There were monsters and guns all over the damned place and he still didn't know where Jerry was. This was not going at all the way he'd hoped it would.

Johanssen fell on his ass and Chris took the opportunity to kick him in the face as he went past. He didn't think it would do much good, but it did knock the man into the big pile of writhing nightmares still trying to get itself together.

Too damned much. He didn't want to think anymore, didn't want to die here in the midst of raw insanity and wanted desperately to be home. He intended to get the hell out of Dodge as it were and fuck anyone who got in his way.

He ran as fast as he could, happily moving downhill this time, and didn't bother to look back. Maybe the detectives would keep the monsters busy, and if that was selfish, he couldn't help it anymore. Enough was enough.

It wasn't a very long run, when he thought about it, but it felt like a few decades right then. Chris got back to his station wagon and damn near pulled the door off the hinges getting inside. He slammed the door and locked it before looking up the hill to see if anyone was following. They weren't.

Maybe they're okay.

Chris started the car, fully intending to get the hell out of the area. He gunned the powerful engine and roared out of the parking lot, damn near clipping a few cars in the process. It didn't matter, he had to get out of there and if he got into a tiff with the cops, at least he would still be alive to get into trouble.

He started up the hill, and made it past Dark Harvest Books before he cursed himself and turned toward where the fighting was going on. It would have been so easy to just leave, damn it, if he could make himself do it. But the two men might still be alive and if they were, even if they were working for his grandmother, he couldn't bring himself to leave them there to die.

He looked for the combatants, for the oversized red wall of ruined flesh trying to rebuild itself, and found it without trouble. It was done reforming. Several people in bloodied, ruined clothes were standing on the sidewalk and looking around in a dazed way. *Maybe building yourself from scratch takes a lot out of you.*

He bit the inside of his mouth to stop hysterical giggles from kicking in. The detectives were nowhere to be seen, and neither was his good buddy Bobby Johanssen. The other two persistent freaks were gone as well, and Chris got a nasty feeling deep in his stomach when he noticed that.

"Fuck it. Fuck everything. I'm outta here."

Chris backed up the station wagon and started driving, heading for home. He heard sirens in the distance and any little part of him that felt like examining what was going on in greater detail gave up the ghost right then and there.

Cops were not his friends. He'd learned that the hard way, even if the cop that tried to kill him wasn't really an officer of the law.

Chapter Eight

I

Brittany managed to sneak out without being seen. She was getting good at that. She had to behave, true, but no rule existed that said she couldn't have some fun in the process. Well, no rule except the stupid ones her brother was forcing her to deal with.

Kelly wanted to go out, so they were going. Chris could come and go as he pleased and fair was fair. She was only four years younger, after all, and everyone knew girls matured faster than guys.

That didn't mean they weren't sneaking out the window. Brittany wasn't that stupid. Chris was out and Courtney and Katie were downstairs watching something on the TV.

Chris hadn't really paid attention lately. He'd been

in a funk about Jerry and so was Brittany really, but there was nothing she could do about that. So it wasn't hard to get out of her bedroom window and down the tree that grew there, as long as she was careful. Kelly hated scaling the old oak, but for Brittany it was old hat.

A quick look around and they were out of the yard and moving across 'the back of the neighbor's property. Five minutes after that, they were in an area where it was safe to smoke a cigarette and make their plans for the night.

"You sure you aren't going to get in trouble?" It wasn't like Kelly to worry, but even she could see that Chris was a little stressed lately.

"Probably." She shrugged and looked around. "But maybe if I'm gone Chris can score some action with Courtney or even call in a hooker."

"That's not the answer to everything, Brit."

"Maybe not, but he definitely needs something." She shrugged and took a drag off one of the cigarettes Kelly had brought along. "Shit. I dunno. I just know if he doesn't stop acting like he's been acting lately he's gonna blow up all over me again and I don't need it."

"Whatever." Kelly pulled out her lip gloss and re-coated her lips until they glistened pink. "Right now, let's just go find something to do."

They moved quickly and quietly. There were far too many neighbors around who were just nosey enough to ruin their plans if they got caught, and Brittany was

178

the first to admit she was already treading on dangerous grounds.

The summer was going away too fast and Brittany wasn't going to waste her chance to have a good time. As far as she was concerned, that was what mattered the most.

They didn't have to look too far to find good times. They just had to enter the Club of the Week. Bryce Darby was playing doorman again, and as always, the guy gave her a weird collision of feelings. There was the fact that he was her brother's worst enemy from school to consider—Darby was a big mean bruiser with a long history of violence—and the fact that he was still deeply pissed off at her brother for causing the scars that ran down both of his arms was both scary and exciting. More and more she wondered what it would be like to get intimate with Darby. There was something about the menace he exuded with his every gesture that she found titillating.

Added bonus, Chris would have a seizure.

She opened the blouse she was wearing another button as she pulled out her three dollar admission, and smiled up at Bryce as he took her money. Eyes extra wide for the coy look, and an extra sway in her walk. Bryce didn't say anything, but she saw the way he looked and knew if she wanted to push it, she could probably have him before the night was over.

The club was playing a song by Hoobastank. She still couldn't decide if she liked the band, but they were normally pretty good to dance to. The crowd was solid, lots of faces from school and most of them just exactly too young for Chris to run into and talk with. They might all be from the same neighborhood, but that didn't mean everyone was all chatty with each other all the time.

Kelly led the way and in no time they were in the thick of things. It was nice getting away from the house and from Chris's endless fuming. It was all he did since their mother died—and that was a gut punch she was trying hard not to think about, thanks very much—and she didn't want to deal with it. She had enough troubles of her own.

Brittany hadn't quite managed the art of ducking away from her feelings of guilt, but she was learning to. That was important. If she didn't learn, she'd be just like Chris, and that was the last thing on earth she wanted.

Well, aside from dealing with her grandmother.

Even thinking about the woman was enough to make her want to scream. This nasty old bitch who had never bothered with them was doing everything she could to make Brittany's life suck even more than it already did.

And what was stopping her? Chris. Downer, brooding, pissed off Chris.

And what was she doing? Making it harder for him.

Just like that, Brittany decided the night's excursion was over. She tapped Kelly on the shoulder and her best friend looked at her with one arched eyebrow.

"I gotta go back home."

"Yeah?"

"Yeah. I need to make sure I'm not busted again. Chris is going through enough."

Kelly just nodded and started with her toward the door. Brittany put a hand on her shoulder. "No, it's cool. I'll get home. You go ahead and hang if you want."

"You sure?" Kelly sounded dubious.

"Yeah." Brittany forced a smile she didn't feel. "It's all good. Give me a call tomorrow, okay?" Kelly nodded and in a few seconds she was mingling with the crowd. Brittany watched her for half a minute, wishing she'd taken her up on the offer to go back to the house and then turned to leave.

It sucked, really, listening to the angel on her shoulder instead of to the devil whispering in her ear. She stepped back outside and saw Bryce's broad back. Instead of doing what she wanted and seeing how much effort it would take to get him hard as steel, she turned to head back home.

Simple math. Go home, be good and stay at home. Go out, screw up and go to live with the wicked witch of the west. Not much of a choice, really.

She made it home with no troubles. It was dark out and though there were a few neighbors who might have reported seeing her if they got the chance, Brittany already knew the best ways to get out of the house and back without ever being spotted.

She looked up at her bedroom, where the lights

were off and the screen had been carefully set against the inner wall, and looked at the tree that would get her back up where she needed to be.

She should have looked around the side of the house. Then she would have seen the man who stepped out into the darkness and moved over to her before she could begin to scale the oak.

His large, callused hand was big enough to cover the bottom half of her face. He pressed his palm against her lips and shushed her with a sound. Her eyes flew wide open and her pulse tripled in her chest. She opened her mouth to scream or to bite, whichever worked best, but the man's hand clamped down harder and she swallowed any action she might have taken in fear.

He spoke softly, but his voice was low and grated against her nerves when she recognized him.

"Quietly, Miss Corin. You and I need to have a few words." Detective Martin Callaghan was not a small man by any stretch of the imagination. She nodded her head slowly, realizing even as she did it that she was screwed.

II

Chris got home later than he meant to, and found Courtney and Katie in the living room, both sound asleep. Guilt washed through him in a slow-moving wave and he clenched his fists together, pissed at himself for being such an asshole.

He looked at the two of them, and studied everything about them, drinking in the details of their faces and bodies as they slept. He loved them for being there. He didn't deserve them as friends, especially with the thoughts that both of them generated in him. And still they came back and waited for him to come home, looking after Brittany.

And he hadn't found Jerry. Not a single sign of him. After trying the bookstore he'd gone off again in search of where his friend might be and came up with nothing but the faces of strangers and people who looked at him like he was something the cat dragged in.

He touched Katie's face lightly, savoring the feel of her soft skin under his fingertips. She let out a small sigh and opened her eyes, looking up at him with sleep still muddling her thoughts.

"Hey . . . What time is it?"

He squinted and looked at the clock on his VCR. "A little after ten."

"Did you have any luck?"

"None of it good." He looked away, hating that he knew the expression she'd be wearing. Hurt and confusion and fear all blended onto her face. He'd seen it way too often lately. A side effect of letting her down. Again. "I couldn't find him, Katie. The store was closed up tight and I had a run-in with the detectives my grandmother sent out." He bit his tongue. He didn't want to tell her the rest. Didn't want to remember the rest. He was doing his best not to think about it whenever that was an option, because he already had a few worries about what was left of his mind.

"Why don't you guys go ahead on out?" He looked at the floor, anywhere but at Katie and Courtney. "I'll call if I find anything out, okay? But you two both need a little time to just avoid being here."

"What? What do you mean by that?" She almost sounded angry. He didn't look at her. He was too tired and knew if he did there would be a fight as surely as he knew that if he thought about the things out there that seemed to want him dead, he'd start screaming and never stop.

"I mean I'm a fucking jinx these days, Katie. Everyone around me is having their lives turn to shit. Go home and get the hell away from me before anything else goes wrong." That wasn't what he'd meant to say. He'd meant to tell her it was nothing, just him being a moron. "Just go, okay?"

He walked upstairs and into his room, tired and sore and once again beaten on by the events of the day.

He peeled the shirt off his back, flinching as the material bunched up around his neck and ran over the bruises he was accumulating like trophies to his own stupidity. The pants were next and pulling them off was a painful operation. His knee was throbbing from the extra strain and felt four times its usual size. The good news was it only looked twice the regular width.

"Shit. Look at you." Katie's voice came from behind him and Chris turned his head fast enough to damn near break the sound barrier.

He was practically naked, and very, very glad he was wearing clean underwear. "What?"

"It's hard to knock your teeth out when someone keeps beating me to it." She walked out of his room and into the bathroom across the hall, coming back a few moments later with two wet towels. "Put that on your neck, asshole." She threw a soggy towel at his face and he caught it, placing the cold cloth against his throat where the bruises were the worst.

"Sit on the bed." She shoved at his chest to make him listen and much as Chris wanted to protest, he stumbled and sat. Katie dropped to her knees in front of him. That portion of a fantasy coming true was much more than he needed to see at the moment. He looked away, his face flaming with embarrassment.

Katie stood up and shook her head. "I'm getting you a couple of ice packs." She left the room, not looking at his face, not looking at him at all, really.

He sat where he was, feeling lower than pond scum for what he'd said and lower even than that for the thoughts going through his head. A few minutes passed in silence before she came back into the room, a bundle of paper towels—presumably filled with ice—in each hand. Sure enough, it was ice. She handed him the one for his neck and then lowered to her knees again, unwrapping his leg and placing the ice inside the towel before rewrapping it.

"I'm sorry for how that came out downstairs, Katie . . ."

"You're not the only one, Chris." Her voice was

barely above a whisper and filled with brittle hard anger. "You're not the only one whose life has turned to shit and not everything in the world revolves around you."

"I know that. I do. It just feels that way sometimes and I—"

"Right now? I don't care what you feel." Her fingers brushed his thigh as they pulled the towel back around his knee and he felt heat moving into his groin. "You don't get to be a martyr here, Chris. I'm here because you were supposed to be looking for Jerry. Brittany can't be left alone or she'll do something stupid. Courtney's here because she's my best friend and wanted to keep me company. So don't go thinking it's all about you and your poor little feelings." Her hands yanked the towel tight on his knee and he winced. If he was expecting anything like an apology for the pain from Katie, he was disappointed.

If he was expecting his body not to respond just because he was getting more and more embarrassed, he was in for a double dose of let-down. Much to his absolute horror, he was getting a serious erection. His face felt hot enough to melt the ice he set in the towel and placed against his neck.

He wanted to apologize. He really did. But just when he thought he could open his mouth and say the words, Katie lifted her gaze from his knee and looked up to where his underwear had tented. She looked away quickly and a moment later was standing, turning her back to him and leaving the room. She closed the door on her way out.

Chris shook his head and lay back, humiliated. He closed his eyes, wishing that the world would go away. Less than a minute later he was asleep.

In his dreams, Katie did more than tend to his knee.

III

Coffee wasn't really what Brittany normally drank, but it had to do. Detective Martin Callaghan wasn't very likely to give her a shot of scotch to soothe her jangled nerves.

He was a scary man. Genuinely frightening on many levels, the most obvious being that he could throw her stupid ass in a jail cell if he wanted to. A little less obvious was the look on his face, which was about as friendly as she imagined Jack the Ripper might have been. His eyes almost seemed to suck in the light, and his short crew cut was so precise she was tempted to think it was actually a toupee made from wire.

He sat ramrod-straight across the table from her, his own coffee black and growing cold while he studied every move she made.

"So what did you want to talk to me about?"

He looked at her for a full thirty seconds before he answered. "About your brother. About the house fire on Tillinghast Lane. About Detective Crawford." He shrugged his broad, muscular shoulders. "About everything that I've been looking into that still doesn't make any sense to me, Miss Corin."

"What makes you think I can tell you anything?" She hated that her voice was shaking. That was a sign of guilt as far as she was concerned. And while she might have a few zillion things to feel guilty about in her life, none of the stuff he was mentioning was on her list for those sort of feelings.

"I don't know anything I haven't told you before." She sipped her coffee, looking at him over the rim of the cup.

He looked right back, his eyes as dead and unreadable as those of a fish. "I think you're lying to me, Miss Corin."

"I think you look like a Jehovah's Witness in that suit. But that doesn't change that you're a detective."

"We can do this the easy way, or we can do this the hard way." Callaghan's voice was almost perfectly monotone. He was a living, breathing human being, but from what she could see he had about all the passion of a tree stump. On the other hand, he was as scary as hell and she had to make an effort not to let her panic show.

"We can also do this the way where I tell your superiors you were trying to cop a feel off of me." She shrugged and looked back just as seriously. "Don't threaten me and we're going to get along a lot better."

Callaghan actually smiled. His lips curled up at the corners and his eyes narrowed just the slightest bit.

She wished he'd go back to looking like a statue. "Let's get something straight right now, little girl. I'm not playing games with you. I have better things to do. I want to know what happened to Walter Crawford. He was a good cop. He was also my friend. I've been patient, but you and your brother and your friends have given me the runaround long enough."

The man leaned forward and placed his massive hands on the top of the table in the diner where they were sipping their coffees. "Now let's cut to the chase. I know what you've been doing every night for the last three weeks when you were supposed to be at home. I know where you've been going and who you've been with."

Okay. That got her attention. "You do?"

"I even have pictures." His face was back to cold and dead, but that faint hint of a smile hadn't quite gone away. He reached into his jacket and pulled out a thick envelope that was well worn. "I have a powerful suspicion your grandmother would love to know what you've been doing. I think that would cement her case against your brother staying your legal guardian. Don't you?"

"How do you know about that?"

"I'm a detective. It's what I do."

"So what do you want from me then? You can fuck my life up, right?"

"The pictures could go away, Brittany. And so could all of the information that I have. Everything I witnessed. I don't care about how you live your life. I care about finding out what happened to a good friend of mine."

She stood up, nodding her head woodenly. "So let's go."

"Where to?"

"Tillinghast Lane. Take me back there and I'll tell you everything I know."

Callaghan threw a ten-dollar bill on the table and walked her out to the car.

Brittany swallowed her heart and sat in the passenger's seat. She didn't want to look at the pictures. More importantly, she didn't want Chris to know what was on them. She didn't think she could face him again if he ever caught wind.

They drove in silence, even the police scanner turned down to the point where the words spoken by the dispatcher were too soft to identify. The silence wouldn't last. Brittany knew that. The silence never lasted long enough.

IV

Katie woke Courtney as quietly as she could. Court let out the sort of moaning noise that would have had half the men she knew trying to get into her pants and then sat up. "Come on. We have to go."

"What?" The first word out of Courtney's mouth made Katie flinch, and she immediately toned it down to a whisper. "What's wrong? Where are we going?"

"Brittany snuck out again, goddamnit."

Courtney slid out of her nearly fetal position on the couch and sat up, blinking her bright blue eyes repeatedly. "I swear, I'm gonna beat that little ho to death."

"I'm gonna help you, too." She moved toward the door. "But if Chris finds out he's gonna beat us both to it."

"Stupid little bitch is on my last nerve." Courtney was not amused. Courtney was very seldom amused when it came to someone interfering with her sleep.

"Yeah? Well, you're the one with the hots for her brother. Get used to it if you want him back in your life." They slipped out the front door and down to Courtney's Miata. It was small, but it was fast and in better shape than Katie's little car.

They were halfway down the street before Courtney turned on the lights. "Where the fuck am I going, Katie?"

"Straight to hell, probably." It was an old joke and one that comforted her. Courtney had always been wilder than she was, and a few years back Katie had worried about her friend's soul. They'd had several long talks that had backfired miserably. These days Katie thought a lot less about heaven and the afterlife than she used to.

"Smart ass. No, I mean where are we going to go looking for the teenaged monster this time?"

"Let's hit the Club of the Week. Maybe Bryce has seen her."

"The big ape outside? That dude is seriously terrifying."

"Well, he isn't exactly a teddy bear, but you have to sort of push him before he tries to kill you." Katie looked over at Courtney. "Just do us both a favor and don't mention Chris. He's sort of got a hard-on for breaking Chris into little pieces."

"Why isn't Chris dead?" Courtney sounded suitably worried about that notion.

"Bryce is a little too smart to actually kill anyone with witnesses, but I think it's mostly because Chris is doing his best to avoid getting near him right now."

"Smart boy."

"Sometimes." Katie looked out the window and felt the flutters start in her stomach again. She was worried about Jerry and instead of looking for him she was looking for Brittany again.

Bryce Darby was still outside the building when they pulled up. He scowled his usual greeting, his eyes looking over both of them with a quick flicker. If he was attracted to either of them, he managed to hide it well. Then again, in all of the time she'd gone to school with Bryce, she'd never known him to date a single girl. Made her wonder, but not aloud.

He nodded a noncommittal welcome. "You ladies want inside?" Darby's voice was a raw growl.

"Only if you've seen Brittany Corin tonight, Bryce."

"She was here earlier. Might still be. I didn't see her leave."

"How much is it to get in again?" The last time Katie had been to the club was also in search of Brittany. That particular night had ended with death, fire and mayhem in another part of the town. She'd been doing her best not to think about it ever since.

Darby shook his head. "Just go in and look. You stay more than half an hour you can pay on your way out." He opened the door for them, his face already looking back out at the street.

"Thanks, Bryce. Really. Thanks, very much."

He nodded and closed the door behind them. It only took a few minutes of looking through the room at the myriad teens to realize that Brittany wasn't there. There were plenty of other kids, including several males ranging from five years younger to the same age as Katie and Courtney who tried making plays for them, but no sign of little Miss Corin anywhere.

Courtney scowled and shot a look at one of the boys in the crowd that made him hastily back away. She was very good at looking like a bitch when she wanted to and right now her glare was particularly potent.

Five minutes later they were outside and thanking Bryce again. He nodded his acknowledgment without a word as he took money from seven more teenyboppers.

"I have no idea where we should go from here." Katie spoke mostly to herself as they headed back to the little Miata.

"I think if Chris had a brain he'd go ahead and give the little slut over to her grandmother."

"Don't be a *complete* bitch, Courtney. She's the only family he has left."

"Well, think about it. She's doing everything she can to screw up her chances of staying around. Maybe she wants to go live with the old biddy."

"Would you want to live with a relative you never met before?"

"Would I be fucking around every night if I wanted to stay home?"

Katie couldn't really argue with the logic there. They drove off in silence, even the radio in the little car turned down.

A few moments after they left the Club of the Week, another car pulled out. Katie barely even acknowledged it at first. The only reason she really paid it any attention at all was because one of the headlights was off-kilter and pointed to the left like a lazy eye.

"Where the fuck are we going to look for her, Katie?"

"Huh? Oh. You know what? Maybe we should just head back to Chris's place."

Courtney looked at her, took her eyes completely off the road and looked at her as she drove. Katie resisted the urge to pull herself into a fetal position and scream, but only because she was used to Courtney pulling crap like that and never getting into any trouble in the process. Courtney seemed to have a built-in guidance system that stopped stupidity from killing her and it had never failed her yet. Of course, like everything else right now, that made her think of Jerry, who swore that on the day Courtney's blind luck ran out it was going to be the Hiroshima of shit storms.

He wanted to be far, far away when that day came. Thinking about it made her eyes sting. She hated that it hurt so fucking much for him to be gone.

"Okay, so why would I want to go back to Chris's without Brittany? So he could be in an even worse mood when he wakes up?"

"I think we're being followed."

"My ass."

"Seriously." Katie shook her head. Courtney could be impossible sometimes.

"By who?"

"The little car back there. The one with the messed-up lights." Katie knew she'd made a mistake even as she said the words. She should have expected Courtney's response. She should have known she'd be stupid. But hope springs eternal.

And friends like Courtney existed to crush those hopes. She had to start remembering that and made a promise to try harder when she felt the car abruptly lurch to a stop even as Courtney unfastened her seatbelt and reached down to pop the trunk.

"What the hell are you doing?"

"Finding out who the fuck is following us this late at night!" The words were cast back hastily as Courtney moved to the trunk and reached in, pulling out something long, dark and metallic. The car behind them had come to a complete halt, and the askew lights glowed fiercely. Courtney was little more than a silhouette with short blond hair. Katie climbed out of the car, prepared to apologize for her friend and stop Courtney from doing something unbelievably stupid.

"Court! Stop it!"

A closer look let her see that Courtney was wielding a tire iron. "Get out of the fucking car!" Courtney walked up to the driver's-side door and pulled on the handle of the old car. The door opened with a slight metallic squeal in counterpoint to the much louder scream from inside the vehicle.

Courtney screamed at the driver again, and a thin blond girl stuck her head out of the open door before climbing out, her hands held up to protect her face and skull from any forthcoming blows.

Katie knew the girl from somewhere. She racked her brains trying to figure it out. Courtney didn't waste time fucking around with thinking—which had never really been her strong point anyway, as far as Katie was concerned—she just moved forward and pushed the girl against the side of her own car. "Why are you following us? Make it good or I'll knock your fucking head in!"

The girl was pretty, sort of, if you liked the anorexic type. She was also shaking with adrenaline. "I came here to tell you about Jerry." Her voice was soft, but it carried. Both of the girls at the car looked toward Katie. Katie looked at the girl Courtney had pinned and felt her vision go a little red around the edges.

"What about him?" Her voice didn't sound right, but that might have been because she could barely hear herself over the pulse slapping the insides of her ears.

"He's okay. He's safe. But if you look for him, he won't be."

Katie stared long and hard at the girl. She wanted to do a lot more, but was afraid if she even tried moving, she'd rip the little bitch's face off her skull.

Courtney came to the rescue. She used her free hand to slap the girl hard. Even from ten feet away and over the sound of two cars idling, Katie heard the sound of flesh on flesh.

The girl let out another little squeak, and this time Courtney leaned in close, hissing words that Katie couldn't make out. The girl shook her head violently, and Courtney lashed out, grabbing a handful of hair and pulling hard. Her other hand waved the tire iron around like a baton and the girl got moving, stumbling over to Katie, who still hadn't quite figured out how to move without wanting to kill the little blonde.

Katie looked hard at the girl and recognized her. She had been at Chris's party not that long ago—or a few centuries ago depending on how you looked at it. She'd been the one thanking him for helping her little brother. From what little Chris had said about everything he'd been doing, she was almost certain this was the same girl from the rare bookstore he'd spoken about. The same bookstore that Jerry had gone off to earlier.

"Where's Jerry?" Her voice was shaking, the adrenaline in her system kicking into high gear as she looked at the scared girl in front of her.

"You tell Chris . . . You tell him that his friend is back at the place he burned down."

"Why is he there?" Katie clenched her hands into fists, feeling her short nails cut into her palms. "Why would you take him back there?"

"I don't know why." She looked away as she spoke and Katie felt her mouth twitch.

"You listen, you lying little piece of shit." Katie leaned in closer, still afraid of what she might do, but almost welcoming the chance to test out her own potential for violence. "You tell me what the fuck is going on, or I'm going to take my friend's tire iron and knock your goddamned brains all over the street."

"My father has him. That's all I know."

"Courtney?"

"Yeah?"

"Get this stupid bitch away from me before I kill her."

The girl opened her mouth to speak. She shut it again when she saw the look Katie shot her way. Courtney let the girl go, but took the liberty of removing the keys from her ignition and pocketing them.

Katie climbed back into Courtney's little car and sat down on the passenger's side. A few minutes ago she'd been absolutely appalled by Courtney's actions. Now she wished she had the damned metal stick in her hands and was beating down on the little mousy blonde.

"Where to?" Courtney spoke as she climbed into the driver's seat, tossing the tire iron into the back.

"Tillinghast Lane."

"Where?"

"Just drive. I'll tell you where to go."

"We gonna pick up Chris?"

"No. I'll take care of this all by myself."

"Yeah. You'll have plenty of help."

Chapter Nine

I

Chris woke up when the phone rang. He didn't want to wake up, God knows, because every part of him hurt. But when no one else answered the annoying thing he was forced to stand up and limp his way across the room.

"Hullo."

"Chris . . . ?" He recognized the voice, of course.

"Laura. What do you want?" Was that venom in his voice? Yep. No doubt about it. He might have had a crush on her, but the girl had gone way too far.

"Listen. My dad has your friend, Jerry. He wants you to go to the house you ruined. He says he can make everything all right, but he needs you to do it."

"Your dad can fuck himself."

"Chris. He said if I didn't tell you to come, he'd kill Jerry."

Chris closed his eyes and clenched the phone hard enough that either the plastic or his bones creaked in protest. "Don't be there when I get there, Laura." He hung up before she could make a comment.

Ibuprofen. Half the people he knew swore by it, so he took four before he left the house. He also took an ax, a four-pound sledgehammer and three kitchen knives. He also promised himself a trip to the local gun shop when his money came in. Enough was enough.

The car sputtered, argued, and finally started just as he was contemplating beating the engine to death. And wouldn't that have made a lovely noise for the neighbors to complain about?

For a place he kept trying to forget about, the remains of the house on Tillinghast Lane were still relatively easy for him to find now. There was an old sedan there. He took one look at the crappy brown color and figured it for a cop car. He was right, the tag gave it away, but he didn't see anyone in or near the vehicle.

He pulled the ax out of the back seat and slung it over his shoulder. The small sledgehammer he shoved into his belt so that the head rested against his abdomen.

"Hey! I'm here!" Down the street, the dogs he'd had encounters with before started barking. He made an obscene gesture in their direction and headed for the ruins of the house. The ground was still burned and scorched. What was left of the building was worse. There was a thick layer of soot on the ground that had become part of the soil itself. Even in the darkness, Chris could see where it had been disturbed.

"Chris? What are you doing here?" Katie's voice was just about the last thing he'd expected to hear. He looked toward the source and saw Katie and Courtney both heading in his direction.

"I got a call from Laura. What the hell are you doing here? You should be at home, in bed."

"Said the gimp." That was Courtney, as tactful as ever.

"I'll handle this. Okay?" He rolled his eyes and started for the ruins again.

"Don't even start that shit, or I'll beat your ass myself." That was Katie. He kept forgetting that chauvinism wasn't really accepted by her personality. Frankly, he was too tired to care. He waved her aside and kept going.

"Don't you walk away from me." Her voice dripped menace. Jerry could be afraid of that. He didn't have to.

Katie slapped the back of his head and he turned fast, glaring at her. She didn't flinch back but stared just as hard. "He's my boyfriend. I'm going in there."

"You weren't invited. Go away."

"Fuck off."

"I'm serious here, Katie. Go home."

Katie shook her head in disgust and walked right past him, heading for the burnt remains of the house.

Chris scowled and looked back at Courtney for help. Courtney just shrugged.

Chris wasn't going to knock Katie on her ass. He couldn't if he wanted to. So instead he walked faster, trying to get past her and into the remains of the house before her.

The freak squad stopped him. He didn't recognize a single one of them. But he knew who they were. There were an even dozen of the monsters in front of him, each looking far less human than the last time they'd come after him.

The night was dark, but not so heavy he couldn't see them clearly. They had either lost the ability to look completely human or had just decided to stop trying. The one that was closest walked forward with hands held out and made a deep rumbling noise in its chest. There were large, lumpy growths sliding up one of the hands and running up the arm all the way to the side of the man's face. His left eye was buried under bulging skin. His mouth was stuck in a sneer.

He took two steps forward and Chris whacked him with the flat of the ax, no longer willing to wait to be attacked before he defended himself. The man grunted and pushed on, knocking the weapon aside as he grabbed for Chris.

Thick, powerful hands grabbed his shoulders and shook him hard. Whatever they had become, smarter wasn't a part of it. Chris shifted his grip on the ax and buried it in the monster's chest.

At least they could still feel. It let go of him and

roared out a ululating wail of pain. Chris swung again, this time taking a chunk out of the man's normal-looking arm.

That seemed to be all that was required to open the floodgates. The whole group moved forward as the first of them fell screaming. One of them casually knocked Katie out of the way, sending her staggering. Before Chris could even think about going to her side to help, he was overwhelmed. They came from all sides, and all of them seemed to have a passionate desire to beat him to death.

Chris felt the first fifty or so fists and boots that landed blows on him. After that, there was nothing.

II

"How the hell did you kids get out of here alive?" Callaghan was holding a flashlight that could have also been used as a baseball bat in case of emergency. The thing was solid and heavy and gave off a powerful beam. Brittany was very glad about that, because she was already sweating like a cold glass on a hot day and it had nothing to do with the heat. It had everything to do with what she had seen here in the past. The smell of burnt wood and plastic was powerful, but underlying that she could still catch the musty, moldy odors from the things they had encountered. The things that had almost killed her and had been making frequent visits to her sleeping mind ever since.

"I don't know. I guess we were lucky." They were in the basement, which was really the only part of the structure that was still standing. The rest was a pile of broken and burnt debris that was currently sitting over their heads and making unsettling groaning noises from time to time.

"Lucky doesn't cut it. I think you must have a guardian angel."

"Yeah? He could do a better job." She spit onto the ground as she spoke: not to be rude, but because the smells from the place had permeated her mouth and now everything tasted like mildewed ashes.

"Don't be like that. God has his plans."

"He can keep them." She reached out a hand without thinking and grabbed the detective's arm when he almost stepped into the abyss near his right foot. "You might want to check on His plans yourself and look where you're going."

Callaghan stepped back hastily and bumped into her. "Where in the hell did that come from?"

"I was outside when that happened. I guess the floor fell in."

Callaghan ran the flashlight over the entire area. "No. Something came from below or it exploded here. Maybe a gas line . . ." He crouched lower and looked at the hole. It was huge, big enough to run a bus through. If he hadn't been stopped, he probably would have fallen a long way down.

"How deep you figure it is?" Callaghan looked over his shoulder as she spoke.

"I'm not planning to find out, but the flashlight doesn't reach all the way to the bottom."

Brittany nodded. "Like I said. Weird shit went down here."

"I'm getting that." He stopped speaking when the ruins above them groaned threateningly. "I'm also getting that leaving here would be a smart move."

"I was for not coming here at all."

"Yeah. I know. But I wanted to see what was what."

They'd been talking for almost an hour and walking around the place. Then bright boy decided going into the cellar would be a good idea. He was wrong, of course.

"I want to go home now."

"Sure. We can go." Callaghan stood up and started for the gaping hole where the cellar's entrance had been before it all went to hell.

Something let out a deep groan that was carried up from the pit behind him. Callaghan froze and Brittany cursed. Of course he was going to check now. Really, why would he want to be smart and just leave well enough alone? She could see it in his body language, the way he tensed and then reached for his gun's holster. He was going to check.

"Just leave it alone, I'm warning you." She didn't mean to speak. It just happened.

"Can't do it."

"Pretend you're a chickenshit and leave it. I promise I won't tell anyone."

"Go outside, Brittany. I'll handle this."

"No. You won't be able to. Whatever you think you might see, it's worse. Believe me."

"I'm a cop."

"No shit." She looked at him and pointed to the hole in the ground where more sounds were now emanating and getting louder. "It's a monster. You won't win."

Callaghan looked at her. His eyes were as expressionless as ever and she had to wonder if he had a death wish. "Won't know if I don't try."

Brittany moved closer to the man, her anger rising. "Look. Don't be an asshole, okay? You don't know what you're dealing with here and believe me, it was luck that got me and Chris out before. Don't trust in a fucking gun."

She grabbed at his arm again and he shrugged her off. Brittany backed away, her face scowling out her displeasure. "Fine. Do whatever you have to. I'll be up top waiting, and you better fucking be up there in five minutes or I swear I'll tell your police chief you tried to rape me." She started to stomp up what remained of the built-in ladder that led to the surface, but decided to take it nice and slow after the second rung broke under her weight.

Brittany crawled out of the hole where the cellar doors had been and tried not to hear the screams that echoed to her from the past. She wanted nothing more than to be in bed and dreaming the whole damned thing.

When she heard Katie's voice, she flinched. "You gotta fucking be kidding me."

"What the hell are you doing out here, little girl?" That was Courtney. She sounded more scared than angry. Brittany looked at the girl and saw how pale she was, her color almost as bad as a dead person's.

Katie stood nearby, looking all around the area. She wasn't pale. She was bruised. "What happened to your face, Katie?"

"I don't know. I don't care. We have to go. We have to find Jerry and now we have to find Chris, too."

"Chris?" Brittany felt her stomach drop. "What happened to Chris?"

"I don't know. There were a lot of guys and they grabbed him." Katie's voice sounded weird, almost monotone.

"Katie, damn it. Where did they take him?"

"I don't know." Katie shook her head. "I don't know anything any more."

Courtney was looking around, a strange smile on her face. She looked almost drunk. Brittany looked at the two older girls and grunted with disgust. She reached out and got a good fingerhold on Katie's arm before pinching as hard as she could.

Katie jumped back, yelping nice and loud. "Ow! What the hell are you doing?" She rubbed at her arm.

"Waking your ass up! Where's Chris and what happened to him?"

"Oh shit . . ." Katie looked around, her eyes growing wider. "They took him. They dragged him away and we couldn't even get close. I don't know what they hit us with, but it was nasty."

"Where did they go?" Brittany was trying to stay calm and failing miserably.

"They were on foot . . ."

Before Brittany could express her dissatisfaction—perhaps by ramming her foot straight down Katie's throat—the ground bucked beneath them. No one lost their balance, but it was close.

The sound of several gunshots exploding in the ruins of the house caught their attention.

"Damn it all!" Brittany looked at Katie and then at Courtney, hating them both just a little right then. Not because they were bad people, not at all, but because she was hoping one of them would tell her what to do.

Leaving Callaghan down there would be so easy. All she had to do was not walk over and see what was going on. All she had to do was ignore the sounds she was hearing and let the man succumb to whatever fate awaited him and she knew for a fact that he would never be able to blackmail her again. There would never be a chance in hell of Chris finding out what she had been doing and there certainly wouldn't be any photographic evidence.

Of course sleep would never happen again and then there was the whole I-Let-A-Man-Die-So-I-Could-Feel-Better-About-Myself thing. But no pressure.

Brittany ran back to the dark opening of the cellar, cursing a blue streak as she went. She got there just in time to watch Callaghan trying his best to climb out of the place using only his feet. His hands were far too busy reloading his pistol.

She didn't clearly see what was down there. She didn't want to and she sure as hell didn't need to in order to know it was bad. She could hear it over the curses of the policeman and she could smell it over the scent of burnt gunpowder.

Her fingers caught his jacket and she felt him pushing, trying to get up the stairs. She hooked her nails deep into the fabric and pulled as hard as she could, throwing her weight into it. The firearm was blasting away as he fairly flew out of the cellar and back on top of Brittany. He was exactly and precisely as heavy as he looked, which meant she had no chance in hell of moving his body off hers.

"Shit," she squeaked. "You weigh a ton." She pushed hard at his muscular back and after a moment, he actually shifted his weight off her.

"What the fuck was that thing?" The good detective was shaking and pale, his skin covered with a fine patina of sweat and his eyes doing their best to look in several directions at once. She wanted to feel sorry for him, but he'd done it to himself.

"I don't know." Brittany shrugged. "I don't care. Right now I have to go find my brother. He just got himself kidnapped."

Without another word, she walked in the direction that Courtney kept staring, hoping to see some sign of where Chris had been taken. Behind her, Katie called out and so did the detective. She didn't have the time to bother with them. Chris was more important. Brittany walked and after a few seconds, the others followed.

III

The darkness around him was complete. The only sound he heard was his own heartbeat, which was decidedly not regular and seemed muted even to his own ears, despite the pulse bouncing through his skull.

The old man, the freak, was much stronger than he'd expected, and Jerry was not happy about his current situation. Then again, he hadn't been happy for a few months now. When the fevers weren't on him, the muscle cramps were. Only he knew they weren't muscle cramps. Never had been. They were changes going on in his body.

Changes. Small steps away from being human. He realized that now. He wished he didn't. Ignorance really was bliss.

His body felt cramped, locked into a small tight space that would have left him gasping for air if he'd ever had any sort of claustrophobia. He wanted to move, wanted out of the place, but so far his efforts to do anything at all were proving fruitless.

He thought he closed his eyes. All he could do was guess, really. He tried to stay calm, to be rational. Chris was the one who went off at the drop of a hat. Katie was the one who went off whenever it struck her fancy. And best not to think about Brittany, who seemed to just randomly explode into a rage these days. Jerry was the one who was best at staying calm. He always had been.

Until Chris left him. Ran off like a frightened fucking mouse and left him alone to be taken, torn and bled and infected with whatever the hell it was that had been growing inside of him like an intelligent cancer. Thinking about the way Chris had abandoned him, about he possible reasons for it, was enough to make him seethe. Chris, his best friend, his brother, really, had been making eyes at Katie for years. It didn't take a genius to know Chris was at least halfway in love with his girl, and had probably been sporting a hard-on for her ever since they met.

He'd have to remember to thank Chris properly. Maybe he'd just take it out on Brittany and settle that little problem once and for all. The little bitch was getting too big for her britches anyway, and he could think of a few ways to take her attitude down a few levels. Hell, it wasn't like he hadn't noticed—

Jerry shook violently. He forced his body to move, forced it through sheer will, and wrenched at the darkness that surrounded him. It hurt to move, things pulled inside of his body that he knew had never been there before and he felt tugs and sharp pains as he struggled against what felt like glue sealing his muscles together.

The pain was cleansing: the more he felt it, the better he could think and push the alien thoughts out of his head. Did Chris have a thing for Katie? Maybe, but he would never act on it. And the thought of what he'd just been toying with doing to little Brittany was enough to make him want to gag. The damned thing growing inside of him had grown subtler, better at hiding inside his own thoughts, and he had to remember to pay better attention to which notions that bounced around in his skull belonged to him and which to the Whispers.

He thrashed, finally convincing his arms to stretch away from his body. They met resistance but he kept fighting, pushing against the barriers that sealed him into an area smaller than a coffin.

How the hell had he gotten here and where was here in the first place? He didn't know but he'd find out as soon as he could, and if that old fuck was still hanging around, he'd just have to break him into a few hundred pieces. That thought was all his and he knew it.

"Well, that's taken care of." The words were muffled, but clear. The old bastard was still somewhere nearby. The sound of the man's voice only added fuel to his anger and he pushed harder, wishing that every straining blow could be directed at the bastard on the other side of the damnable barrier. "Some fool with a gun was nosing around. We wouldn't want him interrupting us now, would we?"

His hand punched through whatever was holding him and in spilled faint light along with the stench of raw sewage.

From outside whatever held him, he heard the phlegmy voice of the bookstore owner. "That's right, boy. Push! Fight! You have to be strong if you want to survive this. You want to be free, and I'll help you. But you'd best pray that Laura comes back soon. You'll need her. And you'll need your friend, Corin, too."

"I'm gonna fuck you up when I get out of here . . ." His voice came out deeper than he expected, and his throat felt freshly sanded when he spoke. That made him angrier, too, and he caught the edges of the stuff surrounding him, ripping and pulling as he kicked with his feet.

And outside of the place where he was struggling to get free, what had once been an old man with a bookstore chuckled and waited with the patience of a saint.

Chapter Ten

I

His head hurt. Not really a surprise. Chris could vaguely remember one of the doctors at the hospital who made a comment about him having a stone skull and guessed that was a good thing. In the last few months he'd taken more blows to his cranium than the average heavyweight boxer takes in a lifetime.

His arms felt like they had been pulped in a car crusher. They were also well above his head and bound tightly to something, The rope was cutting into his skin and cutting off his circulation. He could feel his legs, but he couldn't move them. They were under his body weight and from the knees down—including the knee that now felt like the size of a watermelon, thanks—all he could feel was the hot tingle of limbs deprived of circulation.

And the smell was back, along with the nausea that was damned near crippling him these days. Stale beer and mushrooms was the way his mind always processed the odor of the things around him. He opened his eyes. The left one was burning and didn't want to open all the way, but he forced it.

Yep. Dark place. Nice and wet and smelly. But there was enough light for him to make out that he was in the sewers, or in a pretty good facsimile of them. There was water, rats, filth and, of course, a few of the mutated freakazoids hanging around. Whatever had happened to them was only getting worse. Some of them looked like they were growing tumors on their skin and others looked a little like they were melting, but not a one of them looked much like a human anymore.

They were looking back at him. Every single one of them was looking back, staring hard out of eyes that more often than not belonged in his nightmares. Some of them were almost reptilian, with the slit for a pupil. Others were glowing in the darkness, a vast array of odd, unhealthy colors. A few of them still had only two eyes on their faces. Most had grown extras. The worst of the lot had a thick bubbling mass of eyes seeping down one side of her face. He couldn't guess what she'd looked like before this, but now she was enough to make him want to retch.

"What are you staring at, assholes?" Oh yeah, that

was gonna make the situation much better. Sometimes his mouth was not his friend. The one with the nest of eyes walked closer and tried to smile. It didn't work so well with half of her mouth overgrown by the spider-like cascade of eyeballs.

"Took us some time. We had to figure out a lot of this without the help of the others."

Chris scowled at her. "Figure out what?"

"Why we're changing."

"Okay, I give. Why are you changing?" He didn't much care. But if she was talking, maybe she wouldn't feel the need to beat on him anymore. He'd had about all the ass-kickings he wanted to take, thanks very much. His eyes were stinging from the damage they'd already done to him and from the tears that wanted to start falling. He blinked hard, determined not to cry. They could beat him to death, but he refused to let them see him cry.

Part of him wondered if he'd just gone insane at last. The nightmares were supposed to be over. Maybe this was all a dream, a warped sort of survivor's guilt coming back to fuck with his mind after he let so many people die. As much as he would have loved to believe that, the pain lancing through his body wouldn't let him off the hook that easily.

"You are why."

"Bullshit. I didn't do a thing to you."

"You let them live. The ones that are left. The ones that made us. And now we suffer their sickness." Her words weren't really angry, which was puzzling. The expression—what he could recognize of it on the parts of her face that still looked human—was almost expectant. What? He was supposed to call out with a hallelujah or two?

"Whatever. Just do what you're going to do and then fuck off."

The woman turned away from him and shook her head. At first he thought she was crying. Then he realized the hitching noises were laughter. "Oh, we're not going to do too much. We're just going to return the favor."

Okay. That can't be good. "What do you mean?"

"Everything has a purpose." The woman waved her arms around wildly as she spoke and for the first time he noticed the lump sweeping from her chest up her right arm. It was moving under the skin, slithering slowly up from the region of her armpit and pushing itself further across her bicep. He had to focus on her words, because, no matter how important what she might say was, the thing slipping under her skin was surreal.

"Everything in the universe has a purpose. But sometimes that isn't enough. We were all created for the same reason. We know that now. We were given seed by the . . ." And here she faltered, uncertain as to what it was she had been seeded by, apparently. "Let's just call it the Gatekeeper. That's good enough. We were given seed so that we could bear fruit."

"Wonderful." His muscles spasmed in his shoulders

and he tried to pull free, but whatever they'd used to bind him was holding fast.

She reached out and slapped his face with an open hand that felt like an iron skillet. "Pay attention!" As if to apologize for her actions, she smiled. It wasn't a pretty sight. "Only one of us gets to bear the fruit properly. The rest of us will be like oranges for eating, but one of us becomes the new tree. The new Gatekeeper."

"Excuse me?" She was talking gibberish.

"Let me get you up to speed, asshole." He knew the voice. Bobby Johanssen's tones he would know anywhere. Chris looked over to see the bastard as he came closer. Johanssen's face was just as smarmy as ever. Unlike most of the people in the sewer, he looked mostly unchanged. If anything, the man seemed almost healthy.

"That thing that held us captive? The one that made imitations of us? It's dead. You killed it when you blew up the house we were all stuck in." He came closer, and paused to light a cigarette. "Your heart was in the right place, man, but you screwed us all when you took us out of that dump." Bobby looked far too tall. That probably had to do with the fact that he was standing up and Chris was bound and sitting on his own feet.

"Remember how you found us? All inside those big drum things? Well, they were all connected to what Lucy over here was calling the Gatekeeper. It's as good a name as any, I guess." Bobby took five fast hits off the cigarette, igniting a good deal of the tobacco until the glowing tip was half an inch long. "Anyway. Here's the thing. When you started the fire, the Gate-keeper came out of the ground and tried to finish what it started, which was opening the way between worlds."

Bobby looked at him for a second and then took the cigarette out of his mouth. He brought it down hard and fast, crushing it out against the side of Chris's neck.

Any doubts that might have remained about being awake or asleep went right out the window at the same time the cherry of the cigarette exploded against his throat. The pain was too intense to ignore and far too real to be a dream. Chris yelped and bucked and tried desperately to get away. Every rational thought left him for several seconds as the group of nightmares around him laughed and applauded.

Eventually the pain subsided, almost in perfect pace with the dwindling laughter of the mob around him. Chris bit his own lip and tasted blood. He also broke his promise about not crying.

"Sorry. Sometimes I get these urges . . ." Bobby smiled at him. There was nothing kind or apologetic about the grin. It was pure pleasure that spread across his long face.

"Where was I?" Bobby squatted in front of him, his face inches from Chris's forehead. He was just far enough away that Chris couldn't head-butt him into the next week. Then again with the way his skull felt, that probably would have been enough to break a few bones in his noggin. "Oh yeah. You killed the Gate-keeper thing. Only, death doesn't always work out the way we want it to." Bobby stood up again and looked down at Chris. He'd have given a testicle to be able to kill the man right then. "It didn't really die all the way, just sort of went into a coma and hid.

"And those little reminders of what it did to us? The vines or whatever the fuck it put into our bodies? They started growing."

"Yeah. I got that part."

Again with the mouth, as his mother used to say. Bobby Johanssen grabbed his chin and made him look up. The color of the man's skin was dark red and his eyes—still looking human—glared with fury.

"You got shit, Corin. You don't know anything. What's growing inside of all of us is supposed to be a replacement for the Gatekeeper. It's not dead, you ass-hole, it's hibernating somewhere inside of us. Only, it doesn't need all of us to get a new body. Just one. The rest of us are supposed to be used as food to help it grow bigger when the time comes."

Chris looked the man and rolled his eyes, casting glances at the ones he could see behind Johanssen. They looked back, every last one of them seeming to accuse him with their mutilated expressions.

"So what the fuck do you want from me? An apology? Gosh, Johanssen, I'm really sorry my life turned to shit and I took the time to try to save your sorry ass." He jerked his head away from Bobby's fingers. "Next time I have the chance to save you, I promise not to. Okay?"

"You probably think we want to kill you, don't you?"

Chris had nothing to say to that. For once he kept his mouth shut.

"Well. Surprise. We don't."

Johanssen looked around at the others and they nodded their agreement. Chris slipped his legs out from under his body, wincing at the pain as his circulation got busy below the knees.

"But I'm not so sure about your friend, Jerry. He might want to kill you. That's part of what he gets to go through, because he ignored the summons when the Gatekeeper called on us to finish what you started. You killed it bad enough to make it die, but it was a slow death. It needed to find us, to have one of us eat from it for it to finish changing us. We had to tear it apart and eat it to trigger the final changes."

The thought was almost enough to make Chris gag. The notion of eating the flesh of the thing that he'd seen come up through the burning floors of the house was beyond nauseating.

"Don't look so shocked, asshole. You'd be amazed how tasty the flesh of a god is."

"What? You think you're going to be a god?" Chris started laughing. He couldn't help it. He knew it was a mistake, but he couldn't stop. Bobby nodded knowingly, and behind him the woman with the patch of eyes on her face grinned, revealing her teeth, even as the growth under her skin slipped past her chin and started moving up her face.

Bobby shrugged. "One of us will be. The rest of us . . . we're just a midnight snack for the other one."

"You gonna beat up all your new friends and make yourself a god?" Chris felt the crazy laughter fade away. His stomach hurt too much for the laughter to continue.

Bobby shrugged. "We don't know. We just know that something will happen."

One of the ones behind him dropped down with a groan. Chris could sort of recognize him. He thought it might be the bum he saw the others beating on when he and Katie had lunch. The shape of his head was all wrong, but the clothes looked about right.

Johanssen didn't even bother to look around. He just closed his eyes for a second and smiled. Meanwhile the bum was twitching and shaking and as Chris watched, something long and black pushed through the bum's skin and slapped at the wet ground.

Whatever it was, it hissed as it slid around in the filth. Chris tried to make his legs work, but all he got for his trouble was a flash of hot pain. The circulation hadn't come back yet. *Besides, my arms are stuck to something.* His shoulders throbbed at him as a reminder, and the scar where he'd taken a bullet at the beginning of the summer gave a few extra tweaks to his nerves. *This blows. This blows and that dude is growing something nasty.* The man with the new limb let out a moan as something else punched through the skin of his back and stretched lazily toward the ceiling.

Johanssen let out a dry, nervous chuckle. "Well, that's new. Haven't had anything come out that way before." He looked at Chris and winked. "Most of the bad stuff just comes out as puke or diarrhea."

"I do *not* need to know that, man. That's just disgusting."

"You don't know the half of it." They both turned to the sounds that came from the Living Eruption. The skin on the man was blistering everywhere, and sloughing off like wet plaster off a marble statue. Only in this case the statue kept moving, writhing and groaning. More new additions kept splitting away from him, but none of them moved independently. They were all attached to whatever was still hiding behind the human layers.

"Well. I think I see what most of us get to look forward to . . ."

Bobby walked away and talked with the others for a moment, and Chris tried to loosen the bonds that held his wrists. Somebody was a Boy Scout. Chris wished that somebody very dead, but made no progress in his efforts.

II

The moment he was out of the bindings, the thing that was waiting in the darkness came closer. It was much bigger than when it had been a bookstore owner. About four times bigger, actually. The flesh of the thing was black and warty, and in a few places it looked like the warts had been torn away to reveal the light gray inner flesh of the beast.

At least Jerry thought it was the old man. It spoke with the same voice. "Come on. Let's get this over with." The voice was amused. It came from somewhere in the region of the chest as best Jerry could figure. It didn't really have a head. What it had was a wide torso and short, stumpy legs. And four arms, which were over four feet long and ended in a Swiss Army knife variety of strange-looking appendages.

Jerry closed his eyes for a second and prayed hard that everything around him was some sort of sick joke. When he opened his eyes again, nothing had changed.

"What the hell happened to you?"

It shrugged, which was a little disconcerting, all things considered. "I have been blessed. I have a second chance."

Jerry staggered back, the room around him slowly coming into focus. Well, not a room, really. More like a pit. He could make out vague light far above him. Mostly what he saw was a rounded tunnel that went up for what looked like a few miles.

"Just get the fuck away from me, okay?" he looked for any way in which he could get out of the deep well.

"What? You don't want to be human? Completely human?"

That stopped him. Jerry looked over at the thing squatting across from him. "You can do that?"

"Yes, you damned fool. All I need is your friend, Chris Corin. After we get him, I can cure you."

"You said there was no cure . . ." Jerry eyed the thing. He didn't want to get his hopes up.

"There's a cure. But Chris Corin has to be involved or it won't work."

He couldn't judge the man. He didn't know him well enough to guess if he was being truthful from the look on his face. For that matter, as there was no face to really study, he was pretty much screwed.

"What happens to Chris?"

"He loses a little blood, but he lives." Again, he couldn't tell if the damned thing was telling him the truth.

"Well, I don't even know where Chris is . . ."

"I do." It moved closer, and the way it moved hurt his eyes to watch. Nothing about it made much sense. The motion of each of its legs was off-kilter and seemed to involve at least a dozen different joints.

"So go get him if you're so hot on making this happen." Jerry watched it come closer, still almost mesmerized by the funky walking motions. He was so busy looking at the legs on the thing coming his way that he forgot to pay any attention at all to the arms.

That was a mistake. He was grabbed and lifted from the ground before he could react. Thick, hard appendages—he couldn't justify thinking of them as fingers—wrapped around his shoulders and hauled him into the air. Jerry kicked and tried to struggle, but it was a waste of time. He may as well have tried to chew his way out of a sarcophagus.

"Listen carefully, boy. I have no patience left for you. You'll find your friend a few blocks from here. Down in the sewers. Head toward the north of where we are. You'll find an open manhole cover. I can't go there myself. It's going to be light out soon, and I might draw a little attention with my current appearance."

"Get your fucking hands off of me." Feeling that thick skin against his sent flashes of heat through Jerry's body and made him want to scream. The thing dropped him to the ground and he landed with ease.

"Chris Corin is about to have bad things done to him. I don't care one way or the other if he survives them. You might. He's your friend, after all." It shrugged again and skittered back away from him. Jerry stared at the ex-store owner and watched as it changed shape slightly. Whatever was happening to him wasn't finished.

"Fine. I'll go get him. How do I get out of this place?"

In answer the thing reached out again, grabbed him in two arms and used the rest of its limbs to climb up the side of the deep tunnel. Near the top, it threw him the rest of the way. He managed to keep the screaming to a bare minimum before he hit the ground.

"Find him. Bring him here. Believe me, boy. He's the only hope you have."

Jerry climbed out of the ruined building, his head

still feeling like it was off. The night was dark and the meager illumination offered by the one working lamp on the street was barely enough to see by. Still, he walked.

He wasn't exactly sure where he was going, but he figured he'd know when he got there.

He was right. It was hard to miss the screams.

III

Callaghan was looking a little better. The pasty color had left his skin and he wasn't really doing the sweat thing as much. Also, added bonus, the sun was starting to rise.

The biggest problem of the moment was that they weren't finding what they were looking for. Maybe the sunrise would help, but Brittany was beginning to think they just weren't going to have any luck locating her brother and that thought wasn't making her very happy. Okay. It was scaring the hell out of her.

"Look, where did you say they took him again?" She looked over at Courtney, mostly because Katie was lost in her own little world of grief over Jerry and she could understand that and didn't want to add to it.

"They took him this way." Courtney was fretting a lot too, and Brittany reminded herself to be patient.

"Okay. Who's this 'they' you keep talking about?" Callaghan spoke to Courtney, but mostly seemed to look at her ass while he spoke. Brittany lowered her estimation of the man. He was apparently as much of a pig as most of the guys she'd met lately.

Katie beat everyone else to the punch. "Infected people. Some of them were at that damned house when everything went down." She shot a look at Brittany that was almost completely alien on her face. It said she knew that Brittany had been talking about what had happened and even if she didn't really understand the reasons, she understood. Brittany felt a flash of guilt and crushed it quickly.

"Infected by what happened to them?" The detective looked over at Katie. On her he actually managed to find her face.

"Yeah."

"Why would they be after Chris Corin?"

"If I knew, I'd tell you."

The man was about to make another comment when they were interrupted. Arthur Hall came walking their way, his face lost in the darkness and his gait pure menace.

"Because he did this to us." Hall's voice shook with rage. "Because he took our lives away from us and made us into freaks!"

"That's a load of crap and you know it! We were trying to save you!" Knee jerk reaction. Brittany had her mouth open and was firing off comments before she even let herself think.

"Yeah? Well, you failed!" Hall reached out and grabbed her by the neck, lifting her off the ground easily. Brittany would have loved to protest, but she was far too busy being strangled to death. The man's face caught a little stray light, enough to let her see that his eyes were all wrong. The pupils had started splitting like cells dividing and his breath was a rancid mix of beer, mushrooms and vomit.

She was sure he was going to hold her there until she died, and all she could do was look into his eyes and feel a deep cold fear washing through her.

He might have actually killed her right then and there, but Martin Callaghan decided to put a stop to it. The man reached out and drove his fist into Hall's face, knocking him backward. The blow was powerful enough that Arthur Hall, street bum at large, let go of her and stumbled as he tried to keep his balance.

Brittany took a moment to land on her ass and let her head get used to the sudden blood flow.

"What the hell is wrong with you, attacking a little girl?" The detective was outraged, she could see it in his face. The man might come off as a cold fish, but he didn't like seeing anyone picking on a kid. Brittany's estimation went right back up, even as Hall rounded on the officer.

Hall took a swing and landed a solid blow in the detective's stomach. Callaghan grunted, but otherwise seemed unfazed. He grabbed Hall's wrist the second time he swung and moved with his body and both hands, wrenching the bum's arm behind his back. Martin Callaghan had to be the quickest draw she'd ever seen: Before she could do much more than gather

her legs under her body, the cop had handcuffs out and on Hall's wrists. "Don't move, Mister Hall. I know who you are and you have a lot of questions to answer."

Katie and Courtney were at Brittany's sides, helping her stand up. Her neck felt like someone had tried hanging her. Even without benefit of a mirror, she knew she'd have bruises on her throat in a short time.

"Brittany? Who the hell is that guy?" Courtney was sounding a little more like herself. Maybe it was the adrenaline.

Arthur Hall chose that moment to remind everyone that he wasn't human. He swung with both of his arms, groaning and straining against the handcuffs behind his back, staggering as he twisted one way and then the other in an effort to get free.

"Calm down, Mister Hall. You can't get free . . ."

"Shove it!" Hall grunted, fighting off the detective's hands as he tried to grab the bum's arms. He strained hard, his face purpling and his teeth bared, then let out a yowl of pain as the double report of his wrists breaking reached Brittany's ears. She watched the bones give, the arms sag inside of his skin and muscle.

And then he let out a roar and ripped the handcuffs away from his left wrist, tearing off his own hand in the process. There should have been a fountain of red blood and gristle. Instead something dark and foul spilled from the new wound.

Callaghan stared, shocked as the man rounded on him and grabbed his face with his right hand. The hand that should have been uselessly dangling from a broken joint. Brittany saw things moving under the skin where the bones had separated, saw the flesh swelling and changing and heard the detective's muffled screams as the fingers clutching his face started sinking into flesh.

Courtney's screams weren't muffled. They were loud and proud and pierced the fading night as easily as the sun did. She backed up as she let loose with her shriek and her eyes were larger than Brittany thought any person's should be. Katie was the one who moved. She took a running start and did her best to bulldoze through the street bum. Unfortunately, it didn't work out very well. Instead of knocking him on his ass, she just sort of bounced off him and quickly regained her balance.

He barely noticed. Arthur Hall was far too busy digging his fingers deeper and deeper into the skin of Callaghan's face, first just making red marks and then penetrating the skin, drawing blood as his fingers clutched at the detective's features. Callaghan finally recovered enough to retaliate. He pulled back with his entire body, cursing and spitting as the powerful fingers clawed deeper into his skin. At the same time, be brought both of his hands up and slammed them hard into the elbow of his assailant, shattering the bones there.

Callaghan staggered back and reached for his gun. Hall lunged, barely acknowledging the broken arm. He almost made it, but Callaghan was faster. The three bullets left in his clip blew very large holes in Arthur Hall's head, neck and left shoulder.

Brittany watched the man fall down. He didn't stagger around or spasm. He just fell, a thick plume of gray matter spilling onto the broken asphalt behind him. Not far from where it happened, Courtney fell on her hands and knees and retched again and again, her body shaking.

Callaghan eyed the dead man warily. He also rubbed at his face with his free hand in an effort to make sure all of his features were still there. They were, but it was close with his eyes. The skin on his eyebrows was cut and blood was flowing freely down his face. He wasn't looking so emotionless any more.

Katie, ever the caregiver, moved closer to the detective, reaching into her purse and pulling out a handful of McDonald's napkins. Courtney was recovering from her dry heaves, and Brittany kept looking at Arthur Hall's body. There was no way in hell he was dead. She knew that. It was too easy. He'd been killed before, according to what little Chris had bothered to tell her. Why would this time be any different?

"Okay. That was completely fucked up." Despite everything, the man still sounded almost rational. That was more than could be said for Courtney, who was hitching in breaths way too fast for normal conditions. Katie wiped at the blood on the detective's face, wincing in sympathy whenever she hit a spot that was especially tender.

Brittany felt detached from the whole thing. She

233

knew she should be freaking out, but instead she just kept watching Hall's body. Because she knew good and damned well that the very second she looked away, he was going to move.

He didn't wait long enough for her to get bored. While she was watching, the dead man's body rolled over and pushed off the ground, the one good hand and the ragged wrist stump of the other taking on his weight. One elbow bent the way it was supposed to, the other bent the wrong way. Both of them seemed to work well enough for the job though, and the nearly headless corpse stood up.

Brittany wanted to scream. She wanted to run. She wanted oh so many things that weren't happening. Instead she just stood there and watched as the man she had seen die stood and swayed, his face and head spilling all sorts of nastiness onto his filthy clothing.

He took a tentative step. When he didn't fall on his face he took another and then a third. And then he was heading right for Katie's back. Courtney let loose with another scream. Brittany watched Katie turn and then back up quickly. She saw Callaghan reach into his pocket, probably searching for another clip for his pistol. The detective seemed calm enough, but his skin was about as white as a virgin's wedding dress.

When he gave up on the extra clip, Callaghan hauled off and punched Arthur the Walking Corpse in what was left of his face. Little bits of dead bum came back with his hand.

The detective stared at the slop covering his knuckles and gagged. That was all the opening Arthur needed. He brought both hands around in wide arcs and slapped them into the detective's head.

Brittany heard the bones give out even from where she was standing. Martin Callaghan wouldn't be examining any more details about her brother or about her or about anything. Not ever again. Unlike Arthur Hall, he wasn't likely to get back up with half of his head pulped. His skull still bled out a deep crimson in addition to the gray of his brain.

Brittany stood perfectly still, her world turning darker, even as the sun rose. She stared long and hard at the mortal remains of Martin Callaghan.

And while she was staring, the thing that had killed him turned its remaining eye on her.

III

Whatever was happening to the man finally finished happening. His skin sloughed off like a tarp blown away from an art deco nightmare. What lay under it was hardly art deco, but it was most definitely nightmarish. There were too many limbs to easily count, and none of them seemed to match any of their mates, but all of them had deadly-looking appendages. Whatever he had become, even in the darkness Chris could see it was designed solely to kill. There was a thick gelatinous looking shell over most of it, and even as he watched that shell was hardening, darkening.

All around him in the sewer, the shuffling freaks

and infected rejects of humanity looked on silently. The woman he'd spoken with earlier walked over and touched the thing. It didn't move save to breathe slowly, laboriously.

Chris thought about warning her to avoid a trap and then decided against it. Screw the bitch. If she got torn apart, that was one less of them that could rip bloody chunks out of him.

Guess I'm getting a little bitter. He snorted to himself, looking at the woman's hand as it touched the creature. Her fingers were long and delicate and he wondered how she'd become infected. He knew for a fact that she hadn't been in the house when he got there.

His brain kicked in a second after the woman started her caress-the-monster game, and he started trying his luck with the bonds that held him in place. In the darkness, and with his arms up above is head and partially behind him, it wasn't easy to see what he was doing, but he could feel the fabric they'd used as he strained and pulled. He could also feel the muscles in his shoulders—which had long since been aching and were now starting to get bitchy about it—protest being moved.

He made a small sound and had the pleasure of seeing Bobby take notice of him again. Johanssen stepped closer and smiled. "It's not that easy, is it? Being tied up. I didn't have the best materials to work with, but the jeans weren't being used by anyone any more, and the denim is pretty tough stuff."

"What happened to him? He wasn't one of you. One of the ones we tried to save."

Bobby squatted until they were face to face. "You know, if it was my choice, we'd leave you alone. You really did try to do right by us." It bothered Chris a lot that he believed the man. "But it isn't up to me. It was a group decision. I have to go along, because, really, we're all sort of a big happy family." He chuckled. "At least for the next few hours. Then we're going to be a big dead family."

"I'm sorry too. I wish I could have made it better." He wanted to be angry, but it was taking too much energy. He was tired, damn it. He wanted to sleep more than anything else.

"I know, Chris."

The woman let out a soft moan and backed away from her pet monster. Even as she did so, her body started trembling.

"Here we go again." Bobby looked at her and smiled. "I wonder what she'll become."

"Can't be as bad as the last one . . ." Chris shook his head. Looking away wasn't an option. Each of the people around him was going to change and whether he wanted it or not, he was going to see them become whatever it was that hid under their human surfaces.

"I don't want to die here, Bobby." Damn it, he didn't. He didn't want to die. He had a lot of stuff left that he wanted to do in the world.

"I thought I already explained that. You're not going to die here." Johanssen seemed distracted. Chris looked at the woman again and understood why. She wasn't becoming something completely alien. Instead her body was changing in subtle ways. Her hair grew longer, fuller, and took on a look that seemed more like plant than animal. Her skin was splitting, but instead of falling off in bloodless strips, it was falling away as dust. For her, the transformation was almost beautiful. Somehow that didn't make him feel any better. What was revealed beneath the shower of flecks was pale and gray, but otherwise seemed perfectly human—until Chris noticed the slits forming all over her flesh. Each of them opened and closed at the same time, like mouths breathing softly. Thin streamers of darker gray crept like ivy from those openings and spread over her flesh in a slowly growing pattern.

He looked away. For one instant she had been almost beautiful. He didn't want to see what came next.

"We're not going to kill you, Chris."

"So what are you going to do then?"

Bobby reached into his pants and pulled out a small flask. It was silver and banged up from years of use, but Chris recognized it as the type designed for easy carrying and probably preferred by middle-aged men everywhere.

"See this? This is revenge. We all shared in filling it."

"With what?" He knew. He already knew. He just didn't want to get it wrong.

"With our blood. We're going to make you drink this, Chris."

"The fuck you are."

"Oh, you'll drink it." His voice was confident. "You'll drink it and then you'll sit here and watch what happens."

"But why?"

"We're calling it justice. You get infected. Only by then, the thing that made us will have finished with us and you won't be a part of the change. You'll just be infected. You'll get to feel it all. You'll get to suffer everything we have. But you'll get to live at least."

"No fucking way!" Several of the others looked his way at the sudden outburst. Chris didn't care. He wanted out and he wanted out yesterday and fuck all of them. He yanked harder on his bonds, but they didn't break. Chris put his feet on the ground and made his legs move. Screw them if they didn't like the notion. Johanssen just watched, that half-amused smile back on his face.

The first time he'd seen that face, it had been when Johanssen's doppelganger had been groping his little sister. He let himself remember that and used the anger that the notion generated. Maybe he wasn't the brightest guy around, but he knew how to work his emotions to his advantage. The last few months had taught him that if nothing else. Chris stood up, his back protesting, his shoulders decidedly pissed off about it, and his knee, his damned knee again, drawing a howl of pain from him.

"Chris, calm down."

"You go get fucked, Johanssen!"

"Chris, you're going to rile them. The changes are

happening and there's nothing I can do about that, but believe me, you don't want to see these guys angry."

Instead of answering, Chris head-butted good ol' Bobby in the face. Bobby dropped the flask from his hand, and without bothering to think about it, Chris kicked the bottle across the concrete floor, where it skittered, bounced and fell into one of the numerous puddles.

What had been a woman once turned and looked his way, her face gone now, buried under a continuing bloom of eyes that glared hatred at him. Below her ever-expanding ocular nest, her mouth opened wide, baring multiple rows of wicked-looking teeth. She screeched out a protest and moved in his direction and, around her, several of the other infected people let out sounds of their own.

They moved toward him as the changes in their bodies finally took hold and overrode whatever control they still had left.

Johanssen stepped out of the way, revealing the full menagerie of nightmares moving in his direction, their bodies shivering, twitching or just plain exploding into flurries of odd transformations.

"Can't say I didn't warn you, Chris."

Chris didn't respond. He was too busy watching his death moving in his direction.

Chapter Eleven

I

Courtney was a screamer. It wasn't a funny situation, not in the least, but Brittany giggled and thought she'd have to let Chris know his ex was a screamer.

Then she let out a scream of her own and forgot all about being humorous. Having something that looks like a dead man walk toward you can take all the good times out of a hysterical fit.

"You're Brittany, right?" The voice that came from the ruined face of Arthur Hall was trying to sound reasonable. Like, because he was being pleasant she'd overlook the gaping hole in his skull and the weird way his body was twitching, and the blood and bits of Detective Martin Callaghan that were dripping from his hands.

Still, conditioning is a hard thing to break. She nodded in response.

"Come with me, Brittany. Let's find your brother . . ." He reached for her and the paralysis that had been rooting her to the ground finally gave way to the wave of adrenaline that blasted into Brittany's body. She didn't run or jump, she did a standing vault that cleared five feet and then she ripped half the treads off her shoes when she took off.

Brittany might have lacked in form when it came to athletic feats, but she moved damned fast anyway. To their credit, Katie and Courtney did a fine job of keeping up. The deceased Mister Hall did not. He was trying, but maybe the holes in his body kept him from really being aerodynamic.

On the other hand, he was a fast learner. When Brittany looked over her shoulder, she could see him starting to change, the clothes on his body ripping away from him in thick shreds that he impatiently yanked from his changing body.

"Shit! I hate these fucking things!" She screamed the words, feeling just a little better for the effort it took.

Courtney put on a burst of speed that had her passing Brittany, her legs covering tremendous distance with each step she took. It was obvious in no time that she'd been on the track team, a fact that Brittany had forgotten over time.

Brittany looked back just in time to see the sleek, predatory thing that had been Arthur Hall reach out with a wicked-looking paw and swipe at Katie. She couldn't tell how well the blow stuck, but Katie went sailing, her body tossed into the air and then rolling across the ground at speeds that left scrapes all over the older girl.

She didn't let herself think about it. She just turned, running in a wide arc as the feline shape moved in closer to Katie. Katie was doing her best to stand up, her eyes wide as she looked at the thing coming her way. There was no fear on her face. That was what surprised Brittany as she moved closer. There was just anger and a deep resignation that was heartbreaking to look at.

Brittany wasn't much in the mood for heartbreaks. She ran harder and lifted both feet off the ground as she cannonballed into the side of the thing. Brick walls gave more yield. What looked almost furry from a distance proved to be damned rough up close. The hide was covered not in fur, but in spines, thin and delicate-looking, that cut through her clothes and into her knees and her left hip. Just like the needles of a cactus, the filaments broke off in her skin. She hissed loudly and bit her lip as she fell to the ground, skinning her elbow in the process.

And the strange thing that had been a bum a few moments earlier turned baring fangs that looked about the right size for swallowing her whole head.

The burning of the wounds was agony, each and every one of the little pins thrusting through the denim enough to make her want to cry. The idea of getting torn in half, however, was stronger. Brittany got up and backed away. It followed, leaving Katie on the ground where she fell. Brittany kept doing a back step, too, when the beast decided to keep coming at her. Up close and personal, it was even uglier than she'd expected. The face was almost feline, but covered with more of the same nasty quills, and the eyes were all pupil, with no color at all save the deep, dark black.

But the face wasn't holding its shape very well. Whatever these things were, they didn't seem to have the same control over their forms that the freaks from the house had shown. The shape of the face, the eyes and even the teeth inside that ferocious maw kept sliding.

She decided to focus less on the details when it leapt at her. Rather than try to dodge to the left or the right, Brittany just dropped straight down, bruising her ass on the road but getting to keep everything above her posterior attached.

The fucking thing was growing bigger, she was sure of it. Her view of its hindquarters seemed to go on forever as it went over her head. Brittany rolled over onto her stomach and practically vaulted herself into a standing position, running as fast and hard as she could. The noises behind her let her know that mister were-thing wasn't at all happy with her. She responded with a squeal of her own and ran toward Katie.

Katie was still flat on her back, her eyes closed and for the first time Brittany could see that part of the older girl's jeans had been shredded away from her leg along with a few inches of flesh. Thick lines of red ran across the exposed skin and turned black as they soaked into the denim on her leg.

Brittany came to a halt, looking in every direction she could for a weapon, for anything that would help her because, damn it, she was not going to leave Katie behind. No way, no how. They didn't always get along, but when you got down to it, Katie was family in her eyes.

Of course, the thing coming back at her wasn't family and probably didn't care about her sense of loyalty. It lowered down to the ground and grinned with that oddly feline face, the smile was unsettlingly human.

For a moment the world slowed down to a crawl and every detail around her became crystal clear. First was the cat-thing crouched low and beginning to lift off the ground. Its muscles coiled beneath the thick hide of bristles, and a string of saliva glistened between the teeth in its mouth as the jaws opened wider, wide enough, she suspected, to remove her head completely. Katie moaned softly nearby, her sweet face wincing as she moved her leg. The simple movement increased the flow of blood spilling from the gashes that marked her thigh.

And then the beast was airborne, sailing across the distance between them and changing even as it leapt. The claws grew wider apart, the changes blatantly unnatural. The mouth opened wider and the eyes, showing only pupils a moment ago, flared with a light that seemed to make them shrink. In fact the entire left side of the creature's body was getting lighter.

Well, that's just stupid. Brittany looked to her side and saw the light coming from down the street. It seemed to be moving slowly, but so did the thing that was about to eat her face.

Then the light was moving fast. The thing was moving faster.

Brittany reached out with her hand and shoved against the face of the thing coming at her, the muscles in her legs straining against the weight and the flesh in her palms screaming in protest as the spines along that roaring visage punctured her skin. One long tooth opened her left palm, but even that was only one of a hundred different wailing agonies that danced through her hands.

The cat-thing roared and scrambled as Brittany pushed against it. Had it been on the ground or trying to leap past her, it surely would have just smashed her to the ground. Instead, she caught the weight of the beast and pushed back with everything she had, and felt the animal stop in midair.

And that was when Courtney's car caught it on the back end and knocked the thing into the air as easily as Brittany could clobber a soccer ball. Metal met flesh with a truly amazing amount of noise. The thing let out a screech and the car's front crumpled against it with a sound like paper being balled up, amplified a thousandfold. The car shuddered and stopped. The monster did not. It rolled and bounced its way across the road and into the yellowed grass of a front lawn where, like all of the other houses around, no one had even bothered to turn on a light to investigate.

The creature stayed still for a moment, its body mangled below the hips and the flesh there pulped into a bloody ruin. Brittany knew that couldn't last.

So, apparently, did Courtney. Brittany got to see the girl's pale face through the glass of the side window, got to see the expression there, the wild eyes, the flared nostrils and the mouth open in a scream, just before the car lurched forward with a shriek of burned rubber and roared toward where the thing lay on the ground. It tried to move, but the car was better prepared. Courtney's head bounced up and hit the ceiling of the car and then she held on tightly as she ran the thing over with the front tires.

It roared, a sound so loud that even the dead would surely have heard it. But it couldn't manage to get up. *Having a car resting on your body probably does that,* Brittany thought. Courtney didn't back up and try again. Instead she put the car in neutral and pulled the parking brake.

The Mazda bucked a bit as the thing under it writhed and pushed, but it wasn't going anywhere fast. Courtney stepped back, eyeing the shape pinned under the front end dubiously. It was already trying on new shapes to see what it could do to get itself free.

"Okay. This is all fucked up. This is so fucked up I

can't even begin to say how fucked up it is." Courtney kept her eyes on the car and started ranting. Brittany understood how she felt, but wasn't exactly feeling very patient.

"Yeah, that's nice, Courtney, but right now we have other problems." She pointed at Katie on the ground and winced when she felt a flash of pain from her hand. The damned quills were too small to pull out easily. Courtney kept on mumbling to herself for several more seconds before Brittany yelled at her. After that, she snapped out of her little fugue.

"Shit. Shit!" Courtney ran over to Katie and looked at the wounds on her leg. Brittany joined her, biting her lower lip to stop from crying out. The wounds were not as deep as she'd feared they were, but they were deep enough to be a problem.

"We have to get her out of here and we have to get out of here ourselves." Brittany rolled her eyes. At least the dumbass was actually thinking again. That was an improvement.

The two of them crouched over Katie and Brittany wound up peeling off her shirt in order to wrap the cuts. The area was filthy, she didn't want the wounds getting infected and, frankly, her tits were smaller than Courtney's and less likely to attract even more unwanted attention. Besides, she still had her bra on; it wasn't like she was naked or anything.

They both looked over their shoulders a lot, to where the thing under Courtney's car was still trying to get loose. If they'd looked elsewhere from time to time, they might have avoided the thing that came at them from the remains of the house where so many of their problems had originated.

II

Jerry walked, following the instructions that he'd been given and eventually heading down into the sewers. The manhole cover thrown off to the side helped him figure out which way to go. After that it was all guesswork, but the man had said to head north and he was pretty sure he was going in the right direction. He was amazed at how calm he felt, and blamed most of the sensation on the simple fact that, for now at least, the voices had stopped. For what seemed like the first time in months—and actually was the first time in months—the only sounds he heard were the ones outside of his thick skull.

The sewers were not well lit. In fact, they were about as dark as a place could be, but he could see well enough. His body was changing, and there seemed to be little he could do about it.

Jerry looked at the lump of flesh sliding under his skin as it writhed from his elbow toward his wrist. *Sometimes you just have to go with the flow.* The thought made him chuckle a little bit. It also brought a sting to his tear ducts. He was depending on a monster to be telling him the truth. If the thing he'd been with down in that tunnel was lying, he'd not only be killing himself but he'd be damning his best friend at the same time.

And was it worth it to take the risk? Oh my, yes. Because, when he got right down to it, he didn't want to live if he couldn't be human. The very notion of going through any sort of life without Katie at his side made him want to just lose it. And he was close enough to getting lost already.

Or maybe he'd lost it already. He had to consider that possibility, and seriously. Maybe he was just as normal as anyone else, but a psychosis was making him think he was changing.

He shook his head and scowled. If he was that crazy, they'd have committed him to a nut ward a while back. The waters in the sewer were rising a bit, and tepid liquids of dubious origin ran over the tops of his shoes and across his feet. Though he was fairly certain he was heading in the right direction, he heard nothing out of the ordinary and saw only the waste left to fester in the pipes and an occasional rat.

The changes kept happening, strange little sensations making themselves known in his body, but Jerry did his best to stop them whenever he became aware of the alterations to his physical body. Like a man trying to work off a cramped leg muscle, he would stretch and contort the flesh where he felt it shifting, even as he continued on his way.

He stopped thinking about the changes going on inside of him when the first body parts came drifting his way in the rising waters. Oh, they weren't really complete body parts, more like chunks of skin and hair and occasionally a few scraps of clothing. But they were definitely enough to get his attention.

He just plain had to stop and look when he saw what looked like a rubber mask go rolling by in the stream. It wasn't rubber, and the back of the head had been torn away, but he could make out the features well enough and even see a few pimples showing on the thing.

Jerry chuckled. It just sort of crept out of his mouth before he could stop it, a nervous laugh that echoed in the sewer and got a chittering complaint from a black rat that glared at him from a few feet away.

He glared back at the rat and it decided to find something else to bitch about.

The laughter wasn't stopping, and Jerry found that he didn't much care anymore. Despite the insanity around him and the fucked up things going on inside his body, he felt invigorated. Upstream from him, something new and different was happening to the other freaks that had been infected by whatever was screwing with his mind and body. Like it or not, he'd find Chris up there.

Jerry started walking faster, his feet sloshing through the rising tide of sewage and shredded human flesh. Unless he got there soon, it would be too late for Chris. And if it was too late for Chris, it was too late for him.

He felt too good to want to go down without a fight.

251

Johanssen didn't stay down, damn him to hell. He got back up, a smirk on his face despite the split lip and the new angle his nose was cast at. Chris had beaned him a good one. He should have been whimpering on the ground and moaning over the broken nose at the very least. Instead he was standing up and grinning as the things around him shuffled, flopped and hopped in Chris's direction.

It isn't really fun, looking at your demise as it comes toward you. Chris backed up, his arms still hanging behind him off of whatever Johanssen had tied the jeans to.

"You're pissing off all the wrong people here, Chris." Bobby shook his head.

"What? You mean you'll just kill me instead of making me a freak?" Chris was scared, but he was also really, really tired of Johanssen. "Either way I'm fucked and I don't like the options."

"Cry me a river!" The smile fell from Bobby's mashed face in an instant and his eyes damn near glowed in the faint light. Every action, every gesture that he made indicated his powerful desire to beat Chris to death. Considering the options, Chris was almost willing to let him.

Behind Bobby, and looming around him, the menagerie of obscenities was fidgeting. They all wanted him, every last one of them, as if he were responsible for what had happened to each and every one.

He sighed and made himself look into the eyes of the ones whose eyes were still obvious and weren't too disgusting to stare at. "Listen. You're gonna tear me up, and I know that. But at least have a little common sense here, okay? Bobby over here and maybe one or two of you were rescued from that fire a couple of months ago. I can see them blaming me for what happened. But the rest of you? I wasn't the one who made you drink anything or forced you to eat something or for all I know raped you until you got whatever this sick fuck—" he pointed with his chin toward Bobby, "—did to make you sick. I had nothing to do with that."

It would have helped if he could have read the expressions on any of their faces, but that just wasn't going to happen.

"So you want to give it to me? Fuck you. I didn't do a damned thing to any of you." He looked around for a few heartbeats and then he started walking, with absolutely no idea in hell where he intended to go.

Bobby Johanssen applauded him, his face still set in the same smirk, but with just the faintest hint of actual admiration in his eyes. "Oh, that was just lovely. Really. I couldn't have said it better myself." He walked to keep pace with Chris and the things behind him kept moving along the sewer with him. Really, that was all Chris had wanted. He didn't figure he was likely to get out of this alive, but if he could avoid drinking the blood that was now festering merrily away in a puddle behind the entire congregation, he was just fine with that notion.

"Go get laid, Johanssen."

"Yeah. Not a bad idea. Bet your little sister would be a good little romp." Just like that, the man used the one tactic that could have made Chris stop walking. Once again the image of Johanssen groping his little sister while her hand slid into his pants flashed into Chris's skull, and even knowing that it hadn't really been the man behind him, and knowing that it was a baited comment designed to make him do something stupid, Chris couldn't stop himself from acting exactly the way Bobby wanted him to.

Chris looked over his shoulder—and past his hand, which was still feeling like a lead weight and was almost as useless—sited his target and swung his entire body around as hard as he could. Whatever Johanssen had strapped his wrists to was solid and had a good edge to it. It slammed into Bobby's skull with a loud noise and sent the man down into the shallow waters.

Chris didn't let himself think much. He just did his best to go to town all over Bobby's sorry ass. He couldn't use his hands, but he had two feet and his knees. He took full advantage of their existence. His left foot hit Bobby square between his legs, and whatever else he might be, he was male. The impact across his testicles had the desired effect of making the man whimper. Chris took a chance on his bad knee supporting him and landed with the other one on the side of Johanssen's neck. He felt the bones inside the thin pillar of flesh break under the impact and felt the explosive pain of his good knee trying to give out.

Johanssen backhanded Chris across his chest—it would have been the face and head, again, but Chris managed to half duck the blow—and sent him backward with the blow. Before Chris could stand up on his own, someone was grabbing his arms and lifting him. He let out a gasp as his shoulders were moved, and then a second sharp breath when he felt the jeans being cut away from his wrists.

The claws that severed the denim let him know it wasn't a human getting him free, and while he was puzzled, he wasn't so curious that he was willing to take his eyes off of Johanssen.

Blood flowed back into the muscles in his arms. Maybe later he would be grateful, but for the moment it felt like someone had decided to pour boiling water through his veins and arteries. Chris sidestepped away from Johanssen as the man got back up out of the water. His head hung at an angle for a moment, and then good old Bobby looked his way and snarled. The older and sleazier creep used his hands to hold his skull at the right angle and the very sounds that had come from his neck when Chris landed on it were repeated as the bones fused back together.

And that was Chris's cue to deck the bastard again. He took two steps forward and put everything he had into a roundhouse punch.

And missed. Bobby ducked without even trying. Chris's arms were screaming in protest, and moving like they were suspended in gelatin. Bobby didn't seem to have the same problem with his own fists. He brought both of his hands down from his own head and landed a couple of solid blows on Chris's face. One fist slapped into the side of his right cheek. The other boxed his left ear, sending another shiveringly exquisite flash of pain through his nerve endings.

Chris fell back, not so much as a retreat but because his head was ringing. True to form, Bobby followed, his face frozen in an expression of undiluted rage. For a skinny guy—though granted not a fully human skinny guy—Johanssen could hit like a mule. His third blow was a flawless delivery to Chris's chin that took all of the strength from his knees and dropped him back to the ground. He bruised his ass on the piece of lumber that had held his hands and arms above the level of his head for a while. It wasn't exactly comfortable.

Bobby walked over to him and brought a knee around to reshape Chris's face. Chris managed to block it with both forearms and then grabbed hold of the offending leg joint before Johanssen could pull it back. His arms were still aching and his fingers felt like someone was deep-frying his hands. The feeling of blood flowing back into starved extremities was not gratifying, but rather extremely inconvenient. That didn't stop him from using all the strength he had to crush the kneecap in his grasp.

Chris Corin was not exactly bulky, but he was not small either. He'd done his time in high school sports and he'd worked for three summers to make enough money to go to Europe before his plans were changed out of necessity. He thought about Bobby and Brittany and shoved his hands together as hard as he could while wrenching his body to the left.

Bones cracked and soft tissues tore. Bobby Johanssen let out a squawk and tried to get away. Chris wasn't having any of it. He kept one hand locked onto Bobby's knee and with the other one delivered a volley of blows into the man's crotch.

Something was different this time. When his foot had crushed Johanssen between the legs, there had been something to hit. Now, there was nothing there, no soft tissues, no testicles, not even a penis tucked away for safety. It was like hitting a man with washboard abs in the stomach.

Johanssen kept screaming above him and Chris looked up to see the man's mouth opened in a wide grin as he kept making noises.

"Not getting it, Chris. I'm not human any more." Bobby pulled his leg back and pointed at the ruined knee. While Chris watched, the ruined bone and flesh righted itself and then thickened. "Wanna see a really neat trick, Corin?"

The dark wet denim on Johanssen's leg split apart, and the skin underneath turned a dark gray. The pants tore off of him, falling away as so many dishrags.

Bobby's body kept changing, shifting, but not like the transformations that had happened with the creatures around him. There was no random shifting, no uncontrolled changes that did as they pleased. Instead, the changes were deliberate and fluid.

All around them in the darkened sewer the other freaks were backing away or sort of half dancing agitatedly. Chris looked at them from the corner of his eye and said nothing, letting Bobby do all the talking.

"I'm not like the others, Chris. I'm pure. First generation and undiluted by anything else. I can control this, just like the ones that took our places in the first place. I can change the color of my skin, the shape of my face, even the location of my balls, which believe me is a bonus."

Chris shook his head. "Damn, Johanssen, you're a stupid man."

"What are you talking about?" Bobby wasn't worried, just amused. He'd become convinced of his own invulnerability. With his help, Chris had gotten over any delusions along those lines a long time ago.

Chris pointed past his enemy and indicated the creatures all around them, who were, by and large, looking uglier than should have been possible and about three times as pissed. "Dude. You just told all of your enemies that you have an unfair advantage. What would you do in their place?"

Realization took a while to get past the smirk on the man's face. Chris pushed himself off the ground and hugged the side of the round wall as the things around Johanssen thought about what he had just said. They all wanted the same thing, they all wanted to be the head honcho and survive the culling. And he had just pointed out for the slower members of the studio audience that their still human-looking counterpart was cheating and could kick their collective asses in a fair fight.

He had about enough time to get out a hearty "Oh, shit" before the monster squad surged forward in a wave of claws, tentacles, pinchers and teeth.

Chris didn't stay around to watch what happened. He ran as fast as his now two bad knees would let him. The noises that came from behind him were not healthy to think about.

Chapter Twelve

I

Brittany had just finished with the bandages when Katie came fully awake. The tight knot tied around her thigh was enough to make her eyes finally open and her mouth expel a sharp breath. "Ow. What the hell are you doing?"

"Patching you up. Now be quiet."

Katie looked at her with a strange expression on her face. Finally she nodded. Courtney in the meantime was still looking at the thing under her car and probably trying to figure out how she could get the Miata back home without a snot monster stuck in the tires and grille. Poor Courtney was having a little trouble accepting the changes in her reality. Brittany sympathized and so did not fire off a few rude remarks.

"What happened?"

Brittany shrugged. "Monster. Courtney parked her car on it."

Katie let out a chuckle as Brittany helped her to her feet. "Why are we out here, again?"

"Looking for your boyfriend. So far we haven't seen him."

"Okay, so at least I'm still up-to-date on that." She was forcing a smile and Brittany knew it. But as with Courtney before, she chose not to call Katie on that fact.

"So let's go find him. Or, hey, we could get you to a hospital."

"No." Katie shook her head. "I want to find Jerry." Her voice sounded petulant, which Brittany expected far more from herself than from the older girl.

"Jerry will be here soon. He just has to find his friend first." Courtney didn't have a voice anywhere near that deep and whoever had been speaking wasn't Brittany or Katie, so Brittany figured it had to be yet another unpleasant surprise.

She was right. There was an older man standing nearby, a sheaf of pictures in his hands. He had salt-and-pepper hair, a wide, friendly face, eyes that glowed with the same sort of icky green she had seen in the cat-porcupine from hell and the photographs that Brittany had been desperately trying to get from Callaghan before.

This was not turning out to be her night. Not at all. She felt her blood pressure rise and her skin flush with red. Screw the old man seeing the pictures. If Katie or Courtney saw those pictures, her life was as good as over.

"Who are you?" That was Courtney, who was now looking at the man and frowning.

"Lawrence Chadbourne, at your service." He smiled. He had the sort of grin that just screamed salesman.

"At our service? You have a tow truck and a really, really big gun?" Courtney was direct. That was one of the things Brittany had always admired about the older girl and the number one reason she sometimes wanted to knock the blonde's teeth down her throat.

"A big gun?" He frowned for a second and then his face lit up. "Oh, for the little thing under your car. Don't you worry. I'll take care of him."

"Mister Chadbourne, what do you know about where Jerry is?" Katie focused on the man and stared hard. He stared back just as intently, studying her.

"I know where Jerry is, because I sent him to fetch Chris Corin. If he can get Chris, I can cure him."

The look of relief that washed over Katie was enough to make Brittany want to cry. It was possible that the man was telling the truth and it was just as possible that he was a complete bastard who was trying to pull one over. Or worse, he might be one of the things they'd been messing with. Just because he was clean-cut and had probably showered some time in the last few days, that didn't suddenly make him one of the good guys.

She was still looking at him intently when he returned the favor.

"Brittany, isn't it?" Brittany nodded as the man walked over. He waved the pictures—still, thankfully facing him and not the three girls—and raised one eyebrow. "May I have a word for you in private?"

What choice did she have? Those pictures were pure poison and while seeing Callaghan get torn apart had successfully pushed the thought of them from her head, she had been reminded and needed them. She nodded.

"Are you out of your fucking mind?" That was Katie, and while she was behaving herself and speaking quietly, she was not happy about the situation. Maybe she wasn't quite as far into daydreaming about Jerry as Brittany had thought.

"Just . . ." She was trying to figure out how to be tactful. "Just leave it alone, Katie. I got it."

She walked over to the man and felt her pulse rate start doing a nervous twitch. There was something about him that didn't sit well with her and she'd always been pretty good about trusting her instincts—well, okay, when she wasn't drunk, stoned or pissed off. She stopped just out of his reach zone.

"Young lady," the man looked at her with reproach in his eyes. "I truly hope these pictures don't show the sort of thing that's become a habit for you. You're an attractive girl and I'm sure your brother would disapprove." He handed her the pictures, which she hastily crammed into her jeans pocket, feeling them crinkle along with the negatives that were pressed in among them.

"Thank you!" She looked away and then back at him. "And no, I don't plan on doing anything like that ever again."

He nodded his approval. "Good. Because if I even thought my daughter was considering that sort of thing, I'd have to consider levels of punishment best not thought about."

Brittany turned away, having no idea how to respond to that. "Umm . . . thanks again. I have to try to get Katie to a hospital or something."

"I'm sure Chris will be here soon." The man's voice held an odd edge to it, one that she couldn't quite decipher. Was he gloating? Teasing? Planning on inviting her brother for tea? She had no idea, but as with the man's physical presence, something about the comment didn't sit right with her.

"How's Chris supposed to help Jerry get better, anyway?"

The old guy looked at her and smiled. "Simple, really. When he gets here, I'm going to take a little of his blood and use it to draw the infection from Jerry. Once that's done, I'll have what I need to place the infection into myself and assimilate it."

Her stomach did a slow, steady roll and she blinked a few times slowly before she responded. "How much of Chris's blood do you need?"

"Not enough to kill him if that's what you're worried about." And oh, he was so lying to her. She could feel it. She knew it as surely as she knew her name. The man intended to kill her brother.

Brittany smiled thinly and nodded. "So let's see about getting him for you." She walked back over to Katie and Courtney. Courtney was still focused heavily on the thing under her car, which had successfully broken something under the Mazda and was letting out gurgling growls as motor oil or something just as thick sploshed all over it.

Katie was watching Brittany like a hawk. "What did he want?"

"He gave me something I lost and then he told me that in order to save Jerry, he has to bleed Chris."

"Excuse me?"

Brittany nodded her head. "You heard me. He has to bleed Chris to save Jerry. And he didn't say it, but I think he has to kill Chris to save Jerry."

"Jerry would never go for that."

"Yeah, I'm kind of sure Chris would be against it, too."

"So what are we gonna do?"

"We could have Courtney hit the dude with her car."

Katie shook her head. "No. That would mean moving it off of the nasty screaming thing."

Courtney backed toward them slowly, never quite taking her eyes off of the thing ripping into her car. "Listen, can we just run away now?"

Brittany looked for the old dude who'd given her the pictures and then looked again when she realized she didn't see him. "What happened to the guy?"

Katie and Courtney checked the area out, though for Courtney it seemed to take an effort. "I have no idea." Courtney shrugged.

"Let's just get the hell out of here and find our way home, okay?" Brittany grabbed Katie's wrist and started tugging. She was liking the whole thing less by the second.

"No." Weak as she looked, Katie yanked her hand free with ease. "Screw that. I want to find Jerry and we're going to find him."

Brittany didn't even think about it, she just nodded. Jerry, just as with Katie herself, was practically family. Okay, he was an annoying older brother type who tended to look at her ass when he thought she wasn't noticing, but he was still a big brother type.

Courtney on the other hand made a face like she'd been sucking down the juice from a moldy lemon before finally nodding her agreement. "Whatever. Let's just get this shit done. The sun's getting ready to rise soon and I want to get home."

II

Monsters shouldn't have to answer cell phones. Lawrence Chadbourne was adamant about that fact, but he answered anyway, just as soon as he was out of view of the little girl with the voracious appetites.

"Yes?" If he sounded impatient, it was only because he was. In the last year he'd worked hard to achieve certain goals, among them a new and more powerful form, a new lease on life and the gathering of a very large fortune. Now all of those things were damned near within his grasp and he had to put everything on hold to answer the phone. Why? Because it might be her, and if he didn't answer, she would be unhappy. And when she was unhappy, she made his life absolutely miserable.

Life is never as easy when you have a demanding employer.

"Hello?"

"Mister Chadbourne? How very nice of you to answer at last." Her voice was chilled to the point of leaving frostbite on his ear. "I was wondering how everything is progressing."

"Well, to be honest your timing could be better. I was just speaking with your granddaughter."

"Well then, might I suggest you finish what you're being paid to handle? What you've asked for comes at a high price and if you're not willing to pay it, I can always find someone else to assist with their desires."

Before he could even begin groveling properly, she'd hung up. Of course, by the time he put the phone away, the girls had vanished. That wouldn't do at all. The old witch was not known for her forgiving nature. If he lost the girl he was going to lose everything.

The changes he made were small and subtle, but they did the job. After a few moments of concentration he inhaled deeply and caught the little girl's familiar scent. He had to make sure not to play his hand too soon. The brother might still be alive and that would ruin everything.

He thought about the pictures of Brittany Corin that he had found on the dead policeman. They had been explicit.

"I wonder if she minds damaged goods?" The notion put a smile on his face as he moved quickly and quietly down the street, following the olfactory trails left behind by the three girls.

III

He found the source of the rising waters without even trying. Something had deliberately punched a hole in a water main and the resulting cascade was running in both directions through the sewers. Judging by the claw marks on the pipe, he had to guess it was one of his own kind.

No, he corrected himself. *It's one of the things I'll become if I don't get my hands on Chris.*

It was getting hard to focus again. Almost as if the closer he came to his best friend the less rational he became. And he knew Chris was nearby now, because he could hear the sounds of combat and from somewhere further down he could hear Chris breathing hard and moaning.

Jerry moved through the sewer, hunched over slightly as he made his way down the tunnel and into the proximity of the most unusual fight he'd ever seen.

He made sure he stayed back a bit, because,

frankly, he didn't want to be noticed just yet. Not when the rest of the infected people were so busy killing each other off.

They kept changing, adapting to whatever punishments their counterparts unleashed on them. The only exception was one that had been torn into tiny shreds, ripped apart and then, if he was guessing properly, hastily devoured. His new senses were confusing the hell out him. He could almost see the scents of the things near him, and the one thing they all seemed to have in common was that they were all mingling their own unique odors with the fragments around them.

Almost as if to make sure he was getting it right, a couple of the writhing nightmares turned in unison and attacked another that had misjudged what shape to become and been cleaved neatly in two by something that looked like Salvador Dali's idea of a praying mantis. The head was all wrong, leaning over to the side and changing even as he watched, but the mostly insectoid thing started shoveling still moving pieces of the slimy shape it had ripped open into its mouth, chewing and swallowing at a pace that would have shamed the winners of any food eating contest he'd ever heard of. A serpentine form with mouths at both ends joined in on the feast even as it roared and thrashed at something trying to take a bite out of its far end.

And the whispers that he'd been hearing in his head came back tenfold as he watched. Worse still, his stomach rumbled hungrily. The very thought of eating the foulness spilled across the sewer's rounded floor should have had him gagging but instead it made his mouth salivate with anticipation.

Three more of the things went at each other like rabid dogs with PMS. Jerry backed away as they started getting a little too violent, not just fighting, but slamming each other around the narrow space as they fought each other for a better position for feasting.

It was hard to tell them apart. Whatever was going on in their bodies seemed to have reached a fever pitch. None of them maintained any form for long, but rather shifted almost continuously in the quest for the perfect form to kill with.

Something shifted along his spine, seeking a way out of his skin. He grunted and stepped back against the wall, pressing at the moving lump. It pressed back, which was decidedly unsettling.

He was still trying to figure out how he was going to get past the mutating army of cannibalistic monsters—and remembering all too well that he would be on their diet plans if they were going only for their own kind—when he spotted Chris on the far side of the combat zone. Chris was not looking his best. He was trying to run and failing miserably as both of his legs seemed to be out of whack. He'd manage about five serious steps before leaning against the wall and moving like an old man. Then he'd get another burst of speed and do it again. The only reason he was alive was because the things he'd been running from were too busy ripping each other into bite-sized snacks.

And again, as he looked at his best friend, he felt the irrational hatred start inside his skull. A response to something that had changed in him, he knew that. And if he was feeling it, so were all of the things eating each other.

And if they went after Chris, they would take Jerry's only chance of ever being human again with them.

And that was all it took to get him motivated. Jerry looked at the continuing bloodbath going on in front of him and got a running start, hoping to clear all of it or even most of it before he was noticed.

He made seven long strides before it was too late to turn back. On the first step he was in the clear. The second he had to jump over something that looked like a furry tentacle with eyes. The third was easy and clear. The fourth had him pulling his foot free from something green and sticky that howled when he touched it. Step five, still alive. Step six and his ankle twisted. Step seven and he ran straight into the backside of something that looked almost human and almost female until it turned to face him.

Whatever else he could say about the thing, it was very, very fast. One tapering arm hauled off and cracked him on the side of his face before he could even recover his balance. Jerry went down hard, the back of his skull cracking against the concrete of the sewer hard enough to dent both.

He should have been dead by all rights and he knew it. The feminine monster opened a full-lipped mouth and roared, spraying him with a mist of rancid spittle and diving toward him, both of her arms cocked back and driving for his chest. He looked into her eyes, the nearly countless collection of odd-sized black orbs growing over half of her head, and saw his own face reflected endlessly within them.

Jerry roared back, the sound exploding from his chest before he even realized what was happening. He lost all control as soon as the bitch came his way and all of his plans to rescue Chris went straight to hell at the exact same time.

What had once been hands slammed into his torso and cut into his flesh, shearing away thick layers of his hide. He reached with his own hands and watched them change, thickening and developing blunt, shovel-like claws at the end of each finger.

He sank his powerful hands into her shoulders and grinned as he saw the expression on her face change to one of pain. He liked the look on her face. Liked that she was in agony and beginning to experience real fear. It was a sweet thing to experience and he wanted more of it. So he hauled her shoulders toward him and as she came his way, he opened his mouth to take a bite out of her surreal face.

Jerry tasted her blood, the viscera of her eyes as they popped like grapes against his teeth. He felt her body shudder and felt the organic weapons she'd driven into his chest saw violently back and forth. He felt as well as heard her scream of pain and was vaguely aware of the fact that he was getting an erection. The thought of doing to Katie what he was now doing to this creature in front of him was enough to give him shivers of pleasure. He drank in the fluids that spilled from the head wound and the wails of agony at the same time.

And was horrified. *This is crazy. I'm not human anymore. There's no way I can be human and have these thoughts.* He hesitated, the primal desire to feed knocked off track by the realization that what he was doing, what he was thinking, was completely alien.

And that was when the thing he'd taken a chomp out of returned the favor. He felt the barbs she'd shoved into his chest change, shifting and spreading, the better to hold him still and the very spot where he'd drawn—*Blood? Ick? Disgusting raw sap?* He gagged at the thought of what was in his mouth and throat, even as his stomach and tongue demanded more—from her head and her face opened wider as she generated a new mouth, complete with several razored tongues and teeth that would have shamed a piranha.

Any pleasure he might have been receiving was lost the second she tore away his left shoulder. The pain was worse than anything he'd ever felt in his life, even worse than the hell he'd been through a few months earlier. The teeth in the thing's mouth ripped deeply into flesh and the thin, sharp tongues bored holes into the meat she clenched tightly. He roared screaming and bucking, trying to get away, but she had him pinned and all of his struggles did nothing to get him free.

And from behind him he heard the voice. "Jerry! Goddamnit! I'm coming! Fuck! Got offa me!"

And there was Chris, fool that he was, trying to come to the rescue. Chris knocked something aside, and got a scowl on his face, the pain in his knees apparently forgotten for the moment. Jerry looked at his friend and moaned, tried to form the words to tell Chris to run, and failed. The thing eating his shoulder didn't even stop to notice the newcomer. She just sank her face deeper into the wound she'd already made and cut deeper into his skin. He tried to reach for her, but she'd done something to his hands and he couldn't make them move. Jerry managed to focus well enough to see that the skin on her shoulders had changed, become tarry, and was drawing his claws further into her body without taking any more damage herself.

He kicked with his feet, trying to get in a few good hits, but it wasn't working. Something had a hold of his left leg and his right one didn't seem much inclined to listen to what he was telling it. And damn it, but the pain was doing him in.

Jerry tried to speak again and all that came out was a weak gasp. He saw Chris coming, saw the murderous rage on his friend's face and that was all he saw.

And then there was darkness.

IV

Chris was finally making progress, despite the weakness and pain in his knees, when he heard Jerry cry out. The voice was all wrong, sounded like it had been played on an old 45 record set at thirty-three and a third rpms, but he recognized it. How could he not recognize the sounds of his oldest friend?

And he turned and saw the expression on Jerry's face as the girl-thing started literally eating his shoulder. Chris moved, pushing aside the pain again, pushing aside his exhaustion, and waded into the nightmares.

He didn't try to fight them, just knocked them away when they got too close. It was a damned good thing they were all trying to eat each other alive. He was very grateful, really, but didn't expect his luck to last.

The thing chewing on Jerry was hardly concerned about Chris doing anything. She was too busy enjoying her meal. Rather than try to attack her—which, if he'd learned anything at all, would just about be a waste of time—he grabbed Jerry and pulled hard. Jerry screamed. The woman-thing roared and both of them were hauled in his general direction.

The idea, of course, was to get Jerry free. It didn't work worth a damn. Instead he managed to do what he'd been trying to avoid and got the attention of the monster on top of his best friend. She didn't bother letting go of her snack. She just kicked back and nailed Chris in the stomach with her right leg. The impact rolled him into a ball and knocked all the wind out of him with the greatest of ease. For half a second or so, he'd forgotten he was dealing with monsters instead of just people. She reminded him without any real difficulty.

The feeling of nausea came back again, the one he'd

been doing his best to ignore, and Chris stayed doubled over, uncertain if he'd be able to recover from the blow she'd delivered. There was something particularly annoying about being dropped by a girl. It was a chauvinist reaction and certainly not a rational one, but it was there and it chapped the hell out of his machismo.

He stopped being annoyed around the same time a few of the combatants remembered him. They were still working on each other, but one of the things reached out a four-fingered paw and slapped it down on his chest, pinning him in place.

Chris Corin struggled to breathe, the force of the limb on his ribs almost crushing the last gasp of air from his lungs. Not far away, Jerry Murphy let loose another scream, as the thing that had him nailed to the ground continued to rip at his arm, swallowing flesh as quickly as it could tear it away from his body.

Chris reached toward Jerry with one hand, barely managing to move his arm even a couple of inches. And in the darkness around him, the things that were surely meant to be his death continued to murder and maim each other.

Chapter Thirteen

I

Laura Chadbourne stood in the shadows, something she'd been doing for most of her life. The darkness was comforting to a certain extent, and almost always offered her safety. Tonight was no exception.

But the night was almost over. The sun was starting to rise in the east, pushing past the low-lying clouds and weakening the shadows' death grip on the world.

And that meant her father would soon be able to see her.

And her father seeing her would not be a good thing. He'd ordered her to see to Jason, to make sure her little brother was safe and sound after she delivered her message. She shivered a bit at the thought of how angry he'd be if he found out she'd defied him.

"What are you doing, Dad? What's the big secret?" She had to know, because she couldn't stand the secrets any longer. All of her life she'd been under the impression that her parents were good people. They'd raised her to behave properly, to respect her elders and to do the right thing. All of her life she'd done so, even when she wanted to cut loose and be a teenager. Defiance had never even been a consideration, because she knew the consequence for disobeying her parents was punishment. Severe punishment.

Thinking back on a few of the tricks her father had used in her earlier years was enough to make her want to die right then and there. It was only for Jason's sake that she was still hanging around. If it hadn't been for him she'd have run off a long time ago, at the very least she'd have run off after her mother died because

Laura, honey, sometimes your mom doesn't feel well and sometimes my needs would make her feel worse. You want Mommy to feel better, don't you? Come here. I'll show you a few secrets . . .

the idea of her father touching her ever again was worse than almost anything else she could imagine. Like everything else about him, his desires were not even remotely human. She ran her fingertips over the scars along her sides, unconsciously touching the memories she wanted to forget.

"Jason's not here, Dad." Her eyes narrowed as she watched her father stalking the three girls she knew were friends of Chris Corin. "He's not here to use against me." She reached into her pocket and dialed three numbers on her cell phone. 9-1-1.

Three rings before the operator answered. In that time she thought her heart would explode about ten times. "Hello?"

"911 emergency. Please state the nature of your call."

"I'd like to report a murder . . ."

She answered questions as the man on the other end of the phone asked them, and all the while she watched her father moving with a grace that simply shouldn't have been possible. A week ago he'd been an invalid in bed. Now he was alive and active. That didn't fit in with Laura's plans, and if she wanted him out of the picture, it had to be now.

She hung up her cell phone and moved away from her father. He was after the three girls, and as luck would have it, there was something else that had been after the three girls.

It wasn't that far to get to the Mazda where it sat, pinning down something decidedly inhuman. The entire car rocked as the thing pushed and grunted. She'd seen enough of the action to know that it could change shape, but apparently that didn't stop a ton or so of car on its body from making it sit and stay.

That didn't mean it was being quiet. The thing grunted and from time to time whimpered as it shoved against the car. Laura watched it for almost a minute before she finally got her nerve up.

"Just calm down and I'll move the car, okay?"

She had to repeat herself four times before a voice from under the front axle replied. "Be fast about it. Please."

Laura moved into the driver's seat, half expecting to get her leg torn off. The car keys were gone. She searched quickly, but didn't find them. Exasperated and a little worried about the whole monster-sitting-under-her-ass thing, she slipped the car into drive and released the emergency brake. The Miata didn't move at first, but as the thing under her rear end started bucking, it finally began to roll. After a good four feet, the dark form that had been pinned under the car let out a sound that was one part snarl and two parts glee as it rose up.

It was wet with engine fluids and possibly its own blood. But it looked healthy, even as it changed its shape again, the dark silhouette looked disturbingly healthy.

Laura watched it move away, loping at high speed and continuing its alterations. In a matter of seconds it was gone from her view.

And after it had left the scene, Laura climbed from the car and slowly followed, wondering if she'd just damned the three girls to death, or if her father could handle himself against the nightmare heading in his direction.

II

Katie was making small mewling noises every time she had to set weight down on her bad leg. They were very weak, and if Brittany hadn't been listening for them she'd have never heard a sound.

But that didn't stop the girl from moving. She kept plodding along, with a little help from Courtney. The blonde whiner was actually being useful, and that just after Brittany had given up hope of managing to do anything at all about their current situation.

Well, actually, she still had some doubts about managing to do much, but every little bit helped.

"Look, do we know where the guys are supposed to be?" She had to ask. It was really a little asinine to be walking around the worst part of town as the sun started to rise.

"No." Katie shook her head, her lips pressed into a tight line. "But we'll find them."

"Okay. Fine. Maybe we could call on Jerry's cell phone?"

"Already tried that a few times. Remember?" Katie's voice was annoyed, which made Brittany want to make a few snide comments. She stopped herself. There was a time for being bratty, and this wasn't it.

"So if we can't call, how do you want to find them?" Courtney wasn't making anything easier. She kept asking the same questions again and again and Brittany kept wanting to drop her into a hole in the ground and be done with her.

But there was that whole Courtney-as-a-crutch thing to consider. Brittany wanted her hands free, because they hurt like hell and because if anything else came their way, she wanted to be prepared.

No. That was a lie. She wanted to be at home. She wanted her mother back. She wanted Chris safe and sound where he could yell at her if she got stupid, which she did a lot these days. She thought about the photos rubbing against her side, and bit her lip to stop from making a stupid noise.

I get out of this, no more stupid shit. None. Not ever.

Yeah. That was going to happen. But she'd try, damn it, she would try hard.

And when she saw the thing coming at them from behind, she sort of decided that might not be any time soon. Either the nightmare from the car had finally dug its way out or there was another one coming to finish them off. There were darkened houses on either side of the street and anything could have been hiding there, but the high-speed killing machine came straight down the center of the road, claws scratching at the tar and moving almost faster than she could track. There was over a football field between them, but she knew that wouldn't keep the thing from catching up soon at its current pace.

Brittany pushed herself away from Katie and Courtney. "Run, guys! Now!" She watched the thing coming, terrified to take her eyes off of it, and hoped they listened. In the near darkness she could see eyes and teeth and little else, but what she did see was enough to unsettle her.

Courtney looked at her and screamed. "What are you gonna do? Bite it?"

"No, dumbass, I'm gonna keep it way from you."

She waved a hand at them. "Now run!" Just to make sure they got her point, Brittany ran at the charging shadow, holding back a scream only because she wanted to save her breath for getting away from the thing. When they were roughly fifty yards apart, she veered hard to the left and hoped it would follow her instead of heading for Katie and Courtney.

It had more to do with intuition than it did with heroics. She'd been feeling like she was in the crosshairs of a rifle site for a while now, and she was hoping—praying, really—that whatever was watching her was on her side.

Brittany pumped her legs hard, the soles of her shoes slapping across the ground and then a lawn of dead grass and then across concrete as she moved over the crumbling sidewalk. Her night had not been an easy one and she didn't figure she was going to last very long running her ass off unless someone came to her assistance.

This time her intuitions were right. The creep that had been following them earlier stepped from the darkness between two of the houses and scowled, his features pinched with anger.

She didn't bother to stop. Let the monster eat him instead.

Brittany chanced looking around to see the lay of the land. Off to her left and well behind her, the other girls were hobbling along as best they could, Courtney supporting most of Katie's weight. They were moving, and that was all she could hope for. Chadbourne was still in the same spot, his arms held wide and his mouth moving fast, in a nearly silent stream of words. Whatever he was actually saying made her ears hurt as if there were a pressure building.

Not five feet in front of the older man, the thing with the big teeth was still charging, but now it was paying attention to the guy who was waving his arms around and talking to the air.

And Brittany really hoped he was up to something, because even as she slowed down to watch, the thing in front of him moved forward, both of the front paws lifting into the air and crashing down on his shoulders. Thick brutal claws that had been in pursuit of her a moment before cut deeply into his jacket and the flesh beneath, blood spraying from the wounds. The weight of the thing dropped him to his knees with an audible cracking sound and then pushed his torso against the sidewalk.

The wide jaws grinned open and then the man was screaming, panicking as the thing lowered its head and bit into his face. Whatever he'd been doing hadn't been enough. The dark form over him crunched through his skull with ease.

Brittany felt like she was floating. She couldn't feel her legs, her feet, or even her arms. There was just the carnage in front of her, the beast and the man and the wet noises.

And that was just about all the incentive she needed to start running again, only this time she ran for Courtney and Katie. Sometimes her brain took a while, but it normally got in gear eventually. What she needed, she realized, was something to use as a weapon. And if these were like the monsters she'd met a few months ago, when her world decided to slide far away from reality, she could only think of one thing that would work.

"Courtney! You got perfume in that bag of yours?" She was winded, but her voice still carried over the screams coming from the fight. The older girl looked at her and frowned, taken off guard by the question, and then nodded.

Rather than argue about why she needed it, Brittany just grabbed the purse off Courtney's shoulder and started rummaging, ignoring the protests. Condoms—for just in case, she guessed—lipstick, car keys, wad of cash, two candy bars, a half-eaten roll of Lifesavers, and finally, a bottle of some weird-ass perfume called SeaMist. She grabbed the bottle and dropped the purse, searching her own pockets for the lighter she'd had earlier. She found it in her left back pocket and got it ready, even as she tried to get the top off the perfume.

Courtney and Katie stopped moving and watched as Brittany went back over to the fight. Whatever the man was, he was decidedly capable of taking some damage. He hadn't been killed by the vicious attacks, but he wasn't exactly moving around like a playful puppy, either.

The thing still had the upper hand, or claw, or whatever. It was perched on top of him and still feeding. He was still trying to fight back, which when she considered that he no longer had a head, was enough to make her want to faint dead away.

Brittany stuck the lighter in her mouth, her hands shaking enough to make her drop the lid from the perfume bottle. "Screw it." She shook the contents of the bottle all over the two things and her own hand—which felt like it wanted to run away screaming when the mixture struck her open wounds—until the one on top reared back and hissed, viscera spraying from its bloodied maw, as the alcohol and scent ran into its eyes.

Brittany figured herself for dead, but instead of attacking it went back to its meal, feasting on the still struggling Chadbourne. She struck the pinwheel on the lighter and watched the flame ignite. It then ran promptly up her hand covering her fingers in blue flame. Brittany waved her hand frantically and probably saved her life in the process. The thing sitting on top of Chadbourne was driven by a need to eat, but it wasn't stupid. As soon as it saw the flames it knew what she was trying to do and prepared to remove the threat.

The thing lunged forward and snapped at Brittany at the same time she waved her flaming hand. The black mouth caressed her fingers as it opened, and the flames on her fingers caught the alcohol still on the dark, furry face. Brittany backed away as it roared, Katie screamed and Courtney called out a warning.

Whatever the things were made of they burned well.

That was the only thing she'd seen so far that ever seemed to stop them worth a damn. The creature's flesh began to bubble as the flames started eating, and under it, Chadbourne's remains cooked as well.

The difference was that Chadbourne wasn't trying to kill her. One of the forepaws swatted Brittany across her shoulder and chest, knocking her off her feet, and the thing came out of its crouch, springing for her.

Brittany knew she was dead. That was all there was to it. The massive thing loomed over her, its face burning and the flames forming a mane across its neck and shoulders.

That was when the blond girl showed up and smacked the monster across the face with a tire iron. Teeth broke and skin ruptured across the flaming muzzle and the thing roared again, the voice changing, becoming unsettlingly human.

Pain must have finally gotten through whatever anger was building, because it finally turned away and tried to find a way to put out the conflagration eating its body away. The shape wouldn't hold anymore and the thing changed again and again as it started heading down the street, odd shapes and sounds alike spilling from it.

Brittany sat on the ground, her eyes wide and her heart thudding hard enough to give her a headache.

Katie and Courtney came up next to her and looked at Laura Chadbourne. Laura looked back for a second and then walked away, dropping the tire iron from

Courtney's Miata in the process. She moved only a few feet over to stare at her father's remains, her face expressionless save for a stream of wetness that fell from her eyes.

III

Chris Corin was going down for the count. Jerry couldn't do a damned thing about it. A psycho-bitch-monster was still eating his arm and chest, and that sort of took all the fight out of him.

Chris was pinned to the ground and the things around him were almost done tearing each other apart. There were a lot less of them now than there had been at the start. Most of them were dead or dying, himself included.

He'd have been a lot more upset about it, but the whispering noises in his head were doing everything they could to soothe him now. They were telling him that it was all right, this was his destiny, to become part of something greater than he could ever be on his own. They were comforting voices, really. They'd been interfering with him for so long that he couldn't imagine what it was like without them anymore.

It's the other ones. It has to be. That's why I can hear them now, understand the separate words. It's the voices of the other ones like me. Even knowing where the voices came from didn't change anything. He was still content to let the thing on top of him keep tearing away at his shoulder and neck.

Jerry rolled his face enough to let him look at Chris. "Hey, bro. I'm gonna miss you." The words were slurred: *Heybra . . . nnamizzyu*, but he knew Chris understood. They'd been drunk together enough times. And that was what dying felt like to Jerry. Like he had a good buzz going on and it was only going to get better. The pain in his body was missing. He should have been screaming in agony, but there was nothing there, just a void of feeling instead of a roar of agony.

Chris looked his way, eyes wide and wild, face pale where it wasn't bruised or bloodied. His best friend's fingers were digging at the hard, scaly limb that pinned him in place, and he was making moderate progress at pulling the thing apart, but every time he made a wound, it healed itself again. Jerry knew on an unconscious level he was doing that too, because he should have already been dead.

Chris wasn't having as much luck. When he tore off two fingernails trying to get through the arm on his chest, they stayed torn off. Still, even with that, he was digging and cursing, his legs trying to get decent purchase and his bloodied hands tearing at the thing on top of him. A part of Jerry's head whispered the name for the thing on top of Chris, just as that same voice whispered the name of the one on top of him, but he couldn't make much sense of the names and they weren't significant. What mattered now was sliding into a deep, comfortable sleep.

"You in shock, Jerry?" Chris's voice sounded tinny

and strained. Jerry smiled at him and blinked a few times. "Oh yeah. You're in shock, bro. Wake up! Wake up, goddamnit!"

Chris looked silly, his face all tear-streaked and red. Jerry giggled.

Chris shook his head and his face got all ugly, the pale spots darkening as he got angry. Chris always turned beet red when he lost his temper—which wasn't really that often until lately—and his lips pressed down to a hard line.

Chris Corin sank his teeth into the thing in front of him and bit down hard, ripping a larger chunk of flesh away. The thing pressed on his chest in response—the rest of it still eating what looked like a spider melded with an afterbirth—and he groaned, leaning back and spitting out the dark gray crap he'd torn free.

"Jerry, listen, you have to wake up."

"S'cool. I'm all good." Jerry tried to wave the arm that had mostly been torn away. In response, his flesh started growing back with a warm, soothing rush that left him even lighter in the head.

"Jerry! What about Katie?" Chris was screaming now, but his voice was fainter, more strained than before, because the bugaboo pressing down on his ribs hadn't eased up at all. There was something wrong with that, but Jerry couldn't focus on exactly what. He was too busy thinking about his girl.

Katie. A lot of the guys he knew ragged on her because she had a temper, but Jerry knew that her anger was mostly held back for when he fucked up. He also knew how sweet she was, and how good she felt in his arms and how much he loved her. He wondered where she was and sighed, a brief moment of sadness sliding past the growing numb sensations that were swallowing him as surely as the bitch-thing chewing on his re-grown muscles.

"Gonna miss her, man. God, I'm gonna miss her." He felt the tears slide down from his eyes, but barely even noticed them. They were something from his past, something from before this last stage in his life journey.

"Yeah?" Chris was looking at him through blood-shot eyes, his mouth was wet with nasty stuff and his arms were corded with effort. Even as Jerry watched, Chris managed to drive his fingers deep into the joint of the funky arm that held him pinned. The thing on top of him eased up with the pressure, but didn't go away.

Chris panted for a second, sucking in deep breaths. Queen-bitch-monster took a break from chewing on Jerry to swallow her latest mouthful, which included what looked like a few feet of tendons. Probably very hard to chew that shit.

"I'm gonna get out of this, Jerry. You hear me?" Chris sounded insane. He looked it, too, his eyes glittering in the darkness, his teeth bared in a smile that made Jerry think of Ray Liotta as a pissed-off heavy in one of his earlier movies. He'd have to remember to tell Katie about that. He'd never noticed the crazy smile his friend had before.

"With or without you, Jerry. I'm outta this shithole

and if you aren't with me, I'm gonna fuck Katie for you." Chris spat the words, his face turned so he could gloat at Jerry.

Jerry thought about that. It wasn't right. It was a mean thing to say. "No, man. Katie's with me."

"She wasn't with you last night, bro. She was between my legs, sucking!"

Jerry shook his head. "No way." He looked at Chris, really looked at him for the first time in a long while. Bloodied and bruised, yes, but he was gloating.

The bitch-queen reached down to take another chunk of the Jerry-du-jour and Jerry blocked her distended mouth with his hand. It hurt to move, but that wasn't important right now. What mattered was finding out what Chris was saying, because it didn't sound like the sort of thing a best friend was supposed to be saying.

"She what?" Jerry's eyebrows knitted in concentration. Chris had said something else, but the psycho-bitch-thing had been growling and he couldn't hear him.

Chris's grin grew wider, more taunting. "I said she liked the taste. I never knew Katie swallowed, man."

It took a second for that to register. That warm fuzzy feeling was going away as Jerry concentrated. He pushed at the she-thing on top of him and she bit his hand, breaking skin and fingers.

"Ow!" He hissed and used his other hand to slap the hell out of his dinner date. She hissed again and he hit her again, screaming out loud as she pulled her arms out of his sides to defend herself.

Chris laughed. The bastard laughed at his pain. "Better get it going, Jerry! Maybe this one still wants to do you, but looks like she'd rather be the man!" The creature shoved her bladed arms back toward Jerry's chest as Chris spoke and Jerry grabbed her wrists, the hard blades forced to stop their descent into his flesh. The mouth that had been feasting on his flesh let out a warbling note of anger and the whispers in his head flared in a sudden line of outrage.

Jerry shook his head, trying to stop the annoying sounds he'd found soothing earlier, and bucked with his body in a mockery of sex, throwing the creature off his lap.

He saw red. He saw nothing but red and the multi-eyed face of the thing that had been eating him. Jerry drew back his hands and started swinging, landing blow after blow on the creature as it tried to get back up and defend itself.

His rage didn't grow smaller but ballooned, expanded to fill his entire chest, his body, his world. The thing fought back, he knew that, but it wasn't really doing a very good job. The whispers faded away, merging with the pounding of his heart, the sound of his breathing, and he kept swinging, losing himself in a deep fury that felt even sweeter than the absence of pain had managed to feel.

It felt natural when it happened. There was no thought involved, at least not on a conscious level. He just let his body go and it did the rest all by itself. His torso grew thicker and his arms split in two, growing more flesh as needed until he had four powerful arms, each ending in a fist the size of a football. He didn't grow claws, and he didn't want them. He wanted the satisfaction of smashing the stupid bitch under him into putty.

His senses seemed to grow outward, until he could feel the curved walls around him, see the creatures that were left as they fed on the remains of their counterparts and savored the taste of their feasts. The odor was intoxicating, but he didn't let himself think about eating. Right now he wanted this stupid cow dead so he could pay attention to Chris. As long as they'd been friends there had always been a tension between them when it came to girls. They'd never, ever dated each other's girlfriends, and they'd never spoken about it. It was an unwritten but very serious rule they both lived by, and now Chris was talking about fucking Katie? The girl Jerry planned to marry?

"Oh, hell no. You better be joking, Chris, I mean it!"

Chris laughed, shaking his head. Jerry was still facing the pulp he'd been pounding, and couldn't understand how he saw Chris, but he didn't care. He'd worry about that later.

"Jerry! Hey, Jerry! You never told me Katie barked like a dog when she's coming! Is that because you didn't know?" Chris's voice was manic, absolutely crazy, and for Jerry the noise was infectious. He was starting to feel a little like he'd gone off the deep end himself.

"Shut up, Chris, or I swear I'll kill you!" In an effort to make his point clear, he ripped the thing in front of him into tiny pieces. It took a lot of arms, but that was okay. Somewhere along the way he'd grown a few extras.

IV

Chris watched Jerry tear apart the thing that had been eating him with almost casual ease. He knew it was Jerry because he'd watched the transformation, but he couldn't have proven it to anyone else.

Somewhere along the line, Jerry had lost every single physical quality that made him Jerry.

Chris just hoped the mind of his friend was still in that body, because if not, he was a dead man. Jerry was as mellow as they came, but Chris had known his friend long enough to know exactly what buttons to push, and this time he'd just about hit the right ones with a sledgehammer.

And now Jerry was letting go of his human form. That was good and that was bad. Good because getting him pissed off had finally made him react. Bad for the exact same reason. Jerry was ready to kick Chris's ass. Chris was in no shape to survive a kicking quite that epic.

The thing that had been Jerry grew bigger, looking at Chris with eyes that were no longer remotely human, and the nausea came back tenfold. He thought he'd adjusted to feeling queasy, but this was a new level of upset and he couldn't even begin to form a word.

James A. Moore

His best friend reached out for him, but was stopped by the one that had been holding Chris in place. It was bigger than Jerry. It had been feeding and had a lot more mass.

Jerry didn't seem to care. His body was still changing and as Chris watched, the last shreds of human clothing and skin peeled away as Jerry expanded and warped further away from the memory of anything humanoid. What remained was pale gray flesh, weeping sores that spilled foul green ichor and a massive bloom of snaking tentacles of every imaginable size and shape. Deep inside that mass there might have been a mouth, because the sounds coming from what had been Jerry had to come from somewhere.

Chris didn't want to know and surely didn't feel like checking out that information himself. The thing that had pinned Chris in place was forced to move when Jerry hit it. Both of them—Chris couldn't think of Jerry as a monster, wouldn't, because he was still hoping for a cure—rolled a bit as they impacted and Chris was suddenly free from the weight that had kept him skewered to the bottom of the sewer. He slid out of the rising waters and crawled as fast as he could, hoping he might manage to get a little distance, might be able to find a weapon.

Or even just escape. He had his doubts on all fronts.

"Fuck this, fuck this, fuck this . . ." All he wanted was a nice, normal life. This wasn't even close to qualifying. He'd had about all he could take of the insan-

296

ity in the last few months. Screw everything, he was leaving.

Somewhere behind him the things were still fighting. *Good. Maybe they'll forget about me.* Chris managed to stand up for all of ten seconds before he fell back down. His knees were swollen and hurt too much for him to stand worth a damn.

So he crawled, slipping from time to time in the sludge at the bottom of the sewer and tasting the foul crap he'd chewed on earlier, even after he washed his mouth with the water around him. Even sewage was preferable to what he'd bitten earlier.

He had no idea where he was going. The tunnels were dark and his eyes had adjusted as best they could, but that meant he wasn't running into walls, not that he could actually make out the details of what was ahead of him.

That was okay. It couldn't be worse than what was behind him.

V

It wasn't that hard to sneak away. Not really. The girls were all busy with their own thoughts and trying to figure out what had happened to Chris and his friend, Jerry.

Laura already knew, of course. They were dead. Or if they weren't they would be soon. She didn't like to think about the things her father had done over the years, didn't like to remember the secrets he spoke about when he was sure she wasn't listening.

He'd never understood that she was always listening, searching for a clue about what he had planned. Because forewarned was forearmed and all of that. If she knew what state of mind he was in, she could be prepared for dealing with him. Surviving every day meant knowing what he had in mind.

Laura giggled to herself and shook her head. "Not anymore, Dad. Not anymore and not ever again."

She knew where Chris and Jerry were, but she hadn't volunteered the information to Chris's sister and her friends. They didn't need to know. They'd just get in the way.

Laura didn't have the keys to the car she'd moved earlier, but that was okay. She had the keys to her own car. Well, the spare set, anyway. The blonde had taken the other set away from her earlier. She dug them out of her pocket as she reached the old Ford and slid into the driver's seat.

The containers in the trunk rattled around and the smell of regular unleaded intensified. That was okay. Even if she spilled a gallon or two from the one can without a lid, she still had ten more.

She didn't know exactly where Chris and his friend were, or all of the other things she'd seen for that matter. But she figured with enough gas, it wouldn't matter.

Finding an open manhole cover was easier than she expected. Laura parked the car and climbed out, careful not to trip over the heavy lid sitting next to the opening. She looked down into the sewer and watched the waters flow. They were moving pretty fast, especially considering the lack of rain in the past few days. As she stared into the increasing tide of debris and murk, she saw what she was hoping for: evidence. There were pieces of cloth and a few things that smelled like her father did after he'd performed his rituals.

It was simple math, really. If she saw nothing, she would have used the sewer opening she found. That meant—unless she was being especially stupid, which her father often accused her of—that the fight was downstream. The water would take care of everything. If she saw evidence of strange happenings in the sewer she knew she had to go further down the road.

Three blocks later she found another manhole and killed the motor. The air was calm and cool and the sun was rising. She had to make this fast. This cover was still in place, and after a few seconds of straining she decided it could stay there.

Laura opened the trunk and pulled out the first two regulation-size cans of gasoline. It wasn't very hard to fit the nozzle ends into the holes in the cover of the sewer opening. She held them in place as they emptied into they sewers below.

Just a few more and she could finish what her father had started.

Chapter Fourteen

I

Brittany heard the sirens around the same time that Courtney did. The three of them had just gotten back to Courtney's car when the wailing began in the distance.

"That's fucking perfect." Brittany spat the words even as she inspected the underside of the Miata. "Now the cops show up. Where were they when the monsters were trying to eat us?"

"Does it look okay?" Courtney stared in the direction of the rising sun and the increasing noise from the police cars. They were still out of sight, but probably not for very long.

"No. It looks like something tried to eat your engine, and it's leaking stuff. If you want to move this car, it better be now." Brittany stood up, wincing as she used her damaged hands to get upright again. At least the bleeding had stopped.

"So let's go." Katie sighed as she spoke, her face a perfect example of misery. "Let's get out of here."

Courtney nodded and opened the driver's-side door. Brittany went around and helped Katie settle into the passenger's side. There were only two seats.

"You guys go on. I'll catch up with you."

"Forget it." Katie shook her head, looking more lively than she had in the last hour or so. "Sit on my lap."

"There's no way!"

"I said sit on my lap, Brittany. I'm not trying to explain to Chris why I left you behind."

Having no real desire to talk with the police, have a screaming fight with Katie or deal with her brother's temper, Brittany finally nodded and settled in for the ride.

They caught a break. After sputtering a few times, the car started. Courtney didn't wait around. She just peeled a few layers of rubber off the tires and bolted away from the increasing racket from the police sirens.

Had they gone in the opposite direction, they might have stopped what happened a few minutes later. Had they gone to the left they would have run into the police already standing around the body of Martin Callaghan. To the right at the next intersection would have been bad solely because they would have gotten lost in the worst part of town, but luck was with them and they managed to avoid any confrontations.

Luck is fickle of course. Their decision cost them more than they ever expected.

II

Jerry fought. He suffered cuts and wounds that would have killed him not all that long ago and he recovered from them, healing the wounds as quickly as they came.

Somewhere along the way he forgot what he was fighting for, what he was trying to achieve beyond survival, and began to enjoy what he was doing. He didn't mind. It was invigorating.

It felt like being alive for the first time ever. He attacked and was attacked in turn, by creatures as unique and ever changing as he was, and it was the most beautiful thing he'd ever experienced.

The whispers finally made sense to him, really completely made sense. He'd thought they were the individual voices of the things around him, but he knew better now. They were parts of a single song, a single note held out as a prize that he wanted desperately to have. It was a song of life and rebirth, of purity and design that went beyond anything he could have grasped before he gave in to the changes.

And he finally understood the song. He was a vessel, nothing more. He was a part of something that was about to become complete. The other whispers had a name for it, but he didn't care about names. He cared about winning the prize. He wanted to be the one vessel left when it was all said and done. He wanted the connection to the universe beyond what he could see and what he knew.

He wanted it so badly that he gave into the desire to eat and he allowed himself to become a part of the violent dance the others continued to perform. He devoured flesh and was devoured in turn. He ate and ripped and tore and bled and felt only the growing power as each of his enemies was finally broken and consumed.

He didn't have time to notice the gasoline as it filled the sewer. The fumes, the scent, the oily feel were all distractions that he chose to ignore. There were more important things than liquid fuel to consider.

He was about to become something far greater than the sum of the parts he was ingesting and that was all that mattered.

III

Chris slowed down only when the grate got in his way. It was old and rusted and he managed to bend the soft mesh enough to scrape past it with only a few new cuts.

On the other side of the grate there was open air. He didn't so much climb out of the sewer as fall out. The water below was cold and slapped at his senses as surely as the first blasting light of the morning sun that rose a few moments later.

It hurt to move. It hurt to do anything, but it was

worse if he just sat in the water. The cold was enough to make his testicles try to hide away and the bones in his legs ache. So eventually he crawled out of the water and lay back against the rough man-made sides of the creek the sewers spilled out into.

In a near panic now that he had a moment to think, he opened his mouth and jammed two fingers down his throat, wiggling them wildly until he triggered his gag reflex. Chris forced himself to vomit, ignoring the burning acid and the taste of bile and worse. The only thought on his mind was to clear his system of the nastiness he'd bitten into earlier. He'd been forced to taste the blood of one of those things and from what Johanssen had said earlier, that was how he and the others had infected their victims. He kept going until there was nothing left to try to expel and then he crawled a few feet higher up on the shore.

"Jerry. I hope you're okay, bro." He barely recognized the voice as his own. Worse, the second he finished speaking he started coughing instead. It hurt his ribs to cough.

Chris closed his eyes and promised himself that he'd get up in just a minute. He just needed to rest.

Just for a second.

It didn't work out that way.

IV

Laura Chadbourne had just finished with the last can of gasoline when the police car pulled up. She

RABID GROWTH

looked at the car and reached into her pocket, pulling out the lighter even as the door of the squad car opened.

The policeman looked at the gas cans and then at her, and then at the lighter she struck with her thumb.

Maybe she wasn't looking her best. She'd had to tear strips off her shirt and slide them through the narrow holes in the sewer covering. A simple twig held the end in place, stopping it from falling too far. The cloth was gas soaked, of course.

"Lady, what are you doing?" The cop reached for his revolver.

Laura laughed. "World's biggest Molotov cocktail, coming up!"

The officer seriously thought about his firearm for all of half a second. Then he decided he'd rather live. He went for the car door instead.

The flame touched the fabric wick.

The fire sputtered for a second and then began to burn properly, sliding down the fabric and lowering into the sewer at high speed.

Despite everything, Laura intended to survive the night too. She stood up and began to run.

V

Jerry groaned, the feelings boiling through his nerves were more intense than anything he'd ever thought possible. His mind opened up to the voice

305

that had been whispers and he felt his world, his whole universe, expanding.

Chadbourne had lied, of course. He knew that now. There had never been a cure, but that was all right. If he'd understood everything that the bookstore owner had understood, he'd have lied, too. Katie was out there somewhere, human and alone. He felt bad for her, but it wasn't really something he had control over and in the long run, she wasn't really very significant. Chris Corin was a dead man. He didn't know it yet, but Jerry now understood that the anger he felt whenever he was around his best friend was caused by what had been done to Chris. Like the old joke about God and Job said, there was something about Chris that just pissed him off. That same something was going to annoy every creature Chris ever met that belonged to the world beyond the mundane, a world that Jerry had just joined once and for all.

And none of it mattered. Not when he compared it to the things going on inside of his mind. His body was only a tool, he knew that now. It was insignificant, but useful. And to think he'd been limiting himself, making himself stay as human as possible because he was afraid of the gift he'd been granted.

No more. There was so much he had to do, so many steps he had to take to open the gateways, to free his brethren from their entrapment. There was no time left, and yet all the time in the universe. He'd never been able to understand that before.

Jerry stretched and felt the walls of the sewer shatter to accommodate his new body. He shrugged and knew that somewhere above him the street buckled to make way for him.

He opened his mouths to speak and felt the air around him shiver. This was what it felt like to be host to a god.

And then the flames hit and pretty much blew his entire power trip straight to hell. The fumes from the gasoline caught aflame and sent a wall of heat, pressure, and fire against the massive bulk of Jerry's new body, searing newly formed flesh as quickly as it could grow and pushing against him with enough force to knock a car through the air.

The burning flesh peeled off of his form and worked almost as well as a lubricant to slide him down the sewer tunnel, forcing his cancerous mass to move as the pressure kept building.

Jerry struggled to stay where he was, generating new limbs to clutch at the concrete, but they too burned in the inferno. Finally he tried moving upward to escape the flames and shoved with his entire mass, screaming in agony as he pushed through the piping and into the earth above.

VI

Tillinghast Lane ran a twisting path down through what was, arguably, the very worst part of town. Few of the local police would have argued that there were places that were deadlier.

Martin Callaghan would have voted for Tillinghast if he'd lived. The county coroner and his assistants would have agreed with him. They were the ones doing a detailed examination of the place where the detective lay while several members of the police force pounded on doors to ask people what they had heard or seen. There were quite a few disgruntled civilians looking around and swearing that they knew nothing. The local cops were used to that and not willing to accept their usual answers. Callaghan had been a damned good cop and they wanted someone to pay for what had happened to him.

Several of the officers who were doing the door-to-doors were actually done with their shifts, but that didn't matter much. There were certain things that took priority over catching a few hours of sleep. In typical fashion, one of the policemen even said to his partner that he could sleep when he was dead.

Not five minutes later he got to prove his point when the ground below him bulged and then exploded outward. Flames rose toward the heavens amid a shower of broken pavement, gas lines and water pipes. It was the gas lines that cinched how bad the situation got. Natural gas added fuel to the already burning unleaded gasoline and blistering mountain of flesh that forced its way out from the sewers.

Two police officers and all of the team from the coroner's office were killed in the cataclysmic explosion. The shock wave leveled three houses that should have been condemned years before and blew out windows in twenty-seven more. The few functioning cars in the area were knocked around and dinged, as were several of their owners.

Exactly one person was in a position to watch the creature that lifted out of the ground in a blazing column. He saw it twist and expand, a grotesque entity that liquefied and burned as it reared higher into the heavens.

Adam Hotchkins had long since been a bum and a drunk. He'd seen worse things in his numerous stupors. Hell, he'd seen worse things back when he was sober.

That didn't stop him from running as fast as he could in the direction of shelter, which was a good thing. A moment later the pillar of flesh fell in upon itself, burning and screaming the entire way down.

Jerry Murphy did not go gently to his death, but he went just the same.

Chapter Fifteen

I

The rescue teams found Chris Corin lying facedown in the grass and dirt near the sewer opening and considered him one of the lucky ones. Despite substantial bruising and two fingers that were half skinned and missing their nails, he was intact.

Of course, he was in a coma, but they believed that was only a temporary shutdown caused by trauma. Several tests were performed that showed multiple contusions, a concussion and a hairline fracture of his skull.

When everything calmed down almost three days later, his sister was located at home with a couple of family friends attending to her and was informed of his condition.

Brittany took it fairly well. She stayed at his side quite a bit and she maintained a calm exterior, even when her stomach felt like it was trying to drop out of her body and run away.

Katie stayed with her a lot of the time. Her leg and Brittany's hands were all healing very nicely. Courtney dropped by every other day or so, normally taking care of a few errands for both of the girls before leaving again.

And that routine stayed the same for close to a month. It was a long stretch of time to be doing the hospital thing. But, really, it beat the alternatives.

Sterling Armstrong made himself a regular visitor, too. Either he or his supermodel secretary called or visited every day. Brittany decided she liked the attorney. She also liked the secretary but was more than a bit jealous of the woman's looks.

They were seldom social calls, though. In lieu of Chris making decisions, Armstrong called on his sister for advice on what he might want and Katie chimed in several times when she disagreed.

The battle for custody was getting ugly. Their maternal grandmother felt that Chris was in no condition to look after Brittany, and Armstrong was fighting tooth and nail to make sure that she didn't win her demand for guardianship. The good news was he was holding his own. The better news was that the first of Chris's winnings from the lottery came in a week before he came out of his coma. The first installment came out to just over one and a half million dollars after taxes.

Chris Corin woke up a very wealthy man. He didn't feel much like celebrating. He opened his eyes in the middle of the night and saw Brittany and Katie in his private room, the both of them unconscious. The lights were dim and he was grateful for that. He didn't think he could stand any intense glare at the time.

He went back to sleep and stayed that way until the following afternoon.

When he finally decided it was time to sit up in bed he felt a little stiff, but otherwise fine. Well, okay, the IV in his arm hurt like hell and his mouth was twice as dry as Jerry's wit, but otherwise, he was feeling mostly human.

Brittany and Katie were both glad to see him, but they were subdued as well. After a few quick hugs and some calls to the doctors to say that he was awake, Brittany left the room to make a phone call—weird in itself because there was a phone in the room, and she also had access to a cellular—and Katie stayed behind.

When they were alone, Katie dropped the news on him. "Jerry still hasn't turned up, Chris."

Chris looked at her and shook his head, remembering more than he wanted to about the shape his best friend had been in when he ran. "I don't think he will show up, Katie." His voice cracked and he stared hard at her face through the prism of tears that had started. "He was in it deep when I left, and he was . . . he was like the rest of them. He changed."

Katie stood up and walked around the small room like a tiger stuck in a cage. "Yeah. I figured that." She picked at a basket of flowers someone had sent and looked out the window for a while as Chris stared at her. Shame made him small. He'd run, he'd abandoned his best friend instead of trying to help him, and the end result was this. Jerry was dead, he had to be, and Katie, one of the sweetest girls in the world and one of his best friends, was ruined.

Hail the conquering hero.

"I ran, Katie. I left him behind."

Katie turned and stared at him for a few seconds before she spoke. "What were you going to do, Chris? Save him from what he'd become?"

"Sooner or later they could have found a cure."

Katie hugged herself and shook her head. It was her turn to cry, but she did it without noise, merely letting tears fall from her face. Chris noticed that she'd lost weight she couldn't afford to spare.

"Chris, you dumbass, it's been almost a month since everything happened, okay? I've had a lot of time to think about everything and there's nothing you could have done."

"You weren't there, you didn't see what was happening."

"I saw enough, Chris. If he was like the others then he wasn't Jerry anymore any way. So stop it, all right? Just stop. Jerry's dead. That's all. I've had time to deal with it."

Chris stared at her until her image blurred away under the fall of tears. Katie had had a month. He'd been sleeping. The wounds were still very fresh along those lines. He tried to hide everything inside when his mother died, but that hadn't really been the best way to handle it and frankly, it took too much effort to hold his emotions in check. He was too tired to be macho.

"Listen, your sister is calling in that attorney of yours, Sterling." Katie moved closer and put her hand on the side of his face. She wasn't smiling, but the tears had stopped. "I'm gonna go keep her company. You and him need to have a long talk."

"Okay." It was all he could say. All he could muster. He didn't want to think, but knew he was going to have to.

After he'd stared at the walls and flowers for a while and was almost ready to go back to sleep, Sterling Armstrong came into his hospital room and closed the door quietly.

"How are you feeling, Chris?" His voice was quieter than usual—probably because it was a hospital room, which was the next best thing to church for a lot of people—but he was just as robust and lively as ever.

"Stiff and tired." He managed a small smile to take out the sting. "Katie said we should talk."

"Well, a lot's been going on." The man sat on the edge of the bed, managing against all odds to look graceful even as he perched his ass near Chris's knee. "And you've got a lot to consider."

"Hit me with the bad stuff first, okay? Just get it out of the way."

Sterling nodded his head and looked him straight in

the eyes when he spoke. "Well, first there's the fact that Jerry Murphy still hasn't shown up. You already know that and I'm sorry. I know you two were very close. His family is torn up about it, but considering his condition when he disappeared, no one is overly surprised."

Chris nodded his head and otherwise stayed quiet.

Sterling continued. "Your grandmother has done her best to make a case for taking custody of your sister, which is nothing new, but she's very, very determined. So far I've got her lawyers on the ropes, but I expect a few surprises from them."

"What aren't you telling me, Sterling?"

"Oh, don't worry, we'll cover everything." The man's demeanor didn't change a single bit. Chris wondered if he knew any other facial expressions or if he just saved them for the courtroom. "Your grandmother is being very thorough. Despite my best efforts, she now knows about your winning the lottery and about the money you have in your accounts. Nothing we can do about that, but it's not the end of the world."

"Why should it matter?"

"Because it's one more thing she knows that I don't want her to know. She also knows that you're in the hospital, but I've been able to prevent her efforts to use that as a determining factor. Your sister has been staying with Katie Gallagher and her family. I hope you don't mind."

Chris chuckled. "I don't mind. I just hope they've all survived it."

"Oh, they have. From what Katie tells me, she's been on her best behavior."

Chris shook his head and sighed as he laid back on the hospital bed. "That figures. She's just crazy around me."

"Probably worried about what you'd do to her if she misbehaved."

"No way." Chris looked at his hands and frowned. He had two more fingernails than he was expecting to and it was a little strange. "More what Katie would do."

Sterling looked down at him and stared into his eyes. He spoke softly when he started talking again. "There've been no signs that anyone holds you or your sister or friends accountable for what happened. Apparently one of the police officers on the scene saw a girl pouring gasoline into the sewers just before the explosions took place."

Chris could guess which girl. She hadn't exactly sounded stable when he'd heard her on the phone the last time. Laura was a basket case.

"So why bring it up?"

"Because a dead police officer, murdered apparently, was found near the explosions and had a substantial file on you." When Chris didn't respond he went on a little further. "I've got motions before a judge right now to let me see what is in those files and to make them go away if possible."

"You can do that?" Chris sat back up, suddenly interested.

"Maybe. There are a dozen legal dances I can do to make the files go away or at least hide them well. But I need your word that you had nothing to do with the death of Detective Callaghan."

"I might have wished he'd go away, Sterling, but I never wished him any harm."

"Well, it's time for me to go. Listen, Chris, seriously, take it easy for a while. I don't know what goes on in your life and I don't really need to unless you have a legal problem, but definitely take it easy."

"I'm trying." Chris clenched his hand into a fist and then relaxed it. Then he clenched it several more times. He closed his eyes just after Sterling left the room.

He'd have liked a nap but the doctor came in a few minutes later, frowning and looking all too serious.

"Mister Corin?" The man spoke with the most nasal twang Chris had ever heard.

"That's me." He sat up the rest of the way, resigned to not closing his eyes for a while. "What can I do for you, doctor?"

"Well, I heard you were finally awake and figured we should give you a quick checkup and maybe talk about a few things." The man still hadn't bothered to look at him. He was reading over a stack of papers on a clipboard.

"Okay. Check me up and get me out of here."

The doctor was a thin man with graying hair and a constantly harried look. He finally seemed to notice that there was a person in the bed and focused on

Chris. "Don't be in too much of a hurry to go home, Mister Corin. Let's talk first."

Chris didn't like the sound of that, but he held on and waited while the doctor checked his pupils, his blood pressure, his pulse and temperature, and then moved his arms and legs for him as if he were an invalid. Chris promised himself that the first sign of the man wanting to check his privates was going to get the good doctor knocked into the next week.

After a small battery of tests—none of which involved anal probes or a need to make Chris turn his head and cough—the doctor nodded his approval and wrote a long scrawl of notes on several pages.

Chris finally sighed and spat it out. "Don't keep me in suspense here, Doc. What's the news?"

"The news?" The man actually looked puzzled. "Oh. You're in remarkable shape, Mister Corin. All things considered."

"What things?" Oh yes, the man was begging to get his teeth knocked loose.

"Well, for starters you've been in a coma for the better part of a month. Even with the regular physical therapy you've been receiving, your ligaments should have tightened and possibly even shortened a bit by now." The man finally set down his clipboard and then crossed his arms, apparently at a loss about what to do with his hands. "That hasn't happened. If it had, you'd be in a good deal of pain right now."

"I would?"

"Oh, yes. That sort of thing can be crippling. Now,

318

I know we've worked on your limbs and kept them stretched and mobile, but still, there should be residual troubles just from the lack of full mobility. Instead you move around like you just took a nap."

"And that's good, right?"

"Absolutely. But it isn't exactly normal. Neither is the fact that you recovered very well from several internal traumas or that your fingernails grew back in only a matter of days. It's good, but it isn't normal. Neither is your blood work, your CAT scans, or your general good health."

"Can you translate that for me, please?"

The doctor looked to be at a loss for words. "I'm trying, but it's not exactly easy." The room was quiet for several seconds while the doctor paced at the foot of the bed and moved his lips silently. "Okay. Here it is. I'll just lay it out for you."

"Please. Because you're making me nervous as all hell here." Understatement. Chris wasn't in the mood for any more surprises.

"Your blood seems to have gone through a chemical change that I can't identify. I've taken numerous samples and sent them to several labs, both here and elsewhere, just in case the labs here are compromised in some way, but they all come back with the same results. You were AB positive blood type, Mister Corin, the same as your sister. Now I can't get a proper pH reading to determine your type. The tests come back inconclusive, and that isn't possible."

"Okay. Well, maybe it's something I ate?" Chris felt

his stomach drop. He didn't know what a change in his blood type meant, and neither did the doctor from what he was hearing. All he knew for sure was that he was getting very uncomfortable with the way this exam was going.

He didn't pay much attention for a few seconds and when he heard the man say something about his brain, he decided it was time to double check.

"I didn't quite get that. What?"

"Your brain, Mister Corin. The activity is perfectly normal, but comparative examinations of our previous CAT scans from your last accident and this one show some changes, and we're having trouble deciding what they mean."

"My brain? What the hell is wrong with my brain?"

II

Chris spent most of the next three days in a stupor. He answered questions, but only because someone asked them. He talked with Brittany and with Katie, and on several occasions he and Katie shared a good cry, both wondering what had happened to Jerry and at the same time feeling certain that they knew.

Sometimes it was just easier to lie. There was less pain that way.

On the third afternoon after he woke up, his grandmother called. Chris answered the phone after a couple of rings, shooting a look at Brittany when she reached for the phone. Brittany let him answer, but she shot him a murderous look. Some things never change. Just not Chris, apparently.

"Hello?"

"Christopher? This is your grandmother. I wanted to see how you were doing, dear boy." Her voice was as stiff and formal as before, and the anger he'd felt when he spoke to her before came back with a vengeance. He felt his jaw clench but made himself respond calmly. Sterling had mentioned that the woman might try to record any conversations, hoping he would incriminate himself.

"What can I do for you?"

"I wanted to make sure you were recovering from your accident. Are you well, Christopher?"

"As a matter of fact, I'm leaving the hospital today." Which was true. He'd already decided to wait on the battery of tests that the doctors wanted to perform. Green eyes, changing brain and unidentifiable blood patterns didn't mean he was willing to be a guinea pig. The doctors were disappointed. Chris didn't much care. He wanted to go home.

"Well, that's wonderful news." She said it with all of the passion of a woman finding out that her least favorite neighbor wasn't moving after all. "Have you considered my offer to care for Brittany?"

"Nothing's changed. You aren't getting her. Leave it be."

"Such a pity. I had hoped the loss of your friend would make you see how short life is."

321

Before he could respond the woman cut the connection from her end.

Chris set the phone back in the cradle with an effort. He wanted to throw the damned thing but didn't dare.

Half an hour later he was discharged from the hospital and heading home.

Brittany never said a word. After almost an hour of silence from her, he looked her way, patted her hand and told her she wasn't going anywhere. It seemed to help.

Courtney and Katie stayed with them until well after midnight. Chris ordered takeout and gave the deliveryman a fifty-dollar tip. Not because the food was that amazing, or because it had been delivered on time, but because he wanted to see what it would feel like. The kid was beyond happy.

It didn't really change a thing for Chris.

Sometime around four in the morning, he finally drifted off to sleep. Katie and Courtney had both left for the night. Brittany was long since in bed—he made it a point to check several times—and the house was as quiet and still as it had ever been. If he hadn't known better, he'd have thought he was all alone in the world.

The notion wasn't comforting, but then, little was anymore.

Chris thought of Jerry, thought of all they had been through together, and hoped that Jerry's death was painless. He knew where it counted that his friend was dead. He had to be. Nothing could have survived the explosion that had, according to the articles he was given by his little sister, leveled several city blocks.

Chris thought of Jerry and drifted to sleep.

And in his dreams, he was happy.

JAMES A. MOORE
POSSESSIONS

Chris Corin has the unshakable feeling that he's being followed. And he's right. But he doesn't know what's after him, what waits in the shadows. He doesn't know that what his late mother left him in her will is the source of inconceivable power. Power that something hideous wants very badly indeed.

By the time Chris realizes what's happening it may already be too late. Who would believe him? Who could imagine the otherworldly forces that will stop at nothing to possess what Chris has? No, Chris will have to confront the darkness that has crept into his life, threatening his very sanity. And unless he can convince someone that he's not crazy, he'll have to confront it alone.

JAMES A. MOORE
FIREWORKS

It begins on a happy day. The small town of Collier gathers on the Fourth of July to watch the fireworks. But in the middle of the celebration, the shocked spectators witness something almost beyond comprehension, something too horrifying to believe. The lucky ones are killed immediately. They escape the true terror that is yet to come, terror that will come from an even more surprising source. . . .

It's quiet now in Collier. The townspeople are waiting, resting, gathering their strength. They know the quiet will soon be shattered. They know the screaming will soon begin. But they don't know what will be left when the screaming stops.

UNDER THE OVERTREE
JAMES A. MOORE

Can you see them, the faint shadowy forms that move through the woods near Lake Overtree? Have you noticed what's happened to Mark, a once lonely young man whose entire world is mysteriously shifting to accommodate his desires? The girl of his dreams is his for the taking, the kids who bullied him are disappearing one by one, and even his stepfather has started treating him like a real son. Can you hear the screams of the damned, of those foolish enough to cross Mark's path? Listen carefully. The world is changing in terrifying ways. It's all happening . . . Under the Overtree.

MESSENGER
EDWARD LEE

Have you ever wanted to be someone else? Well, someone else is about to become *you*. He will share your soul and your mind. He will feel what you feel, your pleasure, your pain. And then he will make you kill. He will drive you to perform horrific ritual murder and unimaginable occult rites. You are about to be possessed, but not by a ghost. It's something far worse.

The devil has a messenger, and that messenger is here, now, in your town. He has something for you—a very special delivery indeed. It's an invitation you can't refuse, an invitation to orgies of blood and mayhem. Don't answer the door. There's a little bit of Hell waiting for you on the other side.
